Just Add Trouble

WhoooDoo Mysteries
A division of
Treble Heart Books
1284 Overlook Dr.
Sierra Vista, AZ 85635-5512
http://www.trebleheartbooks.com

Published and printed U.S. A.

ISBN: 978-1-932695-65-5

Other Books by Jinx Schwartz

The Texicans
Troubled Sea
Just Add Water (Bk 1 Series) *Eppie Award Winner!*
Just Add Salt (Bk 2 Series)

✯✯✯✯✯

What People are saying about this series.

You can take the girl out of Texas, but you can't take Texas out of the girl. Set sail for adventure with Hetta Coffey, a bold and bodacious new heroine who doesn't know the meaning of defeat—or self restraint.
—Shirley Wenzel, Rice University librarian.

Grab your life preserver and settle back in your deck chair as Jinx Schwartz serves up another deftly and well-blended concoction in "Just Add Salt"…worth its salt and promises to leave you anxiously awaiting Hetta at her next port of call, "Just Add Trouble."
— Alisabeth Dobesh, Gringo Gazette

Schwartz is a twinkling, bright star on the mystery genre horizon with her witty and sometimes irreverent heroine, Hetta Coffey.

—Fictionaddiction.net, reviewer B. Bramblett, author of *Sliding Stop.*

Hetta Coffey's hilarious string of misadventures after being suddenly plunged into the "yachtie world" is a great page-turner for the quarter berth!
— Capt. Patricia Miller Rains

Acknowledgements

As always, Holly Whitman is my first line of defense. Holly not only edits my work for the usual stuff, like misspelled words, she also puts me back on the road when I've written myself into a ditch. Thank you, thank you, Holly.

I'd like to thank Dorothy and Art Oberto for the use of their brand name, Oh Boy! Oberto. Their generous contribution to a charitable cause in exchange for using their name in my book was greatly appreciated by the community.

Many ideas in my books come from tales told by friends. I have blatantly stolen tall tales from: David Gray, Geary Ritchie, Jane Stris, Garth Jones, and others who shall remain anonymous, as they are still incarcerated.

And many heartfelt thanks to my very supportive hubby, Robert (Mad Dog) Schwartz.

Dedication

I dedicate this book to Russ "Chingo" Madden, my numero uno fan, and my wonderful husband, Robert "Mad Dog" Schwartz. Chingo and Mad Dog, a pair to draw to.

Just Add Trouble
by
Jinx Schwartz

Book 3
Hetta Coffey Series

WhoooDoo Mysteries
A Division of
Treble Heart Books

Trouble comes from too much talk
—Chinese proverb

Prologue

aco itched.

Checking to make sure Nacho watched the scenery instead of him, he shifted forward on the hard bench seat of the panga and squirmed. What he really wanted was to let go of the outboard's steering arm and claw at the thousands of spiders racing under his skin. They had names, he knew. Meth mites, crank bugs. He also feared he was on the verge of tweaking like some lowlife crankhead.

How many times had he and his homeboys busted a gut over the twitchy, skinny-assed suckers who bought their stuff? With their rotten teeth and scabby sores, his customers might as well wear signs reading, Kick Me, I'm a Methhead.

He'd been careful, didn't smoke or shoot it, like some stupid loser. Smoking meth leaves your teeth black, and no way he'd shoot, he hated needles. All he'd done was parachute a small amount wrapped in a torn corner off a paper napkin when he was really dragging ass. Was it his fault the boss drove him past exhaustion on that killer schedule of his? Okay, so he'd added a little more to the 'chute now and then, but only when he really needed it. He'd lost some weight, but hell, with everyone in the gang working long hours, they all looked like hell. Up until today, though, he'd never, ever felt the bugs. Until today, he thought he was golden.

When the boss sent him to pick up a new man in La Paz, he hadn't given it much thought, but something about this guy set him on edge. Maybe it was the way Nacho raised his eyebrows when he spotted two liters of Mountain Dew in the panga. Paco meant to buy bottled water, but meth craved the heavy sweetness of the Dew. He should have been more careful. Was it too late? Was the boss on to him? Sent this guy as a spy? Or was this Nacho just another LA type, down here checking out their operation?

Whatever, Paco decided he was finished with ice. Done. *Termino.* Wasn't worth it. He just wished he felt as good as he did a few hours ago.

Racing northward, he steered the fiberglass fishing boat over a glassy Sea of Cortez, speculating why Nacho was here, and why he didn't fly Alaska Airlines into Loreto, or on one of their runner planes. Why La Paz and a long boat ride that would take hours— Oh, shit! He looked at the needle pegged at HALF on the fuel tank. How could he have forgotten to top it off? Slowing the engine, he glided to a stop.

Nacho turned around. "*¿Que paso, hermano?*"

Paco felt like screaming, "I'm friggin' on fire here, that's waatsappenin', and I ain't your stinkin' brother," but he didn't. Instead he whined, "Fuggin' guy at the fuel dock. I jes' realized he didn't fill up the fuggin' tank."

Nacho seemed to buy it. "So, what do we do? How far to the next gas station?"

Paco snorted. "Ain't none."

"No? So what are we gonna do? Turn around?"

Paco wanted to off the *cabrón* right here and now for asking so many questions when he was, literally, itching out of his skin. Reaching deep into what little self-control he had left, stuffing the flash of white-hot anger, Paco answered Nacho in what he believed to be a casual tone, but actually held an edge of panic. "We'll get some somewhere. All these fishermen, they got gas." *That we can steal.*

Nacho nodded slowly and turned back toward the bow, a frisson of unease running up his spine. Was this Paco character sampling the goods? If so, the boss sure as hell wouldn't be happy to hear it. Using their own product broke a cardinal rule, and guys who broke code met a violent end.

All Paco could think of was putting the boat on a beach, somehow getting away from Nacho long enough for a fix. His last. There was enough stuff in his pocket to get him through this day, and back to camp, then he'd quit for good. Shifting the engine into gear, he sped northward until, as they neared an island, he changed direction so suddenly he nearly launched Nacho overboard.

Nacho, catching himself before flying ass over teakettle into the sea, or worse, cracking a rib against the side of the boat, shot a dark look backward that wiped the smirk from Paco's face.

Paco gulped, and yelled, "Sorry, man. Gotta piss."

Recognizing all the signs now, realizing he had a tweaking cranker on his hands, Nacho didn't challenge Paco. Not here, not now. He knew from experience how to handle a tweaker. He'd keep his distance, slow his speech, keep Paco talking, and for God's sake not piss him off. "Okay by me," he yelled over the engine noise, "then you can show me how to drive this boat. I'd like to try it out, if you don't mind."

Paco's eyes narrowed, then he shrugged. "Chur. No problem, *hermano*." Looking past Nacho, at the looming anchorage ahead, his blood raced with a burst of murderous exhilaration. Glancing into the fish well behind him, making certain his razor sharp machete was handy, he repressed an hysterical giggle, and thought, *Now I'll show homeboy how it's done down here. Jes' like your friendly neighborhood ampm Mini Mart,* hermano. *One stop shopping. A hit, a piss, and a full gas tank, all for the taking.*

He increased their speed.

1

"John Steinbeck was a sissy."

Jenks gave me a look from under his golf cap brim, smiled a tolerant smile at this outrageous challenge of the legendary author's manliness, and went back to varnishing my rails. Well, not *my* rails, my boat's rails.

Not one to accept mere tolerance, I shook my book at him. "He writes here, in his *Log From the Sea of Cortez,* that the Sea of Cortez is a dangerous body of water and is prone to sudden and violent storms." Waggling my fingers at the calm cove we were anchored in, I vamped, "Ooooh, I'm skeered. Save me, my hero!"

"Sorry, Hetta, I have to finish this varnish. It's drying as fast as it hits the teak. I'll save you later. For the record, though, we've only been here three weeks, and I'm sure Steinbeck wrote from experience. A totally different experience than we've had so far."

"Ya think?" I launched myself from the step I was perched on, and padded through a side door leading into the main saloon and galley. I made us both an iced tea, and returned to the sundeck. The fiberglass was a tad toasty on my bare soles, so I did a tiptoed quickstep into the shade. Jenks noticed and teased, "Cool moves, Red. The Texas *tenderfoot* two-step?"

"Watch it, Yankee boy." He ignored my warning and went back to his bright work—that's nautical-speak for making wood bright with varnish—thereby ignoring my precious self, so I rose and threw back over my shoulder, "I shall retire to the verandah, and I'm taking your tea with me as hostage. Make you work faster." I sashayed up three steps to the covered aft deck, and sank into the soft cushions of a patio chair. Taking a sip of tea I let loose with a deep, contented sigh. The air and water temperatures matched at seventy-five and Jenks was here, with me, on this nearly perfect fall day in paradise. I was as happy as a puppy in tall grass.

Anchored at San Francisco Island, an uninhabited piece of nirvana north of La Paz, we were suspended on glassy, colorless water that was also, mysteriously, a stunning turquoise. Behind us lay a pearly crescent of beach, bordered with lava rock and cactus. Beyond that, barren hills jutted into an almost impossibly blue backdrop. A true-to-life painting of the scene would look artificial, garish. In reality, the diorama was simply stunning.

Off in the distance, I spotted what looked like a small boat streaking north and felt an unwelcome clench of tension. We'd had the anchorage to ourselves for days, and I liked it that way. Except for the occasional distant buzz of a panga racing by, or a shrimp boat chugging along, we could have been boating on the moon. And while I tried not tensing up when I heard or spotted other vessels, it hadn't been all that long ago when every passing boat posed a possible threat. Get a grip, Hetta, I told myself. Water under the keel.

Determined to relax and relish this special spot of heaven

on earth, I took a deep, cleansing breath. Good air in, bad guys out, good air…

Jenks stuck his head through the open door. "Hetta, are you hyperventilating?"

"No, I'm practicing breathing."

"Most of us learn that at birth."

"Wise ass."

He grinned and went back to his varnishing. I followed him, sat down on the top step again, watched for awhile, bit back my natural tendency to supervise. When the urge to comment grew too strong, I returned to my chair, laid my head back on the soft cushion, and closed my eyes. Lulled by the slight rock of the boat, and gulls chatting on the beach, I'd almost drifted off when the drone of a distant engine sat me up. I instinctively grabbed for the binoculars, but Jenks already had them in his hand. I hadn't even heard him sit down in the other chair. "Shrimp boat," he said. "You know, if you're gonna be so jumpy, maybe we should head back into the safety of a marina."

"You mean a safe, noisy marina? No thanks, this is too idyllic. And I'm not jumpy."

"Could have fooled me." He handed me the binoculars, which I casually set aside, even though I was dying to take a gander at that shrimper for myself. He took a test sip of tea to see if I'd added enough sugar and lime and declared it, "Perfect."

"So's this part of the world. I want to live here. For ever and ever."

"Sounds nice, all right."

I let that hang. I'd just handed Jenks a huge opportunity to say something like, "*Let's* do that." Or even, "*We* should." But nooo, what he said was, "Sounds nice, all right." Followed by, "But you have to go back to work soon." He didn't even work a "we" into *that* sentence.

I was tempted to empty my glass over his head, but was running low on Splenda and it was a good half-day cruise to a supermarket. Besides, the setting was much too beautiful to let my insecurity demons spoil it with a fit of temper that would be totally lost on Jenks. After all, he was here, we were together for now, and he *had* flown halfway around the world, for the second time since we started dating, to bail my substantial rear end out of a mess of my own making. Only a month before, he saved me, my boat, and my best friend, Jan Simms, from some unsavory and heavily armed characters on the outside of the Baja who took a distinctly hostile attitude toward us.

For his valor, Jenks deserved temporary amnesty from my own naturally truculent attitude. I left his blondish-gray buzz cut tea-free and said, "Spoilsport. You used the W word. Okay, let's do the math. It's the end of November now, we can stay here in the sea until Christmas, at least, head back to Cabo, celebrate New Year's Eve there, and then cruise on up to California. If I get back to W by the end of January, I'm good." Before I could stop myself, I blurted, "And Jenks, it is very important to me that we have this New Year's Eve together."

Dammit, did I say that? How sappy and clingy did that come out? I shrugged and backpedaled, adding, "It's a silly gal thing, New Year's Eve." I strove for nonchalance while still sending the subliminal message, I *need* to be with you when Auld Lang Syne is sung. We women, for some unfathomable reason, insist on beaming the subliminal to the sublimely imperceptive. Why is a mystery to me, and yet we persist, in vain, as his answer proved.

"I can live with that schedule. Barely. Lars is already grumbling about being stuck on his own in Kuwait City while I'm yachting on the Sea of Cortez."

"Your brother will live. And speaking of Lars, does he even acknowledge that his lusterless, or shall I say, lust-less attitude and lack of commitment drove Jan into another guy's camp?" I meant this literally, for Jan had moved to a Mexican bio-nerd encampment and was living in a little grass shack with a marine biologist by the name of Doctor Brigido Camacho Yee, a.k.a. Chino. Chino specializes in whales. Jan specializes in serial monogamy, and Jenks's brother and business partner, Lars, was her latest ex-monogamous partner. This time she'd come darned close to committing polygamy, but managed a very long distance "Dear Lars" phone call before jumping Chino's bones about three seconds after hanging up. I didn't feel one bit sorry for Lars, though, because it was his indifference that dumped their romance into a ditch.

If Jenks noticed my not-so-subtle allusion that he might be steering us for that same disastrous ditch, he sure didn't show it. "I don't think Lars would tell me, even if he was upset over getting dumped. He plays his cards pretty close to his vest."

Must be genetic. Dense, these Norse. Handsome, but obtuse. I gave up trying to have a meaningful conversation. Men hate those anyhow. I sighed. "So, wanna go snorkeling?"

"Nope."

"Nope?"

"Nope, let's go skinny dipping. Last one in makes lunch." He began peeling off his clothes, then mine. For a guy who can't commit, he sure makes the time we spend together mighty worthwhile.

We didn't quite make it into the water.

* * *

I stretched out full length, basking in the sun's sting on body parts rarely seen in the light of day. Freckles be damned. "I think I've died and gone to Shangri-la, or whatever place represents perfection on earth."

Jenks, one arm under my head, teased, "And here I thought that was Texas, the way you talk about it. However, I notice you don't live there anymore."

That's true. Although I love my native state, I moved to San Francisco years before and put down roots. I have a one-woman consulting firm: Hetta Coffey, LLC, SI, PI. Just kidding about the PI part, but even though I am not a private investigator, my snoopery does seem to land me in dustups far beyond the pale of your average civil engineer. Also kidding about the SI, that's my little play on phonetics for Civil Engineer.

Perpetually single, I live aboard my boat, a forty-five foot Californian motor yacht I'd christened *Raymond Johnson*, after my beloved and departed yellow lab. When RJ died, I sold my house, moved aboard and found a whole new lifestyle. A good thing, too, because my old *modus vivendi* sucked.

My work takes me anywhere I can earn a buck, and I can assure you that the C in LLC doesn't stand for conformity. It was my habit of tackling off the radar projects that recently brought me, and my boat, to the Baja peninsula of Mexico. With that project completed and everyone safely back out of jail—don't ask—I granted myself a short leave of absence between jobs, intent on enjoying the magnificent Sea of Cortez with my whatever he is, Jenks Jenkins.

"I love Texas, but the summers are," I stuck my nose in the air and waved a fey wrist, "much too hot, muggy and buggy for my redefined, sophisticated tastes."

Jenks rolled his eyes at my attempted loftiness. "Yeah, right. Speaking of hot, let's hit the water."

"Oh, *that's* what we were gonna do. I'll get the snorkels and fins. You know I gotta have my fins."

"Probably not. This water has a very high salinity content, so you'll float real good."

"Are you implying that my abundance of buoyancy has something to do with me chunky dunking rather than skinny dipping?"

His blue eyes twinkled. For some reason, incomprehensible to me, he finds me vastly amusing, and *not* chubby. But then, he's myopic, a sterling attribute in my book.

Knowing he'd rescue me if I submarined, I cannonballed into the water before he could find his glasses, and before I remembered that seventy-five degree water is not all that warm. I came up spluttering.

"How is it?"

"Fantastic. Come on in." Okay, so I lied. Chunky dunking is a rare and liberating experience, so who am I to deny Jenks the exhilaration? I mean, if I can risk stripping what's left of the L'Oreal Red Penny from my fading locks, Jenks can withstand a momentary chill. He hit the water, surfaced screaming obscenities and threats in my direction, but after a few minutes even he, of the ten percent body fat, adapted. He was right, I easily floated. For insurance though, I slipped on fins.

For someone who lives on a boat, I have an irrational love-hate relationship with aquatics. While I revel in warm, *very* clear waters, and can spend hours snorkeling, watching jewel-toned fish dart in and out of coral and kelp, I harbor a lurking dark fear of the briny deep. Many years ago, scuba diving off the coast of Aruba, I was escorted down eighty feet by four professional divers who watchfully hovered around me while I swam amongst graceful sea fans, gurgled happily into my regulator and wasted valuable air with giggles. Yep, I'm a real water baby until something goes wrong.

That Caribbean dive ended abruptly when I made the abysmal error of looking out, into the abyss of the unknown, beyond the blue, into the unfathomable black. Short of a toothy megalodon suddenly materializing out of that void, nothing could have terrified me more. It took all four of my instructors to prevent me from a panicky zoom upwards to the safety of the boat, and a long and painful stint in a decompression chamber. I no longer scuba, just snorkel.

The upshot of that Aruban episode is that I will not swim in water that does not reveal its bottom, or in an environment I cannot totally control. I guess that's why I'm partial to swimming pools and hot tubs. And ever since my ex-fiancé turned up parboiled in my last Jacuzzi, I'm not all that keen on *those*.

Isla San Francisco's cozy anchorage was perfect for me. We were anchored in only eight feet of crystalline water, mere yards from the beach. I finned around *Raymond Johnson* once, inspecting the hull for green stuff and other gunk along the waterline, then grabbed my snorkel from the dive platform. Jenks was already swimming toward a rocky outcropping, so I followed, checking out the sandy bottom as I went. Okay, so I was also checking out Jenks's bottom. Is it just me, or does watching the south end of a naked man swimming north strike anyone else as downright comical?

I started to giggle, then stopped dead, all of my water demons coming home to roost. Ripping off my mask and snorkel, gulping salty water in the process, I gasped, "Jenks!"

He turned around and, with his long and lanky legs and arms, was by my side in four easy strokes. "What is it, Hetta?"

I coughed up water. "The," gag, "bottom! The sand. It moved."

"Yeah, I know. Cute little buggers, aren't they?"

"They?"

"The garden eels. As you swim over them they—"

I didn't hear the rest. All it took was "eels" for me to turn tail and streak for the boat. Oh, did I mention that, along with my affinity for panic in water, I can't swim worth a damn? Under normal circumstances I sink like a rock, but in the salty Sea of Cortez, with fins on, and eels on my heels, I probably overturned some Olympic record. All modesty forgotten, I executed a belly whop onto the swim platform in a move likely to put Shamu's famous slide to shame. I'm certain there was a resemblance.

By the time Jenks reached the boat, I was sitting on the swim platform, wrapped in a towel. He treaded water and grinned. "I'll give that exit a ten. What a chicken! My chicken of the sea. And here I thought you were a certified sea wench. Garden eels are totally harmless. They auger their tails into the sand and sway with the current. When you swim over them, they sink, hiding themselves under the bottom. I think they're cute."

"Cute and eel do not belong in the same sentence." I peered down. "They looked bigger underwater."

He reached up and ruffled my damp pixie cut. "So did your retreating butt."

"Watch it, buster. My butt is a touchy subject."

"I like to touch it."

You gotta love him, he loves my butt. "Sweet talker."

"That's me. I'll check the set of our anchor." He swam underwater toward the front of the boat, and I followed on deck. When he surfaced, he saw me, slid his mask onto his head and grabbed hold of the anchor chain. "She's buried good. We ain't gonna move."

"That, in my book, is a really good thing. So, Jenks, you say these eels are harmless?"

"Absolutely." Water trickled from his mask, into his eyes. He swiped at them, only rubbing in more salt, but the resulting tears cleared his vision. As clear as his gets.

"And how about other kinds of eels?"

"Perfectly safe."

"Even really big morays?"

"Long as you aren't trying to take a lobster from them. It's their favorite food."

"Sooo, that six-foot bugger right behind you? The green one with the blue eyes? Perhaps you should remove your lobster from his line of sight."

"I don't have a lob…oh, hell!" I didn't realize a body could climb an anchor chain so quickly. As Jenks practically sailed over the rail, an obviously disappointed monster turned a blue eye his way, still ogling what he hoped was a quick meal.

"Nine and a half," I declared as Jenks scrambled onto his feet. "Half a point off for form."

We watched the eel nuzzle the chain, probably hoping for a lingering taste of Jenks. It gave us a snaggletoothed—emphasis on the *toothed*—grin, and began circling the boat. It was then we saw his big brother.

Not only were my skinny dipping days at an end, it wasn't long before we learned that giant morays weren't the only sea serpents plying the waters of the *Mar de Cortez*.

2

"Says here that we have a couple of *Morena Verdes*, or *Gymnothorax castaneus*," I read, making phonetic hash of the scientific lingo, "on our hands."

I took a bite of what is, hands down, the best sandwich ever: Day after Thanksgiving turkey on white bread, slathered with mayo, and sprinkled with tons of ground black pepper. After our feast the day before of roasted bird, Texas cornbread stuffing, and the works, one would think one would be as stuffed as the turkey. Nope, there's always room for that day-after sammich.

Jenks was in the process of making himself another sandwich. "*Moreno Verdes*, huh? And here I thought they were only your everyday sea monsters."

I moved my marine life field guide back into the sun so I could read without my drugstore cheaters, "Panamic Green Morays. According to this, they only grow about four feet long. Obviously these folks," I wiggled the book, "haven't seen our guys. Also says they are harmless to humans, and nocturnal."

"So they try to eat people in broad daylight? I think you need a better handbook," Jenks grumbled, still a trifle miffed that he'd been driven up the anchor chain in such a hasty and inelegant manner.

The huge eels left after an hour or so that first day, but returned every afternoon, reminding me of the not so distant past when a huge and horny blue whale I named Lonesome dogged my boat in search of romance. We'd finally ditched him off Cabo, where a female of his own species convinced him she was far more appealing than fiberglass. I did worry about her judgment a bit, what with the object of her affections unable to distinguish between a boat and another whale. Talk about dense. Could it be that Lonesome, like Jenks, is Norwegian?

The good news about our orthodontically challenged greenies was that they were on a schedule. If we swam before noonday we were safely back on board before they showed up. We planned lunch around them so we could watch them circle as we ate. After some time we figured they were looking for a handout, but we didn't want to encourage their begging. It's not easy being green.

I was no longer intimidated by the garden eels. Heck, in comparison to their big brothers, they were downright charming. They weren't, however, the only critters hanging out under our boat.

Anchored in such a remote setting, you'd probably expect profound silence, but you'd be dead wrong, especially at night. Our anchor light drew an assemblage of jumping mullet, flying fish, squid, shrimp and you name it, all of them drawn by the glow, thereby attracting the attention of those higher on the food chain. It wasn't at all unusual to be jolted from a deep sleep by a slashing frenzy of chasers and chased, some of which ran smack into the side of the boat, or even ended up in our panga in an attempt to escape or attack. First thing every morning we checked out our antiquated skiff, *Se Vende*, for fish and squid bodies. What the heck, we had to bail out the leaky old tender anyway.

Some thought our choice of dinghy comical. However, I became attached to the old tub while using her in Magdalena Bay. Now we dragged her behind us everywhere we went. Recently, in Cabo San Lucas, I replaced her rusty old Johnson outboard with a new sixty-horsepower model, but the beat-up panga trailing along behind *Raymond Johnson* was still a source of derision by Mexican fishermen and yachties alike. Which, of course, made me even more determined to keep her, as I, too, belong to the sisterhood of less than perfect. Those yachties, with their little rubber dinks, couldn't hold a candle to *Se Vende's* speed when I opened up the new Johnson. She'd do forty or fifty, easy.

Even when we weren't at the center of the nightly aquatic life and death struggle, *something* in the sea was invariably breathing. From the comfort of my bed, I could differentiate between a sea turtle's chuff, a dolphin's huff, and a whale whoosh.

In daylight hours, *Raymond Johnson* was no less a marine refuge, with an ever-changing kaleidoscope under us. I sat for hours watching the show, marine guide in one hand, and binoculars in the other for those times when an exotic looking bird took my attention from my real life aquarium. Parrotfish, sergeant majors, rays, damselfish, pipefish, coronets, and the ubiquitous puffers came and went, but a school of tiny, iridescent blue fish I never identified was always there. Whenever I dogpaddled around, scraping the daily accumulation of green gunk and barnacles from the boat's waterline, I attracted a cadre of hungry scavengers that gobbled the yummy tidbits. I tried in vain to train them to cut out the middlewoman, go directly for the boat gunk, but they couldn't grasp the concept.

I was scrubbing away one morning when, to my dismay, I heard the drone of a nearby engine and despite a vow to brush my fears aside, the old heart skipped a beat. By the time I reached the swim platform, the hum reached a roar and, heading straight for us at mock one, was a fishing panga. From my waterline vantage point, all I could see was white water and hull. I knew I either had to distance myself from *Raymond Johnson's* hull, steel myself for getting whapped by a wake, or get out of the water, fast. I got out of the water, fast.

I shinnied onto the swim platform and pulled an oversized tee shirt over my bathing suit seconds before two jerks in a panga circled us, deliberately throwing a boat-rocking wall of water at us. Then the idiots cut their engine and sidled up alongside, bumping my shiny gelcoat in the process.

Jenks, awakened from a pre-luncheon nap by the violent sluing of *Raymond Johnson*, came outside and grabbed a rail, as I did, for balance. I could tell from the set of his jaw that he was majorly pissed, but a stranger witnessing his bland expression would never guess. Spreading his feet, he let go of the rail, folded his arms and rode out the wake with expert ease.

Alarmed by the overtly rude behavior on the part of the panga guys, I worked myself along handholds until I could get inside for a weapon. With my lousy track record when dealing with thugs in pangas, and the fact that these two fit the hoodlum MO right down to their mirrored sunglasses, I was taking no chances. Real Mexican fishermen are invariably polite when approaching a gringo yacht, and they don't wear no stinkin' sunglasses. My second clue that we were dealing with punks was when one of them yelled, in an exaggerated East LA patois, "Hey, man, you got any gas?"

I wanted to yell back, "Yeah, man, and you ain't gettin' none," but decided I'd let Jenks handle the situation. Historically, my mouth tends to overload my ass, and this situation had all the earmarks of a Hetta overload in the making.

Jenks acted like he didn't hear the guy. Just stared at him.

"Hey, man, don' you speak no English?"

This time, Jenks shook his head, put his hands on the rail and leaned down to within four feet above the jerks' heads. The closest, the one doing all the talking, lost his smirk as he involuntarily scooted back. His *compadre,* further away, remained expressionless and silent. He looked about my age, and even through my rage and fright, it was hard not to notice his handsomeness. Though both were dressed in logoed T-shirts touting off-road races, shorts, and sporting razor cut hairstyles, the older guy looked for all the world like a Calvin Klein ad. More evidence against them. Mexican *pangueros* don't wear shorts, they danged well don't have fancy haircuts, and the less than haute couture of a real *panguero* would give old Calvin a heart attack. If these guys were posing as fishermen, don't you think they'd consider getting a couple of nets?

Smirky pointed at me, his raised arm revealing a tattoo. "Hey, you, inside the boat. You speak English?"

Despite a warning frown from Jenks, I stepped out into the sunlight. Following Jenks's lead, I shrugged.

Mouthy of the Baja 1000 shirt turned to handsome, silent, Baja 500, "Jesus, Nacho, looks like we got us a couple of Europeans or somethin'. Probably Frenchies. Let's take the pussy's gas can and get the hell out of here." He made a move as if to step into *Se Vende*, but found himself staring at the business end of a sharply honed steel gaff that materialized in Jenks's hands.

The other guy, who might or might not have been reaching for a weapon, stopped dead when he saw my flare gun leveled at his stomach. He actually grinned, then straightened slowly and snarled, "Shit, Paco, let's go. The *bolillo's* packin'." He started his outboard.

Paco hesitated—perhaps having a misplaced macho moment—recognized the wisdom of his buddy's words, and sat back down in the panga. As they roared away, he shot us his IQ. We put our arms around each other and stared after them until they disappeared around the end of the island. Soon their engine noise could no longer be heard, and it was then I realized I'd been holding my breath.

"Sheee-it!" I breathed. "What do you figure that was all about?"

"Dopers? Fancy panga, big engine, no fishing gear."

"That'd be my take. One thing for certain, they sure can throw an insult."

"Huh?

"The good looking one called me a *bolillo*."

"Is that bad?'

"Not if you don't mind being compared to a round, white, dinner roll."

Jenks burst out laughing, then caught his breath. "Wanna drink lunch?"

"Oh, jes."

Jenks let me decide what we should do next, and my vote was to get the hell out of Dodge. After all, multiple serpents befouled my oceanic paradise. Rattled by the rude intrusion on our anchorage, I made the call to head north, even though the hoodlums' panga left in that direction.

We planned to loosely track John Steinbeck's route when he and his crew explored what was then an obscure sea back in 1938. We didn't have time to visit all of John's anchorages, nor were we intent, unlike the crew of the *Western Flyer*, on shooting, catching, and killing every hapless animal and fish in our path.

Using my dog-eared copy of *The Log from the Sea of Cortez* as a guide, I'd charted stops at San Jose Island, due north of us, then San Evaristo, an anchorage on the Baja Peninsula across a channel from San Jose, as well as several other places before returning south. I said a sad farewell to my school of blue darlings as we hauled anchor and set off for Amortajada, our next stop. Far as I could tell from my handy Spanish-English dictionary, Amortajada meant *covered in a shroud*. Charming.

We never found out if the cove was shrouded, but it definitely wasn't my idea of a vacation spot. The minute we dropped the hook, we were attacked by a cloud of no-seeums. Actually, I was attacked, as Jenks seemed impervious to the tiny buggers.

Swatting wildly at the biting bugs, I yelled, "Jenks! I'm headed inside. Get this son of a bitch underway." Slamming the door behind me, I turned on the air conditioner, then emptied an entire can of bug spray into the cabin. Jenks quickly raised the anchor and motored toward San Evaristo while I slammed down two antihistamines, jumped into the shower, then slathered myself with Preparation H. Hey, read the label. Stops itching and reduces swelling.

By sunset, I was running a slight fever as itchy bumps popped out all over my legs and arms. I took more antihistamines, glommed on more Prep H, and finally fell asleep. Next morning, lured by the smell of coffee brewing, I dragged my polka dotted self out of bed, and joined Jenks on deck. In a blatant ploy to garner sympathy, I pointed out the bites marring tender skin on my ankles and behind my knees. Lucky for him, he wisely refrained from speculating why I suffered no bites on my face.

I was feeling mighty sorry for my itchy self when my best friend, Jan, called on the Satfone. I'd been trying to reach her for two weeks, but her *amour du jour's* cemll phone service kept repeating the same message, *fuera de servico*, which meant the damned thing wasn't working. No wonder, what with her living on some godforsaken beach with a guy who spends his life counting whales. Okay, so he's a world renowned marine biologist with tons of letters after the Brigido Camacho Yee, but he's still a beachcomber of sorts, just a very handsome one, with a job.

"Hey, Hetta, how are you and Jenks doing? And where are you?"

"Miserable, somewhere in the Baja desert."

"Must be hell on your props."

"You know what I mean. I was attacked by winged creatures," I whined.

"You'll heal," she said, brushing off my snivel. "What else are you doing?"

So much for compassionate best friends. I made a mental note to make her pay for her crass lack of pathos in the near future. "We're cruising along the Baja, gunk holing from anchorage to anchorage. We plan going as far north as Santa Rosalia, pick up fuel there, and head back for Cabo."

"Oh, yeah? Chino's grandmother lives along there somewhere. We're gonna go down and see her one of these days. Get her blessing."

"That'll be…what? Blessing?"

"Chino and I are thinking of getting married."

"You're pregnant?"

"No, silly."

"Then why are you getting married?"

This evidently caught her off guard. We were, after all, products of the feminine revolution, even though I was too young to subscribe when Ms. Magazine came out, and my mother certainly never subscribed, nor did she ascribe to any of what she considered feminist nonsense. My mom achieved everything she wanted without burning a single bra, and couldn't understand how I missed inheriting such a fine southern trait as the art of the feminine finagle.

I thrummed my fingers, refusing to fill dead air time while waiting for Jan's suitable answer for what I considered a perfectly reasonable question. Why *would* she consider marrying someone she recently met if she wasn't knocked up?

Finally, she spoke. "Uh, I'm in love?"

"Jan, you've been in love umpteen million times."

"He asked me?"

"Aha! That *is* a first."

"Why are you being so mean?"

Actually, I don't know why I was being such a crab. Poor Jan called to share her good news, and I was raining all over her love parade. Why? Jealousy? Jenks certainly never used the M word. Oh, we'd skirted around it, made plans for the immediate future, stuff like that. "How about, I itch all over and you don't care? Or that we had a run-in with a couple of thugs, and were terrorized by giant green sea monsters?"

"Thugs? I don't like the sound of that."

"Yeah, been there, done that, haven't we? Those guys that terrorized us in Mag Bay…they are still in jail, aren't they?"

"Far as I know. Chino has ears everywhere around here, so we'll know if something changes. Did you think maybe *your* thugs have a connection to *our* thugs?

"Crossed my mind, but Jenks doesn't think so. He's probably right and these two were a couple of bullies trying to get free gasoline. I doubt there's a connection."

"Well, still, be careful."

Her sincere concern put the guilties on me. "Jan, I'm sorry for raining on your happiness. I have a problem picturing you giving up your successful consulting bidness and living in a thatched hut on the beach for the rest of your life. With a guy who adores whales above all else."

"Actually, we're in Lopez Mateos, living in a motel while Chino and his crew get the *Tanuki Maru* ready for the search for the *San Carlos*. We'll be living aboard while he heads the expedition to find the galleon. He is a marine archeologist, you know, as well as a marine biologist."

"Yes, I know. He worked for me, remember? The *Tanuki Maru*? I thought the Mexican government confiscated that ship when we ratted out the Japanese for a plot to catch and can whales."

"They did. Tanuki Corporation, as reparation for what they claim was a rogue operation, in no way sanctioned by them, of course, generously volunteered their ship and the funds for the expedition. In exchange for an okay from Chino on their water desalination plant, needless to say. So, Chino and I will spend the next two years searching for treasure. How cool is that?"

"I guess living in a rust bucket is better than a palapa on the beach, but not much. Has Chino been back to the site yet, found anything else since we dredged up that astrolabe?"

"A few silver coins, some broken pottery. The expedition really hasn't begun officially, but Chino has made a few dives. Guess what? That astrolabe? Who woulda thought a rusty, four hundred-year-old navigational aide, is worth a cool million."

"What? Chino said it only had archeological value. I want my money."

"Hetta, it isn't yours. It belongs to the world."

"Screw the world. My anchor dredged it up."

"And that will go down in history. "

"I don't want to go down in history. I want to go down to the bank."

"Forget it."

"And so should *you* forget about it. Marriage, I mean. You and Chino have only known each other a couple of months. I'll bet your skin's already lizardlike and your roots are showing," I challenged, quite ignoring that *my* ginger locks could use a tint themselves, or that I was peeling, and not from overpriced microdermabasion. "Do you ever get a hot shower? And more importantly, has his *mamacita* taught you how to make tortillas yet?"

"She did mention that they are better hand-patted."

Her defensive tone told me that I hit the nail on the head as to her future as dive crew, or rather, galley slave. I grinned. Payback. I delivered the *coup de grace*. "Before you do anything rash, dear, do stuff this thought into your love besotted brain. You will never, ever, spend another day at Elizabeth Arden. Have fun."

Before I hung up I heard a sharp intake of breath, followed by a little, "Eeeek."

Axing cupid is an ugly job, but sometimes a friend's gotta do what a friend's gotta do, ¿verdad?

3

After a couple of days I recovered somewhat from Jan's depressing news, and no-seeum poisoning, so we continued north, although I was secretly harboring fantasies of a five star hotel in Cabo. One with a fresh water pool devoid of snakelike creatures.

I did have a newer rule of thumb, though. If an anchorage sported so much as a speck of green on shore, any vegetation in which could lurk even a single bushwhacking sand flea with teeth like Tyrannosaurus Rex, we'd give it a miss. We did visit several very, very brown, remote villages, and were always delighted by how gracious the villagers were, and how few of what we deemed necessities they required. Of course, it's easy making snap judgments from the comfort of a luxury yacht, but as far as we could tell, they were content with their lives. It is my sincere wish that some Hollywood personalities never take it upon themselves to inform these people how miserable they *should* be.

After experiencing a slight overheat indication on our

port engine gauge, we made an unscheduled detour into the small bay of Agua Fria. Arriving as the sun dropped behind the distant mountains, we planned to stay the night and troubleshoot the engine problem the next morning, but it was not to be.

Typical of the other dusty villages we visited along the Baja shore, Agua Fria's beach was dotted with small *casas* and a smattering of pangas. It wasn't until we anchored and I checked out the town with binoculars that the difference from previous villages became apparent.

"Jenks, I see at least five shiny, jacked-up, snazzy trucks along the beach. Ya think maybe it's an off-road expedition of some kind? I know there's lots of them that come down here."

"Could be. Lars took his Harley on a tour a couple of years back, had a blast."

I lifted the binocs and continued sweeping the beach. "Gee, the houses look much newer, and much better than the usual *palapas*. Maybe this is some kind of resort." Visions of Margaritas and broiled lobster danced in my head. "Oh, there's someone on the beach. And he's waving."

"Probably wants to sell us something. He'll have to wait until tomorrow morning."

"Maybe not, looks like he's gonna swim out." I watched as the man waded into the water. He was waist-deep when three other guys, one with a cell phone stuck on his ear, ran onto the beach. The wader looked back, dove under.

"Uh-oh, Jenks, problema. Looks like someone's after our swimmer. Maybe not, could be some guys horsing around. Doesn't look like it, though. Dammit, what if he needs help? What should we do?"

"Start the engines. We are outta here. Look casual, like you didn't see or hear anything."

"What if that poor guy is trying to get to us?"

"He's going to have to swim faster. Let's move."

As soon as I fired up the engines, we quickly raised the anchor and Jenks joined me on the flying bridge. Grabbing the binoculars as we powered out of the anchorage, he ducked down and peeked over the flying bridge rail.

"Do you see the swimmer?"

"He's back on the beach."

"Does he look like he needs help?"

"Can't tell. I do know this, though, we can't do much against guys with guns."

"Guns?"

"Bristling with 'em. Okay, throttle up to max speed, I'll keep an eye on them. If they go for the pangas, we'll put out a distress call."

We went straight out to sea and after a while it was evident no one followed. Because we didn't know the area, navigational markers in that part of the sea are nonexistent, and charts unreliable, we simply headed out into open, safer, water. When in doubt, ship out, that's my motto. Jenks took the helm and handed me the binoculars.

Dusk was making it more and more difficult to see anything as we pulled away from shore, but as far as I could tell, the pangas remained on the beach. Soon we were far enough off shore that I could no longer see the village. I started to put down the glasses, but Jenks shook his head, so I worriedly watched behind us for another hour, in case someone followed.

"Looks like we lucked out," I finally pronounced with a sigh of relief. It seemed that both our entry and exit were of little interest to anyone other than the man who waved and swam toward us. Did we witness a crime, or just a boys will be boys moment, dudes having some fun with guns on the beach? We'd probably never know.

There was something else niggling at me, and after a while it hit me. "Jenks, no dogs."

"Huh?"

"Another thing bugging me about Agua Fria. Not just the fancy pangas, muscle trucks, cell phones, guns, and that swimmer. Could be a bunch of vacationing surfer dudes with too much Tequila under their belts. It's what's missing. Dogs, kids. Not a single *niño* or *perro*. There are always urchins and skinny mongrels on every beach. I always save table scraps for the pups."

"Maybe they have a Humane Society and day care."

"Yeah, right. Let's strike this harbor from our future itinerary, what do you think?"

"Got my vote. Is that your phone ringing?"

I made a dash for the main saloon, but missed the call. On a hunch, I dialed the Trob, my mentor and the fellow who keeps me from toppling into bankruptcy. He works for my former employer, the multi-bajillion dollar, San Francisco based corporation, Baxter Brothers. The brothers and I parted on less than friendly terms years before, but Fidel Wontrobski remained my friend. He threw me the bones the Brothers Baxter turned their noses up at, which tells you something about some of the projects I get, for Baxter Brothers makes Halliburton look like the Salvation Army.

"Hello, Hetta."

"How do you do that? Do you have caller ID?"

"Nope."

Did I mention that conversations with the Trob can be a lit-tle trying? With an Einsteinian IQ and the social skills of a three-year-old, he'd actually made quantum leaps into the real world of we mere mortals since marrying my friend, Allison, but he was still light years away from making small talk.

"Then how did you know it was me?"

"Just talked to Allison."

"And?"

"She's fine."

"I *meant*, Wontrobski, how does the fact that you talked to your wife explain how you knew it was me calling?"

"Only you and Allison have this number."

"Gee, I'm flattered. I think. Anyhow, do you know where my VW ended up after the police fished it from the estuary? I'm gonna need a car when I get back, and I can't use Jenks's forever."

"Compound."

"The cops still have it?"

"Yes."

Sigh. "Can you get it for me?"

"Nope. Allison tried."

If I desired compound sentences, maybe I should talk to Allison. After all, she is my attorney of record on those occasions when I need legal advice, which lately seems to be all the time. A black libber lawyer, she is ideally suited to my problems, which are usually dustups with white, male, conservative types.

"Is Allison at home?"

"Nope."

My patience, with which I'm not overly endowed, fizzled.

"Where. Is. She?" I growled.

"You mad at me?"

Yes. "No, sorry. I think I need to talk with Allison about my car. I'd like to get it restored, if possible."

"Okay."

Two can play this game. "Office?"

"Yes."

"Fine. Oh, Wontrobski, did you call me a few minutes ago?"

"Yes. How did you know?"

"I'm clairvoyant," I gloated, enjoying turning the tables on him.

"Want a job?"

"After that last piece of shit you sent me on? You are joking."

"Big bucks. Fast." The man definitely knows how to get my attention.

"Lemme guess, O.J. Simpson needs a new wife, and somehow my name came up?"

"No. I think you'll really like this gig."

The Trob said *gig*? Being married to Allison was truly having an effect on him. "Okay, give me the lowdown. When? Where? What? How long? How much? And who do I have to kill?"

This is the kind of non-rhetorical quiz the Trob thrives on. He didn't miss a beat. "Now, or sooner. Mexico. Independent feasibility study. Two months tops. Top dollar, plus expenses. No one."

"That sound suspiciously like the last *gig* you sent me on. The one that almost got me killed?"

"This one's legit."

Now *there's* a new concept. But wait, there's surely more. "If it's legit, why isn't Baxter Brothers taking it on?"

"Conflict of interest."

"How come?"

"If the project goes, we plan to bid it. We want an independent and no one will ever suspect Baxters hired *you*."

"Hey! I think there was an insult in there. Don't even try telling me the brothers Baxter asked for me."

"They did. They were impressed with the Tanuki deal."

"Impressed? You're kidding. I damned near started another Mexican-American war."

"You did the job."

True, in an end justifies the means sort of way. I *was* hired to see if a saltwater desalination plant and salt kiln by-product could co-exist with a whale sanctuary, and the project *is* a go. Taken at purely face value, I did the job, took my handsome reward, and sailed into the sunset. Okay, so I have a few bullet holes in my boat, several people were killed, and my best friend ran away with a Mexican whale expert. I guess all's well that ends well?

"Where in Mexico?"

"Guaymas."

"Where is that?"

"Where are you?"

I told him.

"Check your charts. You're probably only eighty nautical miles from Guaymas."

"Fidel Wontrobski, son of a Polish communist and engineer extraordinaire, now delving into the nautical. What can the world expect next?"

He hates sarcasm. "Goodbye."

"Goodbye."

I hung up and called Allison's office. After identifying myself to a three-deep front line secretarial and clerical defense, she picked up. "Hey, how's Mexico?"

"Beautiful. I never want to return to Oakland, but when I do, I'll need my car."

"Can't have it back. Fidel bought it for me fair and square."

"Not my old Beemer. My VW. The Trob said you tried to get it released. What happened?"

"They want to talk to you. Since you steadfastly refuse to call them regarding a certain incident up here in Oakland, they are holding your car hostage."

"Hey, I wasn't even in the country when it hit the drink. Why me?" As if I didn't know.

"As if you don't know. There was a *body* in your car. The Oakland Police Department take a dim view of such things."

"Garrison put it there. The police *know* that."

"I know that, and you know that, but the OPD gets real steamed when someone with your body count history won't return their calls. All they want is to close the stupid case, so pick up the stupid phone so *I* don't get their stupid calls anymore. Can I be more clear, Grey Girl?"

When Allison starts slinging racial epithets, it's time to take her seriously. Or sling something back. "Don't get all uppity on me."

She laughed. "Hetta, just call them. Talk with Detective Norquist, the cutie who interviewed you when they found that other body on your anchor. I'll give you Norquist's number."

So I did. Norquist was not pleased with me, but in truth he couldn't justify keeping my car. I called Allison back and she said she'd get it towed in for repairs. Finally, I joined Jenks on the flying bridge. A sliver of moon rested low on the horizon, and a blanket of stars sparkled in a black velvet sky.

"What's up?"

"The Trob has another job for me here in Mexico if I want it. About eighty miles from here. Place called Guaymas."

"What's the job?"

"What does it matter? Much as I'd like to stay here, I have a commitment back home in January."

"Why can't you do both? You could leave the boat down here, fly home."

"For starters, this boat *is* my home, remember? Where would I live?"

"You can stay in my apartment in Oakland until your project up there is over. I'll be in Kuwait for at least three more months. If we don't have to take *Raymond Johnson* back to California, we can both get on with our projects sooner."

"How about all my stuff? Everything I own is on this boat."

"Take your clothes, buy more. When you're ready to come back down here, drive."

"Speaking of, Allison's springing my VW and having it towed to a mechanic."

"You should get another car instead."

"I don't want another car. I want my VW. It has great sentimental value. I could just kill that Garrison for running it off into the estuary."

"If I were you, with your, uh, record, I'd be more careful about threatening anyone. People *do* have a way of getting dead around you. And if I remember correctly, there is a little tit for tat here. You did, after all, arrange to send his prized Morgan for a swim. He's evening the score, in spades."

"Don't be reasonable with me, you know it doesn't work."

He chuckled and shook his head. "Not worth it, you know."

"That was RJ's car. I want it fixed."

"RJ was a fine dog, and the only dog I've known with his own car, but you could buy some decent wheels for what it'll cost to restore your antiquated VW. Especially after it's been submerged in saltwater."

"You're being reasonable again."

"Sorry. I should know better." He put his arm around me and kissed my forehead.

We chugged a few more miles out to sea, far from shore, cut the engines and drifted throughout the night. We spelled each other, taking three hour watches. Neither of us got much sleep. Staring at windows made black by the dark of night made me wish I'd taken my watch from the flying bridge, but we had a firm rule: While at sea, no one goes outside while the other sleeps.

Mentally replaying the scene at Agua Fria, I tried convincing myself that Jenks was right, and I didn't see what I thought I saw. And so what if it was a crime? There was no way in hell, after my recent dealings with several unsavory Mexican authority types, I'd report it. The best thing was to erase the incident from memory. Why worry over something one cannot control?

4

After a night of drifting, we decided to further distance ourselves from the spooky Agua Fria, so we headed for another Steinbeck destination, Puerto Escondido. He wrote: *If one wished to design a personal secret bay, one would probably build something like this little harbor.*

Jagged mountains, the Gigantes, according to my map, jutted against the western sky, and the harbor was protected from all sides by hills and natural rocky berms. I can only imagine what a beautiful spot this was when Steinbeck and crew arrived aboard *Western Flyer* all those many years ago. But now he must be rolling in his grave; some kind of big construction project involving steel girders and cement was underway, shattering the tranquility and forever marring old John's personal secret bay. In my career as an engineer I was, without doubt, guilty of trashing someone else's perfect harbor myself, but I really hated what was happening here.

Exhausted, we turned in early and were up, sipping coffee, when we witnessed what was probably the most spectacular sunrise of my life. The rising sun hit the jutting, striated Gigantes, painting them a mix of pink, salmon, and purple. Both the mountains and the rosy clouds hugging their peaks reflected on glassy, turquoise sky and water. The effect was stunning.

I oohed and aahed, and asked Jenks, "Have you ever seen anything like this?"

He shook his head. "Pretty neat."

"Pretty neat? Jenks, you are the master of the understatement. I'm getting the camera." I rushed inside and was out in a flash. When I clicked off a shot before everything faded, I realized my batteries were dead.

"You know Hetta, there's a better place to store your dead batteries than in your camera."

"Yeah, I know. I usually keep them in my flashlight. Oh, well, we'll be here tomorrow, and believe you me, I will have fresh batteries in this baby. You know, I've lived in and traveled to a lot of places in the world, but so far the Sea of Cortez is my favorite. Well, except for Agua Fria."

"Uh-huh."

"Last night, when we were drifting on my watch, I decided to call the Trob back today, take that job on the mainland. I looked it up. Guaymas, that is. It's a port city and has a fair size harbor. Maybe there's a marina."

"Worth checking out. Give him a jingle, he should be in his office by now. Like I said, it could work to your advantage. Now, I'll muck out the seawater strainer on the overheating engine before we— Phone's ringing."

I caught it on the third ring, thinking it might be the Trob, but it was Mama.

"Where are you, Hetta Honey?" To everyone else I'm Hetta. To my mother, I'm Hetta Honey.

"Still in Mexico. Up in the Sea of Cortez."

"That's nice. Is Jenks with you?" She sounded hopeful. She likes Jenks and lives in fear that I will alienate him. I do have a history.

"Sure is."

"And Jan?"

"No. Remember, I told you? She's with Chino."

Silence.

"Mom, he's a doctor. He's a good guy, and she's happy."

"He's a *Mexican.*"

"Tsk, tsk. Your Texas prejudice is showing."

"I am not prejudiced. It's just that Mexican men can be so…fickle."

"I don't think Chino is, unless an exceptionally comely whale wiggles her tail at him."

"Huh?"

"Never mind. How's Daddy?"

"That's what I called about. He's got trouble."

My heartbeat stuttered. My parents entered the parent pool a little later than was fashionable in their generation, and didn't get around to having me and my sister until they were in their thirties. Even though sixty is the new forty, and my parents are in excellent health, I tend to worry. "Trouble?"

"It's your Aunt Lil."

I stifled a moan. My aunt, who never had children of her own, spent inordinate amounts of time telling Mom how she should raise me and my sister. As well as being a giant thorn in my derrière, Auntie Lillian is overbearing and bossy, so you can imagine how well we get along. Not.

A retired nurse of Ratchet ilk, she'd been married five times, and met each and every of her spouses while they were drying out at Veteran's Administration Hospitals. My mother, always the peacemaker, puts up with her crap. I never do, although maybe I should consider taking a cue from her modus operandi; she finds her hubbies in rehab, marries 'em, buys 'em a bottle or two when they get out, and bingo! Death benefits.

"She get herself another husband out of the drunk tank at the VA?"

"Hetta Honey, be nice. She *is* blood, you know, and no, she's not married again. At least I don't think so. Also, I'm sure she loved all of her husbands, in her own way."

"Spare me the love. Lil is a miserable human being who does her level best to spread the virus of discontent. She's a happiness terrorist. Sorry Mama, I know she's your only sister. How could two sisters be so different?"

"You and your sister are different."

"Yes, but we come from the same planet. So what has the infamous Lil done now?"

"She's disappeared."

"And that's a *bad* thing?"

"If you're going to be this way, maybe we should talk later."

"Okay, okay. Maybe you'd better tell me the story. Truthfully, however, I can't imagine that my aunt taking a powder would upset Dad too much." Actually, I know for a fact that my father would give his new Tony Lamas to never lay eyes on auntie's sour puss ever again.

"You and your father don't understand her."

Oh, we understand her all too well. She's a bully and a user of both people and substances, who takes advantage of your sweet nature. Because my mother sounded upset, I asked, in a softer tone, "What happened?"

"Well, she called and said she was leaving for a few days and could we feed her bird. She never returned."

"Did she say where she was going?"

"No. No one knows."

"She take her car?"

"No."

Well, there's *a break for all of Texas driverdom.* "She'll turn up. She always does. So, other than the fact that you're worried, why is this a problem for Dad?"

"It's trouble."

"You said that. What kind of trouble?"

"No, dear. Trouble. Your aunt's parrot. His name is Trouble."

"I've known a few men like that. When did she buy a parrot? I thought you meant she wanted you to scatter birdseed for her flock of wild birds."

"She didn't exactly buy him. He adopted her."

"Too bad your mother didn't think of that."

"Het-ta."

"Okay, okay, tell me the tale."

"It turns out," I told Jenks over breakfast, "that my aunt named this wild parrot Trouble, because he sings a song from *The Music Man,* the one about pool? Right here in River City?"

"Preston Foster. Loved that movie. So, there are wild parrots in Texas? And your aunt has one as a pet?"

"Not only that, he's illegal."

Jenks raised his eyebrows and took a bite of toast. "This should be good."

"It is. This parrot, he's actually a parakeet called a Monk or Quaker. I've seen them all around Lake Austin. They're cute little devils and they've survived up north, even in your old home town of Brooklyn, because they are the only nest-building parrots in the world. They make warm homes and hole up in winter."

"So, if they're wild, why does your aunt keep him?"

"For some unfathomable reason, he adopted her. If nothing else, this shows a singular lack of good judgment on his part." Jenks chuckled. He had not only met Lil, he'd seen her in action. "Anyhow, you know she feeds all kinds of birds behind her house. One day she heard a ruckus, opened the door and in flew this parrot, with a blue jay hot on his tail. Auntie slammed the door, knocked the jay out, and when the parrot calmed down, he burst into song. First, *Ya Got Trouble* and then *Yellow Rose of Texas*. She was so impressed, she let him stay and now he lives with her."

"How's the blue jay?"

"Woke up and flew off, but waited outside. Every time after that, when Trouble went outside, the jay went after him, so my aunt puts Trouble in the car inside the garage, goes for a drive, then lets him out. He flies right over the car as she tools down the road. Then, when he's had his exercise, or dad whistles him back, he flies into the car and they drive home."

"Whistles for him? Like a dog? I'd pay to see that. So, your aunt has gone missing and now your dad has to uh, drive, the parrot?"

"Yep. And there's parrot droppings in his pickup truck. You know how he loves that truck. He wants to turn him loose, but Mama won't let him. Not only that, Mom and Dad wanna go RVing and now they can't because they're stuck until Auntie Addict shows up. They wanted *me* to birdsit Trouble for a while. Thank God, I can't because I'm out of the country. I told them to board him out, but no one will take him. He ain't got no stinkin' passport. Without proof of where he came from, pet shops are afraid he's a carrier for bird flu or parrot fever or some such."

"I agree with your dad. Turn him loose. He is a wild bird, right?"

"Actually, they don't really think so. Mother's afraid he's been raised by people and can't fend for himself. And even though Dad wants shut of Trouble, he'd feel terrible if something happened to him. I think he's grown on them, parrot poop and all."

"You have a strange family."

"Yeah, well, I've met your brother, don't forget."

He grinned. "So what are your parents going to do?"

"Just wait and see, I guess. Anyhow, not my problem. I, for one, would like a long walk on terra firma. We could both use the exercise. First, though, I'll call the Trob and see about that job down here. At least if I stay I won't have to make excuses to Mom why I can't take that bird off her hands."

The phone rang again. "Jeez, I'm supposedly on vacation. You take it, Jenks. Tell whoever it is to call back in a month."

5

I didn't make it ashore at Puerto Escondido, because we were headed for Guaymas within the hour.

It took the Trob two up-antes to convince me I should take on a project I'd already decided to take. He averred it was a fairly simple study—oh, sure, I've heard *that* before—as well as lucrative. And, for a change, I would actually report to him. That's what really sealed the deal. No murky middleman to work around, no hidden agendas, just plain old grunt work using OP's drawings and studies. I like it when I can cash in on Other People's toil. Only problem is that he needed me there, on site and sending reports within forty-eight hours because of some meeting the Baxters had planned. With whom he didn't say, and I didn't ask. Sometimes it's better to remain ignorant of details, just in case I end up in court.

Jenks plotted our course for Guaymas, which would require an overnighter. If we loafed along at six knots, we'd arrive after first light, always a good idea when you don't have local knowledge. Upon arrival, I'd pay a courtesy call on the port captain, tell him what I was doing there, sort of. The *sort of* part was that I planned fobbing myself off as a reporter writing a favorable article touting the possibility that Guaymas was destined to become Arizona's deepwater seaport. I'd get friendly, gently feel him out, get his take on the political feasibility of successfully ushering his port from the nineteenth to the twenty-first century. I said feel him *out*, not *up*. I do have my standards, lowly as they may be.

Once underway, Jenks took the first watch, casting a leery eye for panga goons, while I set about printing up new business cards. First, though, I needed the name of a viable newspaper. I fired up the sat system, Googled Arizona, came up with major publications in Tucson and Phoenix. Nope, too obvious, and easy to check out. I needed something small and much more obscure. *Tombstone Epitaph*? Nah. *Yuma Sun*? Too far away. I needed a town close enough to care about the goings on in a Mexican seaport. Then I hit it, *The Sierra Vista Dispatch*, Sierra Vista, Arizona. Population, a little over 40,000. Located in Southeast Arizona, very near the border. Better yet, home of Fort Huachuca, a center for Army Intelligence. A town no one ever heard of, with a daily rag to match, was perfect for my purposes. I downloaded the paper's logo.

"What do you think?" I asked, handing Jenks my newly minted business cards.

"Do journalists actually put *Journalist* on their cards?"

"I dunno, but I thought Hetta Coffey, Girl Reporter, sounded somewhat dated."

"Is there really a paper by this name?"

"Yep, and a town. There's an army base there, Fort Huachuca, so I figure the folks in this berg would be interested in the development of a seaport to their south, in a country we're not on super terms with when it comes to avenues for terrorism."

"Beats trucking everything from the West and Gulf coasts, I guess."

"That's what I love about this project. It's clean."

"I hope so, for your sake. When Mexico smells money, things can get dirty, fast."

"You're telling me? This time, though, all I need do is summarize the feasibility studies of others, adding my onsite survey, so I'm not really breaking new ground. My job is to simply ensure we're not comparing coconuts and mangos. I actually have some professional background on this subject. A mite rusty, perhaps, but a soupçon of knowledge in transportation. Marine transportation."

"Oh, yeah? When?"

"Before I started college, I did a summer internship at Brown and Root, now owned by Halliburton. The guys you and your brother are subbing for in Kuwait."

"Small world, but the world of big boy engineering always has been. So what did you do?"

I let that big *boy* thing slide. "A summary of Alaska Pipeline sealifts, beginning with the early seventies. Every year, all the barges had to be loaded and underway in order to make passage to Prudhoe Bay, through the Bering Strait before it refroze. The fascinating critical nature of that lift led me to specialize in Material Control and Logistics. Coordinating a project, down to the last nail, appeals to control freaks like me."

"And your journalistic credentials?"

"I do the Wall Street Journal crossword puzzle."

"With a ballpoint, no doubt?"

"Mount Blanc."

"Oh, well, then. What's for lunch, Brenda Starr?"

"You're dating yourself."

"Really? Then how do *you* know who Brenda Starr is?"

"I took a course in classic comics while studying for my Masters in Journalism at Harvard. No, make that a PhD."

He rolled his eyes.

Guaymas can best be described as a blue-collar seaport with few redeeming qualities other than a populace of very hardworking people. After we anchored at a place called Playitas, in water best described as fishily suspicious, we dinghied ashore, found a small motel, and asked them to call a taxi so we could scout out the city. We gave them ten bucks to keep an eye on the dink, but I was still slightly worried because, during the wait for our taxi, a couple of rooms changed hands. Twice.

From the looks of it, Guaymas qualified as a seaport only because it was on the sea, and it is a port. From what I could tell from the charts, the harbor was well protected, but aside from a fleet of rusting shrimp boats, not much was happening, boat wise. After living near the Oakland Estuary for years, I knew what a busy port looked like, and this definitely was not it. But then, that's why I was here; someone wanted to turn this small town into a major shipping zone. Fortunes would be made, lives changed forever. I couldn't help thinking, as a bunch of uniformed, clean-cut teenagers crossed the street in front of us, *look out what you wish for*. The kids retained a glow of fresh faced innocence of a bygone era. Not a tattoo, nose ring, or bleached hair among them. Nary a cell phone. Instead of text messaging, they were actually laughing and talking. What a concept. They saw us and became shy. Not many gringos about, I'd wager. That, too, would change.

We found the port captain's office easily, but after my little fracas in Magdalena Bay involving a disingenuous assistant port captain, I was on edge, not knowing what to expect. What we received was a genuinely warm greeting.

Decked out in crisp white with some gold braided scrambled eggs here and there, Capitán Reyes looked fortyish, with slightly graying, thick black hair cut in military style. Shorter than Jenks, he still hit nearly six feet. He cut quite the dashing figure, one that, pre-Jenks, would have definitely captured my attention.

We shook hands, I handed him my card, and his face lit up. "Sierra Vista! My niece lives in Sierra Vista. Julietta Bradley, do you know her?" He pronounced her first name Who-lee-a-ta.

Jenks cocked his head at me and lifted his eyebrows. His deep blue eyes shone with delight as he waited to see how I handled the mess I'd created for myself within minutes of officially arriving in port.

"You know, I haven't lived there that long."

"Oh, you must know her. She works for your newspaper."

Oh, dear. "Oh, well, then. Which department?"

"I think it is the place where one sells things?"

"Classifieds?"

"Yes, that is it."

"I rarely go into the office. I am more of a freelancer. When I return, though, I will look her up." This subject needed torpedoing, *rapido*. "So, where is the best place to anchor our boat? I see you have brand new docks, but they look a little tight for my boat. We'll be around for at least a month."

"Yes, we are very proud of our new waterfront, but as you can see, it is still being built. There will be larger slips in the future, but for now you should go to San Carlos, a few miles north. There are two marinas, many yachts. Guaymas is more of a working port, but we have," his face broke into a beaming smile, "big plans for the future. If you wish a *marina seca*, though, we do have one."

"*Marina seca*?"

"Dry dock. A storage yard where work can be done."

"Ah, a boatyard. Well, I really prefer a marina."

"Then you must go to San Carlos. If you wish, you can bring your boat there," he pointed at a fleet of corroding shrimp boats, and a pier lined with old tires, "and tie to our dock while you made arrangements in San Carlos."

I didn't want to sound ungrateful, but there was no way in hell that *Raymond Johnson*, with a two-hundred dollar wax job done in Cabo, was going to cozy up to that dock, or anywhere near those riff-raff rust buckets. "Thanks, but I think we'll spend the night at anchor in Playitas, check out San Carlos tomorrow, if that is all right with you."

He shrugged. "It is your choice. The wind should remain from the north."

We thanked him and taxied back to our dinghy, which was safe but had already acquired some kind of gummy scum along her waterline. "Don't step in the water unless absolutely necessary, and if you do I'll disinfect your feet when we get back on board. And when we do get back, don't flush the toilet. I have a feeling what's coming in is worse than what's going out. I'll flush the head with buckets of fresh water until we're out of here, okay?"

"Yes, Howard Hughes."

"Hey, I'm cautious, not obsessive. They probably have germs here we never heard of. Speaking of, have you ever heard of this San Carlos? I didn't realize there was another one, here on the sea. I guess Mexico, like the US, has cities with the same name in different states."

"So many saints, so little territory. Anyhow, it's my guess

that if yachties hang out there, it has be a big improvement over this harbor."

As soon as we reached *Raymond Johnson*, and secured for the night, I grabbed my *Mexico Boating Guide*. San Carlos looked like my kind of town, with modern marinas, restaurants, and all gringo amenities. We'd get a good night's sleep here in Guaymas, and tomorrow I'd settle in and get the ball rolling on my new project.

We ate a steak dinner, celebrated embarking on a new venture with a good Cabernet Sauvignon, and turned in early.

It was one a.m. when I woke up coughing and nauseous. Dazed and confused, I wondered just what strain of virulent harbor bug could work so fast.

"Jenks! Wake up. Did you flush the toilet? Something's really," retch, "wrong."

Jenks sat up on full alert. "Shit! What's that smell?"

More than a little queasy, I sprinted for the bathroom and tossed my dinner while Jenks pulled on pants and went to investigate. He was back in a flash. "Shut all the hatches, Hetta, I'm gonna fire up the generator and turn on the air conditioner."

Too sick to protest being ordered around, I meekly obeyed, holding my breath as I went. I heard the genset roar alive and fresh air whoosh from vents. I stuck my nose to a vent, inhaled the conditioned air, then held my breath while I dampened a washcloth and clamped it over my mouth and nose. I took another cloth to Jenks.

"Jenks, what *is* that stench? Chemical plant? I've worked in all kinds of petrochemical plants, and even a sulfur operation. None of them ever made me sick."

"You never worked downwind from a seafood processing plant."

The air conditioner and a full bottle of air freshener soon

took some of the stench from our air, but couldn't completely overcome the malodorous fumes of what we later learned was a tuna packing plant. It would be months before I could stomach another tuna fish sandwich.

The *next* time a port captain shrugs and makes some reference to the direction of the wind, I'll damned sure ask why.

6

I sent in my first report to the Trob two days after getting settled in at Marina Real. We chose Real not for its amenities—Marina San Carlos offered far more—but for the relative quiet. Situated north of town, it wasn't in the line of decibel fire from San Carlos's night clubs. We made this decision after one sleepless night when our boat literally vibrated with the thump of a seemingly impossible bass emanating from a club. You know you're not in your twenties anymore when you flee the action instead of wanting to be in the middle of it.

After a couple of snail's pace trips into Guaymas by bus, I demanded, and received, a rental car appropriation from the Trob. Thinking I'd pocket a little change, and avoid a trip to the airport rental agency, I rented a vehicle from a local realtor. The Volkswagen Safari—called a Thing in the US—had a holey canvas top, no doors, a cracked windshield and alligatored, rump-sprung vinyl seats. Well, seat. The one on the passenger's side cratered in the middle and required a piece of plywood and a throw pillow for minimal comfort. An overturned bucket did duty as a back seat. No seat belts front or back and, in places, one could see the asphalt rushing by through the rusted-out floorboard. On unpaved roads, choking dirt billowed up like volcanic smoke. Still, it beat the bus, so I avoided dirt roads and prayed it wouldn't rain. Not one single instrument on the panel, including the gas gauge and speedometer, worked. To be on the safe side, I never left San Carlos without filling up, because the gauge was stuck permanently on FULL.

The contrast between San Carlos and Guaymas was as startling as, say, the difference between East LA and Malibu Beach. A glance at a map showed them both on the water, but there the similarities ended. San Carlos bustled with new buildings, condos, luxury homes, hotels, and, restaurants. My favorite, Barracuda Bob's at San Carlos Marina, features fresh baked pastries by the owner. I stopped there most mornings, scarfed down a breakfast burrito or croissant, and picked up a scone or muffin for the port captain in Guaymas. Okay, so sometimes he never saw the scone, but my intentions were good.

In comparison to the gringo-ized San Carlos, Guaymas remains a hodgepodge of shabby, if colorful, homes on potholed streets. In San Carlos, signs in stores are in English and Spanish. Not so in Guaymas, where Spanish rules. If history repeats itself, the prosperity of a new port in Guaymas will greatly influence more affluent construction toward San Carlos, while the center of Guaymas will only fester as crime rates rise. Not my problem, though. I leave the ethics of development to tree huggers while concentrating on economics. Mine.

I began by checking out existing studies by various universities, Department Of Transportation entities, and general pie in the sky schemes put out by dreamers on both sides of the border. The Trob, of course, already had all of this info readily available, and e-d them to me. A walk through the port, with the helpful and handsome Capitán Reyes as my guide, garnered enough info to hash out a preliminary report.

I tackled the cons first, and they were myriad. Major questions, obstacles really, of political and strategic significance required addressing. Actually more than addressed—depth charged—if I wanted this project to fly, and I did. The phrase, *conflict of interest*, flitted across what little conscience I harbor, but I soundly swatted it down.

Roads: the border at Arizona, although only two hundred and fifty miles north of Guaymas, is serviced by a decent enough four-lane divided highway for the most part. There is, however, a major traffic bottleneck at Hermosillo where the road deteriorates into a nightmare bypass. A new bypass with bridges and overpasses was underway, but I'd have to check it out firsthand. A TEU and FEU capacity study was already in the works. A ship's container capacity is measured in TEUs and FEUs—twenty-foot equivalent units and forty-foot equivalent units—indicating the number of containers it can carry. The road system would have to match up to the port's capacity for unloading and reloading these ships.

Railways: already in place, but antiquated. Also what might be a major problem if rail traffic increased. Nogales Arizona is already cut in half, because the railroad tracks run right through the middle of downtown. Cross traffic is cut off for long periods of time while a train rumbles through. Emergency vehicles, like fire and police, can't get from one side of town to the other. Best solution? A costly bridge. *Which I will gladly build.*

The other railway, which used to cross at Naco, Arizona, is defunct. A consortium is purportedly attempting to raise money for a new rail line, but is meeting with strong environmentalist protests because the train tracks run along the San Pedro River, one of the last wild rivers in Arizona, and a major source of water for the entire valley. Just the *thought* of a derailed tanker car dumping, say, several thousand gallons of sulfuric acid into the San Pedro Riparian National Conservation Area is sufficient to launch conservationists through the depleted ozone layer. *This owl won't fly.*

The Port: dredging definitely required to make a deepwater port. Docks built and/or beefed up. The existing railway needs a serious safety study, and the cranes are inadequate. The one large travel lift won't do the job. *Oh, yes, let's do it. My kind of project.*

Politics: to avoid a serious bottleneck at the US border at Nogales, US Customs will have to maintain a sizeable presence in Mexico, with the ability to not only inspect cargo in-country, but also to install electronic seals on containers. Since Mexico has a deep distrust of all things involving the United States government, this could get tricky, but money talks. *Especially to me.*

Then the good news, which I played up, while downplaying the bad.

1. This project could be the answer to alleviating the logjam at Long Beach.

2. Arizona, being landlocked, gains a strategic port.

3. Guaymas, and more importantly Hetta Coffey, can use the money. I wanna be in on this project if it goes and if I have anything to do with it, it will.

Lest the Trob might find that last part, and my personal wants, a bit self-serving, and not the objective feasibility report he required, I lost line three and my precious opinions.

* * *

Jenks read the report and chuckled. I'd left the unedited version for his perusal. "You really do like Mexico, don't you?"

"Oh, jes. I've had a thing for Mexico my whole life, and I don't imagine there are many Texans my age who don't feel a kinship. It's in the blood. And, hey, what's not to like? If I can land a spot on this project, I'll live on my boat right here at the marina. Best of both worlds."

"You wouldn't be a subcontractor anymore, though. You'd actually be on someone's clock. An *employee*, for crying out loud."

"I'd at least know where my next boat payment was coming from for a change."

He yawned and stretched. "Some things are more important than money."

"Oh, yeah, then why did you and your brother take that project in a war zone? For fun?"

"There is no war in Kuwait."

"The whole damned Middle East is a war zone."

"It's heating up around here, as well," he teased, "judging by the color of your cheeks."

"Sunburn."

"Uh-hmm."

I felt my blood pressure inch up another notch, but decided, for once, not to let my mouth spoil what might be our last couple of days together. Ever.

Jenks concluded that, since I was working, he should get back to his project as well, before New Year's Eve, I might add. Unable to reasonably object, I didn't want to pitch a hissy and send him, pissed off, thousands of miles away, to a brother whose influence I didn't think was in my best interests.

After all, it was Lars who told Jan he and Jenks had plans for the future that did not include either of them being tied down. I never told Jenks I knew about the brotherly master plan, even though I yearned to breach the subject. Although it is against my nature to do so, I swallowed my chagrin and asked, "Isn't it cocktail hour yet?"

He checked his watch. "Somewhere. I'll make us a drink while you call Jan back. She left a message on the machine today while you were gone. If you're staying down here for a while, you probably need a Mexican cell phone."

"Right you are." I walked to the Satfone and dialed Chino's cell. Miracle of miracle, Jan answered. "*Bueno.*"

"*¿Bueno?* My, my, aren't *we* adapting well? Got any new tortilla-slapping techniques to share?"

"I'm ignoring that," she singsonged. I have to admit, she *sounded* happy. "Where are you?"

"San Carlos, Sonora."

"Where's that?"

"About two hundred and fifty miles south of Arizona. On the mainland."

"You're not in Baja anymore?"

"No, Dorothy, but if I click my ruby slippers and say it three times, maybe I could be."

"Dammit."

"Why dammit?"

"I had a favor to ask. Never mind, too late."

"Oh, no, you don't. You cannot pique natural nosiness and then leave me in the dark. What favor can't I do?"

"Well, like I told you, Chino wants us to get married, but he won't do it until he tells his grandmother about me. We thought we'd drive down and see her, but he received a report of a landslide blocking the road to her village. Musta taken down the phone line, as well. There is only one phone in town anyhow, and it's out."

There is a God. With any luck, Chino's granny won't be found for years. Bad Hetta.

"Hetta, you there?"

"Yes."

"Anyhow, I thought you could stop by her village, bring her to the boat, and we'd talk with her on your satellite phone, but now you're on the other side of the sea. Ironically, we are both in San Carlos."

True, but she was in San Carlos, Baja California Sur, and I was in San Carlos, Sonora. "You're on the Tanuki Maru now?"

"Yep, moved aboard yesterday. They've fixed us up a cozy cabin, but it still smells an itsy-bit fishy. It's not the *Tanuki Maru* anymore, it's re-christened the *Research Vessel, Nao del Chino.*"

"What's that mean?"

"Well, the Manila galleons were called *Nao de la China*, ships from China because even though they left from the Philippines, they carried lots of Chinese goods. In fact, they called Filipinos chinos. Thus Chino's nickname, since his ancestors came over on the galleon they're looking for. *Nao del Chino.* Get it?"

"I gotta give Chino credit. Very clever. Now about granny Yee, where does she live?"

"A tiny place on the Sea of Cortez. A fishing village named...hold one."

"Don't believe I know it."

I heard the rattle of paper. "Ha. Ha. It's called, Agua Fria."

Yikes! "Uh, does granny drive a Hemi muscle truck, by any chance?" Jenks walked by, raised my drink in the air and pointed at the bow, where we'd sit in the late afternoon sun and watch the mountains turn red. He was soon out of hearing distance.

Jan sounded justifiably perplexed. "Muscle truck? What on earth are you talking about, Hetta?"

"We pulled into Agua Fria briefly, but there were a few mean-eyed dudes with souped up pangas about, and you know what I think about *them* after our little Mag Bay catastrophe. We also saw several fancy-assed trucks and jeeps, lifted three feet off the ground. Maybe the road *is* out and that's the only way these folks can get in and out, but I smell a drug rat." I left out a possible murder on the beach, for obvious reasons.

"Oh, dear. I hope she's all right. Now I don't know what to tell Chino. He's anxious to make wedding plans, but not without Granny Yee's consent."

A picture flashed in my mind of a vacant-eyed and wan Jan, grossly pregnant, with a toddler on her hip and several others, dressed in rags, hanging onto her tattered skirt hem. She was bent over a fifty-five gallon fire barrel, making tortillas with one hand while Chino, fat and dirty, lounged nearby, chugging beer with his friends. "Tell him you have to visit me. Now!"

"Why? What's wrong?"

"I think I might have cancer."

"Oh, no. Does Jenks know? What kind of cancer?"

"Uh, brain?"

"Oh, my God. Of course I'll come. Where do I fly into?"

"Guaymas. Don't fly, take the ferry from Santa Rosalia to Guaymas and I'll meet you at the dock. No word of any of this to anyone except Chino, got that? Not a soul. I haven't even told Jenks, since the doctors aren't certain as yet. No reason alarming anyone. Come next week, okay? Jenks is leaving for Kuwait and," I wailed, "I don't want to be alone at a time like this."

"I'll be there. And Hetta, be brave."

I was whizzing down a fast track to hell and damnation.

There was no way this whopper would qualify as a small white lie, a prevarication, or a fib. Fibrication, maybe? Nope, this was a doozy of epic proportions, and one Jan might never forgive me for. The voice of reason, before I could whack her away, whispered, "Hetta, why can't you mind your own business and let Jan make her own mistakes? She never gets in the way of *yours*."

I reached for the phone to fess up, when I realized my head hurt.

Heck, it *could* be brain cancer.

7

I was popping aspirin when Jenks called down from the bridge, reminded me my drink waited topsides. This brain tumor was already affecting my mental capacities; I never, ever, forget a drink. My poison of choice is a Cuba Libres made with diet Coke, because I figure the diet and lime part cancels the booze-distilled-from-pure-sugar part. Handing me my glass he asked, "Everything okay with Jan and Chino?"

"Yep, they've moved aboard the former Tanuki Maru, now dubbed the *Research Vessel Nao del Chino*." I explained the historical significance and clever wordplay of the name.

"When do they start the search for the sunken galleon?"

"Immediately. They even received partial funding from NUMA, Clive Cussler's outfit. I remember when NUMA was searching for the *Zavala*, one of the Republic of Texas Navy fleet that sank, or was mothballed, when we were in our glory."

Jenks's eyes glazed over. A member in good standing of the Daughters of the Republic of Texas, I have a history of proselytizing when it comes to my home state. This time I gave him a break. "Anyhow, Jan's coming over here next week."

"Really? How come? I thought she and Chino were inseparable."

Oh, that tangled web I incessantly weave. "I guess she misses me?"

"I will, too, you know."

"I hope to shout, you will." I reached over and took his hand. "We can't seem to stay on the same continent. Or, for that matter, even on the same side of the world, can we? Maybe we can meet in Oakland soon? I still have that quicky project I signed on for before I left, unless I can think of a way of wiggling out of it."

"You're a pretty good wiggler. Oh, before I forget, if you need my car while you're up there, I'll leave a set of keys."

"Maybe my VW will be all fixed up. I should be getting an estimate soon."

"Do they charge extra for barnacle and body removal?"

"Hey, what's a girl to do when her beloved car takes a dive into the estuary, and happens to have a body inside." The body turned out to be just that, a stiff stolen from a mortuary where Garrison, a sworn enemy of mine, worked. He'd also attached another corpse to my anchor before I left for Mexico. That guy has absolutely no sense of humor, as well as a warped sense of vengeance. I hate it when someone emulates me.

I took a glug of my drink and asked, "What time of day does your plane leave?"

"Depends. If I catch a flight from Hermosillo to Mexico City, I can get a non-stop to Paris, then to Kuwait."

"Paris? Can I go?"

"You know you can. You also know you won't. Jan's coming, remember? And you *are* working here."

"*Merde*. Wanna hear something ironic?"

He nodded.

"Chino's grandmother, Abuela Yee, lives in Agua Fria, and hasn't been heard from in a month. Chino found out there was a landslide, and that the only phone in town doesn't work."

Jenks frowned. "Didn't we see someone talking into a cell phone on the beach?"

I shrugged. "Coulda been a handheld radio."

"A CB, maybe, or a walkie-talkie, because we had our VHF on SCAN and we didn't hear them talking. Is Chino worried?"

"Not really," I said, not wanting Jenks in on the Granny approval deal, or that I was dead set on delaying, if not killing, any hurried nuptials. No use him thinking I *meddle*. "I think you're right about the phone thing. I'll sign up for Mexican cell service soon. Now that I don't have a client to bilk with my Satfone bills any longer, I need a cheaper mode of communication. I'll do it right after you leave."

"Good. Call me with the number and I promise I'll call back often so you don't use cell time leaving messages for me. I do have a client to bilk, as you put it. And let's use e-mail more, now that you're in a marina with wireless."

"Jenks, you're not visiting Baghdad again, are you?"

"Nope."

"Good." I gave him an evil grin. "And if you do, send Lars."

"I will. You make me a promise, as well, that you and Jan stay out of mischief."

"Where's the fun in that?"

"I mean it, Hetta. Keep your nose clean down here. You've already made an enemy or two in Mexico, and this study you're working on now can turn into a cesspool of graft and kickbacks."

"Aye, aye, captain. I shall keep my nose above the crapper. Besides, I can take care of myself."

As soon as I said it, he broke out in a hearty guffaw. I tried feigning indignity, but since he'd saved my ass twice in less than a year, I am forced to confess perhaps I ain't all that handy at taking care of myself.

I'd like to contend that everything that happens to me is someone else's fault, but there is only one common denominator in each disastrous scenario: *moi.*

Due to unseasonably balmy weather, we anchored out on Jenks's last night in San Carlos. We dined alfresco, then decided to sleep on deck. Dragging mattresses from the guest bunks, we fashioned a pallet under the stars, finished off our wine, then made the kind of bittersweet love of two people who are already parting emotionally while in physical denial.

As Jenks softly snored, I lay awake under the diamond sprinkled sky, my thigh against his. I was already in tangible pain, a deep, wrenching ache that would intensify when he was actually gone. I, like a dog I once owned, suffer from acute separation anxiety, and would most likely chew up his boat shoes unless I threw myself into work or something else. It was the something else that worried me, since my predisposition toward perturbation has a way of manifesting impropriety when I'm emotionally maltreated. That's psychobabble for, *when Hetta's pissed off, she drinks too much and has a tendency to go on a man prowl, preferably* in *low life bars.*

On the way to Hermosillo the next day, Jenks reassured me that everything would be fine, he'd miss me terribly, and we'd be together again soon. All the banalities people tell others when trying to save their shoes.

I watched him walk out of the terminal, board his plane for Mexico City, knowing I'd be in a misery of anxiety until I heard he was safe and sound in Kuwait. As safe and sound as any American can be in the Middle East these days.

Back at the empty boat, my melancholy only intensified, which of course pissed me off no end. I've been single, like, forever and am not amused when my happiness is so dependent on another. Now Jenks was not only gone, I faced both Christmas and New Year's Eve solo. The New Year thing bothered me the most. For many years I have been alone on that night, and accepted it as my fate. Okay, so maybe not *alone*, alone, but I never had anyone super special, as in male type, to celebrate with. After meeting Jenks, I thought enduring lonely holidays, and especially New Year's Eve, were at an end. I really must learn to lower my expectations.

I eyed his boat shoes, but decided on busy work. I washed out the morning's coffee cups, instead of chewing on shoe leather. As I dried the dishes, though, the realization that tomorrow I'd only need one coffee cup made me miss Jenks even more. As a distraction, I made a list of stuff I wanted to accomplish within the next couple of days, before Jan showed up.

I knew she'd want a thick steak or two, so a *la carniceria* visit was in order. Also a trip to a *farmacia*, where I was told I could buy hair stuff. Salt water and sun had faded my locks to something approaching brassy blond instead of my signature copper. Chastising myself for not stocking enough of my old standby, Red Penny, I added hair color to my shopping list.

Finally, exhausted from the drive and self-pity, and still facing a few more hours of daylight, I considered getting drunk, vetoed that, and crawled onto Jenks's side of the bed, wallowed in his lingering scent, hugged his pillow, and went comatose.

"*¡Day Hache Elle!*" someone yelled while pounding on the side of *Raymond Johnson.*

I willed myself into what passed for consciousness and staggered on deck, primed to kill. Two beaming men in red and yellow shirts stood on the dock. One held a yellow clipboard.

"*Buenas tardes, señora. Day Hache Elle.*"

"What do you want? Uh, *que queres*?"

"*¿Usted es señora Café?*"

"*Si, soy Hetta Coffey.*" I'd long since given up telling folks I was *señorita* Coffey. Evidently all Mexican women are married before they are, uh, thirtysomething.

He thrust the clipboard at me and indicated I sign by the X. It was then I saw who they were, DHL. Figuring that Wontrobski messengered some project paperwork, I signed and held out my hand for a package, but received the Mexican thumb and forefinger hand signal that means anything from, *Wait a minute,* to *I'll be right back.* It was the latter, for they left.

Thirsty, I went inside for a glass of water, and when I returned, the men were lugging a large box down the dock. Actually, not a box, a crate. Actually, not a crate, a cage. From it emanated an unearthly screech, followed by earsplitting, recognizable, lyrics, "Oh, ya got trouble, folks, right here in River City…"

Trouble was on my doorstep. Starts with a *T*, ends with an *E*.

Flummoxed, I bribed the DHL guys with a beer, and slugged one down myself, all the while trying to figure out how to get rid of Trouble. Several Tecates later, between my Spanish and their almost non-existent English, I finally obtained a phone number in Hermosillo. Since getting a Mexican cell phone was on my list for the next day, I was forced to fire up my million peso a minute satelitte phone.

"*Day Hache Elle,*" a woman answered.

"Do you speak English?"

"*Si.*"

"Okay, here's the deal. I've received a shipment I don't want. I want to send it back."

"Back?"

"*Si.*"

"*Momentito, por favor.*"

Very expensive dead air ensued. I ticked off the ka-chings while watching the delivery guys raid my refrigerator for more Tecate. I signaled for them to get me another. It was half gone when there was a click. I thought maybe the connection was cut and was poised to hang up when a hearty, unaccented voice boomed, "Can I help you?"

"Oh, thank God. Yes, you can. I just received a shipment that I don't want. I want to send it back from whence it came."

"Bill of Lading number?"

I grabbed my copy and read off the numbers.

"Can you hold?" he asked, but didn't wait for my answer. Kaching! More expensive Satfone time, with the added insult of elevator music.

One of my new best friends in yellow popped another top and handed me the bottle.

What seemed an eternity later, I heard, "Miss Coffey?"

"That would be me."

"You are in Mexico?"

"Yep."

"Why is it that you don't want the box of jerky?"

"Jerky? I didn't get jerky, I received a parrot.."

"A parrot? I don't understand. We have suspended bird shipments temporarily, what with the bird flu thing."

"Look, buster, I don't know what the hell you're trying to pull off here. These two guys showed up with a damned parrot and I don't want the little bugger."

"Miss Coffey, there's no need to get upset. What does your manifest say you received?"

I squinted at the blurry writing, rummaged for a pair of reading glasses and finally made it out. "*Caso de la machaca.*"

"What's that?"

"Hell, I don't know, maybe it's the kind of bird. Hold on, I'll get my Spanish to English dictionary." I did. *Machaca*: dried meat. "I found it. A *machaca* is a rare Mexican parrot."

"Miss Coffey, I don't think so. However, you only have to refuse the shipment."

Now why didn't I think of that? "So if I do, will these guys take the, uh, machaca back to Hermosillo? I mean, they won't just put it in a warehouse somewhere, will they?" I conjured a vision of Trouble dying a slow horrible death by starvation, and starvation is something I cannot abide.

"How would I know? I'm in New Jersey."

No amount of beer would convince the guys to reload Trouble into their truck.

After all, they pointed out, I *had* signed for the shipment and they must go, now that I was out of Tecate.

8

"Mother, what on earth were you thinking? That...that...*bird* is here."

"That's nice, Hetta honey. Did he have a good flight?" She giggled at her own lame joke. I, on the other hand, was unamused and my feelings were hurt. The manifest wasn't all wrong, for along with the bird, Mama sent an entire case of Oh Boy! Oberto Habañero Jerky, my favorite, with a note telling me to keep my paws off, the jerky was for Trouble.

"How could you do this to me?" I wasn't sure whether I was talking about the bird, or her callous disregard for my own Jerky fetish.

"Well, dear, we couldn't very well ship Trouble to you when you get back to California. Monk parrots are illegal as pets there. Sooo, what with you being in Mexico, and on a boat, your father and I think you two are a perfect match. Parrots sort of belong on boats."

"I meant the jerky. You are kidding aren't you? None for me?"

"Ask Trouble, maybe he'll share. After all, you *are* shipmates."

"This is not a pirate ship, and it doesn't need a parrot. What am I supposed to do with him?"

"Oh, he likes a banana for breakfast with his jerky and lots of sunflower seeds, in the shell. He prefers shelling them himself, and he doesn't throw the husks *too* far from his perch. Loves jalapeño peppers. Once a day, take him for a drive. He flies, you drive. If you want him back, just whistle, which you might want to do if he gets near any Mexican men."

"I didn't want his schedule and culinary preferences and you know it. I have to go back to Oakland and, by the way, Mommy, that is in *California*. What will I do with him when I leave?"

"Take him with you?"

"Are you kidding? Even if he wasn't illegal in California, it would be easier to get Osama Bin Laden with a suitcase nuke strapped across his chest past the border guardians than a bird. No way in hell will they let him back in, even if they believed he came from the US."

"Oh, dear, we didn't think of that."

"And speaking of, how did you ship him here? I don't know for sure, but I'll bet the Mexicans aren't wild about importing birds either."

"Well, you remember Pancho, who's doing our patio tile? He took Trouble with him when he drove south to visit his sister in Piedras Negras, then shipped him. I think Pedro was glad to get rid of Trouble. They don't get along, you know."

"No, I don't know. Was it something I did as a child? Why didn't you send Trouble to my sister?"

"Your sister lives in Colorado. He'd be cold. So nice of you to call, dearest. Your father and I are leaving in the RV tomorrow, so I guess we won't be talking for awhile."

"Why can't you two get a cell phone, like the rest of the world? Or, here's an idea, get on the Internet? Do e-mail?"

"We don't care for such things."

That's the truth. It is a miracle they learned how to switch channels on the satellite system I talked them into only a year ago. Until then, they were living with a roof antenna, rabbit ears and five whole channels of snowy TV. Now they are hooked on the BBC. Dad is especially fond of *Antiques Roadshow* and *Absolutely Fabulous*.

I sighed in resignation. I know when I've been nailed by the velvet hammer. "No word from Aunt Lil, I presume?"

"I received a postcard from Mexico."

At first I was dismayed to be in the same country as my least favorite auntie, but then I perked up, thinking I might dump the winged varmint back into his rightful owner's lap. "Where in Mexico?"

"Hold on." I heard a rustle of paper. "It's a hotel on a beach."

"Gee, that should be easy to find down here. Let's see, I'll put out an APB for an silver haired tourist in some beach hotel in Mexico. That should take us right to…hey, what is Aunt Lil's last name these days?"

Silence.

"Lemme guess, Mom, you don't know."

"Yes I do, but I don't like your tone of voice. Her name is Lillian Seagren, and if you're going to be sarcastic, I'm hanging up."

"Seagram? That's appropriate. Sorry, don't hang up, I'll be good. Is there a postmark and date?"

"Let me get my glasses. Looks like…two weeks ago from M-a-z…"

"Mazatlan?"

"Yes, that's it."

"Hotel name?"

"El Cid."

"Who's she with?"

"Why do you assume she's with someone?"

"Mo-*ther*. Who's she with?"

"I think his name is Frank. No, here it is. She writes, 'Sorry I left so fast. How is my baby bird? Having a wonderful time, water is warm and margaritas are cold. Should be home in a few weeks, since Fred's due back in rehab. Love, Lil.'"

I choked back a guffaw, barely managing to gasp goodbye between spasms of laughter. Sometimes it's either laugh or cry. Or both. I let loose a melange of tears of self-pity, and laughter at the situation.

The next day I rode the crest of a soaring learning curve. Right off the bat I discovered what my mother meant when she said to keep Trouble away from Mexican men.

I let Trouble out of his cage, maybe secretly hoping he'd escape through a conveniently open door. Through the door he went, all right, not to escape, but to perpetrate a vicious attack on a hapless dock worker. Trouble turned tail feather and soared into the boat when the worker attacked back. A couple of hours later, however, the tiny terror went after the dock dog, Marina. I heard the ruckus and whistled for Trouble. He sailed back into the boat, but poor Marina, who innocently nosed around for her daily handout, was so traumatized she didn't return for days. What I had on my hands was an airborne bully who harbored a deep-seated dislike for Hispanic men and dogs. So, quite naturally, my mother sends the pint size anti-Hispanic dog hater to Mexico? Maybe figuring that all the Mexicans were working in Texas?

Another thing I learned? Hair coloring in Mexico is different.

After studying dozens of boxes at the local *farmacia*, I

finally zeroed in on one that possibly might do the job. I like my hair a coppery, peachy sort of hue, with golden highlights. Lucky for me, I found just the thing. According to the box, the color, *durazno*—peach—was also, *rubio oscuro cobrizo*. In my Spanish-English dictionery, that translated to dark red copper. I figured the *peach* part offset the *dark* part.

I guess I overlooked the words, *rojissimos* and *extremo*.

After a sleepless night of listening howling wind, clanking sailboat halyards, and a parrot screeching, "Let 'er blow!" I groggily climbed into the Thing and headed out to meet Jan's ferry in Guyamas. I made Trouble fly all the way as payback for keeping me awake. As I waited on the ferry landing, he settled onto my shoulder and promptly dozed off. Jan was the last passenger off the boat, and looked plumb tuckered out herself.

I waved and yelled. She headed for me. "You didn't have to yell, Hetta. I could see that florid hair from two miles out. And what, pray tell, is that attached to your shoulder?"

I took her bag, gave her a hug, and Trouble roused enough to gently peck her cheek. "Oh," Jan trilled, "how sweet. Aren't you just about the cutest thing I ever saw."

"Why, thank you."

"I meant the parrot. He *is* cute."

"Actually, he's a para*keet*, and he's a royal pa…" I caught myself as an idea formed. "Parrot. Everyone calls them parrots. Very smart, and up for adoption."

"Really? Who wouldn't want such a baby doll?"

All of Mexican maledom? All dogs? Maybe the thirteen states that, according to the Internet, ban his species? Me! I held up my finger, Trouble roused and jumped aboard. I transferred him to Jan's shoulder, where he nuzzled her neck. Good, let them bond.

"What a darling boy. Is he a boy? And what's his name?"

"Trouble. Oh, but he's no trouble at all, not really. I think he is a male because of his bright coloring." While Jan tickled the grey feathers ringed with white on his neck and chest, I continued my sell. "That bib look, that's why he's called a Quaker or Monk parakeet." Jan gave Trouble a kiss, and I upped my praise. "And guess what? He can talk, sing and dance."

Trouble nuzzled himself into Jan's hand, making contented chirping noises. Jan seemed positively smitten. Yes!

"So, how was your ferry trip?"

"Horrible. It was really, really rough and everyone was sick. The toilets backed up right off the bat. Thank God you told me about getting a cabin with it's own bathroom. I holed up, read, and dozed."

"Port Captain here clued me in on that cabin. Looks like he knows what he's talking about."

As I guided her towards the parking lot and she asked, "Hetta, how's your head?"

"Very, very, red."

"I mean the, uh, brain thing?"

"Oh, that. You know, now they think I simply need better reading glasses."

Jan's eyes narrowed. "Let me get this straight. Five days ago "they" thought you might have a brain tumor, and now you only need glasses? My, my, incredible diagnosticians, these Mexican doctors."

In mock high dudgeon, I sniffed. "One would think you'd be overjoyed that I was not going to die."

"Umm-hmm. One would, wouldn't one?"

It was time for a diversion. "Hey, here's my car."

Jan stared at the Thing. "If you say so."

Jan threw her bag into the back and we piled in. She did her best to fold herself comfortably into the caved-in passenger seat, but ended up with her knees up against her chin. Giving me a brave smile, she said, "Let's boogie."

As soon as we left the parking lot, Trouble flew out the window opening.

"Oh, my God, Hetta! Stop. You lost your parrot!"

No such luck. "Let him fly. He'll be good and tired by the time we get home. We want him that way, trust me on this one."

"I think I've done that a few times too many, Hetta Coffey, and have paid the price."

Friends. Ain't it marvelous how they can make you feel all warm and fuzzy?

9

Trouble quickly figured out that the fawning blonde was a patsy for attention—and jerky—and shamelessly sucked up by minding his **P**s and **Q**s. Which in his case involved remaining on his **P**erch, **Q**uietly. He didn't dive bomb a single man or dog on the way home and, when we settled in for a Bloody Maria on deck, didn't even steal our celery stalks. After serenading us with *The Yellow Rose of Texas*, he preformed a little ditty I'd taught him.

"Hetta, Hetta, she's our gal. If she can't do it, nobody shall," he chanted, then after one ear-splitting demand of, "Oh Boy! Oberto," he devoured the two strips offered by Jan, and settled in for a nap. No doubt resting up for a late afternoon blitzkrieg on the local marina staff. Jan remained enchanted. *Yes, yes, yes.*

We spent the next few hours catching up. I filled her in on the so-called Puerto Nuevo Tucson-Guaymas Corridor report I was working on, then asked her about the search for the Spanish galleon, *San Carlos*. As the afternoon wore on, we switched from Bloody Marias to Cuba Libras while discussing family news, our men, our lives. Much had changed for both of us over the past year, plus we shared a twenty-year history to rehash.

As the sun set, Jan gushed over the Sedona red color of the Tetakawis, the volcanic peaks resembling goat teats that is San Carlos's crowning glory. Happy at being reunited, but tipsy, we were in no shape to drive anywhere for dinner. We watched the sky color fade and stars come out before moving inside in search of food.

I was putting together our favorite meal of macaroni and cheese with Rotel tomatoes and extra Velveeta cheese, when my new Mexican cell phone chimed *La Cucaracha*. Trouble awoke up from his third nap in three hours, and sang along, which stuck me as uncommonly funny. Grabbing the phone, I singsonged, "Hi, you've reached the voicemail of Hetta and Jan. If you met us in a bar, we didn't mean it."

Jenks laughed. "Gee, you're in a good mood. Obviously missing me terribly."

"Actually, I did. Do. Jan arrived today, and you know how we are."

"Oh, yes, I do. What's that racket in the background?"

"We got Trouble."

"Why am I not surprised?"

While I strove for a suitably rude reply, a crackle filled the dead air. Or was that a cackle? Perhaps we were amusing someone in the CIA or FBI, or whoever listens in on calls from the Middle East?

"What kind of trouble?" Jenks broke the silence, sounding slightly anxious. He knows me all too well.

"The feathered kind. Mother sent me Aunt Lil's damned parrot and both he and his name are Trouble." I saw Jan eyeing me, so I added, "Just kidding, he's actually a darling little thing."

"You *are* kidding, aren't you?"

"Yes. And no. Later for that. How's Kuwait?"

"Same old."

"Tell that idiot brother of yours that Jan has a fab allover tan. Looks like she stepped out of a *Sports Illustrated* calendar shoot." I smiled at Jan, who was in her panda bear pj's, with cold cream slathered on her face and curlers in her hair. Purple ones.

"I'll do that. His loss. How's her love life with Chino?"

"Getting married as soon as his Granny says yes."

"Still seems awfully fast. Then again, I never rush into anything."

You can say that again, buster. "Hmm-hmm."

"And Granny?"

"No word yet from her. Guess the phone's still out. Think old Grans is being held prisoner by those panga thugs we saw? Maybe Jan and I should go over to Agua Fria, kick some thuggy butts, and free Granny."

Jan began to chant, "Free Granny. Free Granny," as did Trouble.

"Hetta," Jenks raised his voice over the racket, "that is a really bad idea. You'd best stay right where you are, at the dock, where you belong. *Out* of trouble."

I broke into my own song, with, "Ha! Ya got trouble, right here in River City." Trouble harmonized, Jan cracked up. Jenks gave up on having a sensible conversation, and ended the call with a lame, "Love you."

"What a spoilsport," I said into the dead phone.

"Yeah, no fun at all," Jan agreed. "What'd he say?"

"We should stay here, out of harm's way."

"Hey, if we wanna go find Granny, we'll by-golly do it."

"You bet we will. Soon as we eat all this macaroni and cheese."

"I'll open more wine."

* * *

Trouble was sitting on my head when I woke up, chewing on my fuchsia bangs. His beak made little grating sounds, which syncopated with the thump between my ears. The lingering taste of macaroni and cheese, and red wine coated my mouth. I checked the clock. Ten.

Ten! Damn, damn, damn." I sat up, dislodging Trouble from my forehead. Screeching loudly, he flew a few feet. "Oh, shut up, before I ring your scrawny little neck," I screeched back. And he did.

I headed for the shower. I had a meeting with some port authority guy from Topolobampo in fifteen minutes, and Guaymas was a thirty minute drive. I didn't want to make the port captain, who'd gone through a passel of hassle to set up the meeting, look bad. I was headed for the phone to give him a call and a lame excuse, when I noticed it was dark outside. I checked the ship's digital clock. Ten o'clock, *p.m.*

Relieved, I coaxed Trouble into his lair with a fresh jalapeño pepper, covered the cage with a beach towel as per one of the many instructions, written in my mother's hand, that accompanied the little bugger.

I checked on Jan, who was passed out in the guest cabin, then went around closing doors and hatches. The wind had died during the day, but it was still chilly outside. I cast an eye on the mess I'd made in the galley, but gave it a mental rain check. The melted cheese was already hardened, glued to the plates, and probably my arteries. I vowed I'd dig out the dreaded resistance band and DVD that Pam, or as I call her, the Paminator, sent from California, along with a cheerful note that if I stuck to the routine even I could get into shape. Gee, I didn't realize that once you hire a personal trainer, they never let you escape their clutches.

I was crawling into bed again when I remembered Jenks's call, and that I'd best call him back the next morning, apologize for being so silly. Or not. I am woman and therefore reserve the right to silliness at will.

Jan, sipping her third cup of cappuccino, moaned, "What in hell were we celebrating last night?"

I shook my head, very gingerly. "Damned if I know. But then, have we ever needed a reason to drink and eat too much?"

"Nope. You going to work?"

"Gotta. I requested the meeting when I heard this guy was visiting Guaymas, and so far the port captain has been a doll, so I don't want to piss him off. Wanna come?"

"I'd rather eat the newspaper from the bottom of Trouble's cage."

"I understand *that*. We shouldn't be gone all that long. Take it easy. Get some sun. Check out the docks. Wash the dishes."

"You takin' Trouble out for a fly on the way?"

"Oh, yes. He gets cranky if I don't let him go with me."

A loud, "Oh Boy! Oberto," split the air. I opened the cage and gave him a strip of jerky.

"How can you tell the difference?"

"Oh, believe you me, he can be…" I remembered my endeavor to fob the bird off on her, "…so sweet, but like the rest of us, he needs his exercise."

"Hetta, you hate exercise."

"And I am generally cranky. I rest my case."

"If you say so. Want some breakfast?"

"Oh, yes. There's a great place in town that serves

breakfast enchiladas, just like the ones we used to eat in Austin."

"Well, I *was* thinking granola."

"Well, I *was* thinking of putting you back on the ferry."

She grinned and we went in search of cheese and onion enchiladas with that wonderfully bitter red sauce that we were raised on. Heaven.

10

The man I wanted to meet with worked at the port authority at Topolobampo, a busy little port on the Sea of Cortez. Not only did they have a thriving port, but one with a successful railway link called the Texas-Chihuahua-Topolobampo Corridor. The similarities to the project I was scoping out were too good to pass up, and besides that, I just love saying Topolobampo.

If I could get a feel for their overall operation, and especially how freight and paperwork flows, or doesn't, I could use the info for recommendations in my own report. My contact, who turned out to be a wizened little Aussie who'd lived in Mexico for forty years, was very cooperative, probably hoping I'd mention him favorably in my newspaper article. We journalists sure do wield power.

After the meeting I asked the port captain if he thought someone taking Trouble on the Baja ferry would pose a problem. He frowned, not a good sign. "The bird would be required to stay in a car. I know it is so with dogs and cats. Without a car, I do not think pets are permitted."

Rats. So much for that idea. On to plan B. "*Capitán*, do you know of a small village on the Baja called Agua Fria?"

"Oh, yes."

"You been there?"

"No. The road is very bad, I hear, but some say it is worth the trip."

"What do they do there?"

"Do?"

"Yeah, you know, how do they make a living?"

"Fishing. And they raise goats. Like most villages along the shores of Baja, they get along as best they can."

"No industry?"

"Industry? No. Why do you ask?"

I shrugged. "We anchored there briefly before coming here. The little village seemed, well, prosperous, compared to others we saw."

He shrugged. "I have not heard of anything that would make it so, but sometimes gringos discover these small, charming places and move there. With them comes prosperity. I can inquire of the port captain in Loreto if you wish."

Charming? Not in my book. "Oh, that's not necessary, I just wondered, that's all."

"It will be no problem to inquire. I must call him today on another matter." He seemed to be mulling over something, then asked, "You were sailing near the Baja coast recently?"

"Yes."

"Did you see other vessels?"

"Not many. Mostly pangas, a few shrimp boats, a sailboat or two."

"Do you remember seeing a blue panga. It is named *Maria*."

"Maria? No, I think I would remember a blue panga, since most are white. Why?"

"The panga was found on a beach, without the *panguero*.

There have been other, similar, incidents of late, as well, on the Baja side of the Sea of Cortez."

"Incidents?"

"Missing fishermen. The boats are found, but not the men."

"Did someone steal their motors?" Outboard motors are a prized possession in the Sea of Cortez, and many a cruiser has lost his to thievery in the dead of night.

"No, only the gas containers."

I must have looked shocked, because Captain Reyes reached out and grasped my shoulder. "Miss Coffey, are you ill?"

"No, just surprised. When we were at Isla San Francisco, a new panga, with a large engine and two men, approached our boat and asked for gasoline."

He shrugged. "That is not unusual."

"Maybe not, but these two? I think they were planning to…I don't know…they were threatening. They frightened me."

He asked a few more questions, but what more could I tell him? Only that the men headed north.

As I was leaving, Captain Reyes shook my hand and we agreed on a meeting later in the week to get more details for my story. "Oh, Miss Coffey, will you be bringing your photographer?"

My photographer? Jeez, what was I thinking? What's a newspaper story without the photos?

"Uh, yes. As a matter of fact, my photojournalist is arriving today."

* * *

"All you do is aim and shoot, Jan, like you know what you're doing."

"Like when you fobbed me off as a marine biologist?"

"Yeah, like that. Hey, think of your resume. Marine biologist. Photojournalist."

"Idiotic follower of a psychopath."

"Not nice." I swooped into a parking space. "Okay, we're here. Reel in the bird."

Jan whistled and Trouble swooped onto the front seat, stretched his wings and panted. I gave him water from my bottle, and a pepper. We left him shredding jalapeño all over what served as upholstery on the Thing, and went into the Capitanía, where Jan presented Reyes the business card we'd printed out that morning.

Captain Reyes read the card and warmly welcomed her to Guaymas. "Do *you* know my niece?" he asked.

Jan gave me a wide-eyed look. I'd forgotten all about the relative who worked at The Sierra Vista Dispatch. "Jan, Veronica, in classifieds, she's Captain Reyes's niece. Isn't that a coincidence?"

Jan recovered quickly. Being around me for all these years has honed her improvisational skills to the level of a Jerry Seinfeld. "Oh, yes, of course. Veronica. Sure."

"Julietta."

"Excuse me?"

"My niece, she is Julietta, not Veronica."

Jan gave him a dazzling smile and the benefit of her big baby blues. "Oh, *that* Julietta, of course."

The port captain, happily married man or no, seemed to forget he even *had* a niece. He puppy-dogged around after Jan while she snapped shots of everything in sight, especially him. In minutes, she had him practically drooling. I wish I knew how she does that. I send men scurrying instead of salivating.

After an hour we departed, leaving an increasingly pixilated port captain in our wake. We let Trouble out for his flight home, then Jan climbed into the passenger seat and studied my camera.

"Ya know, Hetta, I'm not sure this thing has film in it."

"Ya know, Jan, it doesn't. It's digital."

"So, you think I actually took some photos you can use?"

I shrugged. "Probably. We'll check them out, and if there is anything, I'll send them to the Trob. I figure a couple of more weeks here, then I'll go to the Bay Area, give him my final, collect my dough, and kiss some ass so I can get on the project. I still have that other schedule and logistics study for those guys in Oakland, but I can knock it out *muy rapido*."

"You want to stay at my place while you're up there? Well, actually Lars's place. Since he's still in Kuwait, he hasn't gotten a chance to change the locks on me. I have to go up there and get my things out of his house one of these days. And your stuff."

When I sold my house and moved aboard *Raymond Johnson*, I put my antiques, paintings and heirlooms in Jan's care. Now we were both houseless, and Jenks's tiny studio apartment didn't have room for my belongings. Not that he'd offered to store anything. That, I'm sure, would sound way too much like a *commitment* of some sort.

"I'll crash at Jenks's, but if you want, I can collect your clothes from Lars's place, put them in storage. We'll handle the furniture and art later."

"That'd be great."

"So, how will I tell which clothes are yours?" I teased. Lars has to weigh two-fifty and is over six feet tall.

"Anything that's too small for you."

"Oooh, aren't we sharp this morning? Living on the beach, eating all that fish, must be good for the old brain power. And I'll have you know that inside of this body is a skinny woman yelling to escape, but I've quite successfully pacified her with Fritos. Speaking of, how's the tortilla making lessons going?"

She shot me the finger. "Oh, Trouble, Miss Jan is not only sharp, but very defensive. Think I hit a nerve? Maybe she's having second thoughts about living in a hut on the beach when the treasure hunt is over? Perhaps considering that counting whale sperm might not be a suitable replacement for *Oprah*?" *Oprah* is Jan's favorite show.

"Hey, at least I'm not the one conversing with a bird. Besides, I'm sure we'll have satellite TV one of these days. Before you make your usual snap judgments, you should *see* where we live. Nothing but miles of beautiful water and beach. At night you can hear the whales calling each other, and now the babies are there. They come right up beside the panga so we can pet them. One mama whale actually turns on her back and hugs the boat. Lifts us right out of the water, ever so gently."

"Wow! Can you send pictures? That is so cool." I immediately regretted my enthusiastic outburst. After all, I lured her over here to talk her *out* of marrying Chino, but the truth is, I'd never seen her so enamored with either a man, or her situation. Maybe I was wrong? Maybe Jan belonged in a fish camp? Maybe I *should* mind my own beeswax? Nah.

"I hear gears churning and smell smoke, Hetta. Could it be that you are actually thinking you might be wrong about Chino and me?"

The woman is positively psychic. Either that or we have spent way too much time together when we probably should have been getting married and having babies like normal folk. "Okay, maybe you two do belong together, but why rush things. You *said* you weren't pregnant."

"Has it occurred to you that people actually get married for love, and not only because they're preggers?"

"I guess it could hap—*tope!*"

We went airborne. And only one of us can fly.

A *tope* is the Mexican version of a speed limit. Since no one pays any attention at all to signs, drastic measures must be taken to slow folks down. Even a stop sign and red light are viewed as only a suggestion by most, but the *tope*, an axel breaking speed bump of mountainous proportions, is *muy* effective. Figuring that if one speed bump works, then thousands must work better, Mexican roads are strewn with them.

By some miracle, after we landed with a rib-jarring thud, the Thing stayed intact, as did the tires.

Back on the boat, we counted our blessings while checking for broken bones, and looked over Jan's photos of the Port of Guaymas. Another miracle, they were very good, which gave me an idea. Perhaps not an excellent one, but an idea, nonetheless.

"Jan, let's actually write an article, submit it to the Sierra Vista Dispatch. Who knows, maybe they'll print the damned thing and I won't feel like such a bodacious liar."

"Never bothered you before."

"True, but Capitán Reyes has been such a sweetie, and since his niece *does* work for the newspaper I'm fraudulently representing, he'll surely learn the truth sooner or later. However, if the article actually gets published, it's a win-

win. I want to come back down here and live on the boat for awhile, until Jenks and I can take it north. Having the port captain pissed off at me is never a good thing."

"Probably not? Okay, I'll pick out a couple of good pics, especially of your hunky captain, and you can improvise, lift info for the article from the report you've already written."

Hetta Coffey, star reporter? Perhaps I was launching a whole new career.

I began cutting and pasting stuff for a fifteen hundred word article. I'd gone online and read the *Dispatch's* submission guidelines, and we followed them studiously. Jan picked out three good photos, one of which was me, looking very reporterly, interviewing the port captain. In the background, there was actually a ship, the only one I'd seen dock since I'd been there. According to Reyes, the ship contained a load of fertilizer, much like the gloss piece I wrote on the port.

When I finished, Jan read it, and giggled. "You make it sound like the project is signed, sealed, delivered, and the best thing for Arizona since the Gadsden Purchase."

"Aha, someone did her homework."

"I know my US history, not solely Texas history, like you."

"Hey, I know about the purchase of Arizona from Mexico, but I prefer the way we Texans stole our land, fair and square."

11

I e-mailed the article, with photos, and by some miracle it was accepted the next day by the *Dispatch*. Slow news day, no doubt. They also offered me ten bucks for the piece. I told them where to mail my check and, quick as a wink, I was a bona fide professional writer. And they say it's hard breaking into the business. Jan, spoil sport that she is, warned me not to get too carried away with the Hetta Hemingway bit, as I was way too full of myself already. She also demanded half the loot, as she, the photojournalist, received credit, but no money. Jeez, I'm glad I don't have an agent. I'd end up owing money for something I'd written.

Jan was making noises about returning to the dive ship and Chino. They talked long and mushily on a daily basis via cell phone. Still no word from Grandma Yee, and Chino was becoming alarmed, but he couldn't leave the expedition at this point. With his family mostly on the mainland, there was no one else to check her out. He called the police in Loreto and was given a lukewarm promise they'd try contacting Granny, but that was about it.

After one of those longwinded, saccharine conversations, Jan announced, "I'm gonna take the ferry back to Santa Rosalia, rent a car, and drive to Agua Fria."

"I thought the road was out, or at least so bad that the only things that can get in and out are those lifted-up trucks Jenks and I saw."

"Well, I can at least confirm the road is out. Got a map?"

I reluctantly dug one out. A dirt track passing for the Agua Fria road turned off of Mexico Highway 1— affectionately and otherwise referred to as Mex One, or Baja One, the narrow paved ribbon that runs the length of Baja— south of Loreto. Even the map, which showed every goat path in Baja, declared the road as, "Unimproved Dirt." From what I've seen of the roads in Baja, even the *good* ones, this kind of designation is ominous. "Think they rent Hummers in Santa Rosalia?"

"Oh, come on, Hetta. It can't be that bad. You should see the road out to Ignacio Lagoon. Chino goes through tires the way you go through boyfriends."

"Hey, you're the one with the boyfriend *du jour*. I came off a five year hiatus when I met Jenks. Of course, he's not my boyfriend, really. Aren't we getting a mite long in the tooth to have boyfriends? Maybe *man* friend is more appropriate."

"In your case, cell mate is more appropriate."

Ain't friends grand? Always there, reminding you of yesteryeas, especially when there's a taint of smut involved. "Maybe, just maybe, I need a new *girl*friend."

"Who would put up with you?"

She had a point, but I had an idea percolating on the back burner of my brain. "I have an idea. What if I take you to Santa Rosalia, we'll go in search of Granny, then you can go back to Chino, and since I gotta go north soon, you can take Trouble home with you. It's a win-win." *Especially if I dump the critter.*

"Might I remind you that Chino is a Mexican? And who, on this boat, attacks Mexican men on sight?"

Trouble fluffed up his feathers proudly.

"And," she added, "how in the hell does he always know we're talking about him?"

"It's a gift? Listen, I think that, at some time in his life, Trouble was mistreated by a Mexican man. Chino, being a veterinarian and all, can surely retrain him." *Or lose his life trying?*

Jan looked askance, but I could tell she was considering my proposal. I moved in for the kill. "Come on. We'll have a quick cruise across the sea, leave the boat at Marina Santa Rosalia, rent that car, and go find Gran. Who knows? Chino and Trouble might become best buds." *If Dr. Chino fancies living in full body armor.*

Jan tipped her head and squinted. "How long have you been planning on dumping this bird on me?"

"Let's see. When did you arrive, Trouble?"

When Jenks called, Jan was off the boat, so I told him of my troubles with Trouble. For some reason he was quite amused with my chagrin, right up until I revealed my scheme to divest myself of the pesky parrot.

"What? Let me get this straight. You and Jan are taking *Raymond Johnson* across the Sea of Cortez?" he practically yelled. Okay, so Jenks doesn't yell, but it kind of *sounded* like yelling.

"Jenks, it's only seventy-three miles to Santa Rosalia. If we leave at first light, we'll be there, easy, for cocktails."

"You do remember that there is no Coast Guard to bail you out if you two have engine problems, or some other disaster? And, knowing you, that is inevitable."

"Oh, come on. The boat is running fine and Jan is trained crew by now. I can always put out a cry for help on the ham radio if we get into a jam."

"You still didn't get your license."

"No, but they announce, every morning before the weather report, that in an emergency they'll talk to anyone. I'm anyone."

Jenks's silence screamed: lazy, lazy, lazy. I had a French tennis coach like that once, only he yelled, "*Paresseux*, Hetta, *paresseux*." How about that, I'm bilingually lazy.

"You still there, Jenks?"

"Yes."

"Are you mad at me?"

He sighed. "No, I'm not, but I just don't understand why you constantly put yourself, and others, at risk."

"Oh, come on, Jenks, I'm hardly taking our lives in my hands, you know. It's a simple cruise over and back in a very seaworthy vessel."

"Across the Sea of Cortez. Remember what Steinbeck said about the sea?"

"That sissy?"

"Okay, what about this? If Jan is coming back with you, what are you going to do with Trouble? Chino coming to get him in Santa Rosalia?"

Oops. "Uh, maybe."

"Aha! Jan *isn't* returning to the mainland with you, is she? Please tell me you don't plan on re-crossing alone. That's a long day for singlehanding, even on a powerboat with an autopilot. What if you have a mechanical problem?"

"Okay, okay, I'll see about crew."

"Now you're talking. Who?"

"I'll call Fabio." Fabio is the Mexican boat captain I'd hired to bring *Raymond Johnson*, Jan and me down the Baja from San Francisco to Cabo San Lucas.

"Captain Fabio made it clear he never wanted you to call him again, if I recall. Last time he crewed for you he ended up in jail."

"Look, I'll find someone, okay? I have to get rid of this damned parrot and this is the only way I can think of to do it. Maybe I'll leave the boat in Santa Rosalia and take the ferry back, stay in a hotel for a week or so, then fly home. Lots of options." *None of which I plan to do, however.* "You worry too much."

"You don't worry enough."

"Yeah, well, if you're so concerned with my welfare, how come you keep taking off and leaving me all alone?" *Yuck, that sounded way too whiney.*

"I thought I left you safe and sound, settled in at a dock, with a project to keep you busy and out of harm's way. Evidently, I was, once again, wrong. I have a meeting to go to. Do what you want, but don't expect me to always bail you out."

This conversation was deteriorating quickly, sounding for all the world like a lover's spat. I hate spats, especially when you don't get to do the making up part. It's hard to make up with someone who is half a world away. Of course, that didn't keep me from saying, "You know, Jenks, I was doing just fine before you came along, and I can bloody well take care of myself. Do me a favor and keep your friggin' worries to yourself. *Hasta la vista*, baby."

I hung up and, as always when I do something stupid, immediately regretted my stupidity.

Jan, back from her walk in time to hear my last retort, sauntered into the main saloon. "Gosh, that sounded mature. No wonder Jenks keeps running off."

"Oh, stuff it."

She grinned. She loves it when I go off on someone, especially when she's not the one taking the heat.

We had a glass of wine and mulled over how we might lure crew for my return trip. "We could ask for crew on the local boaters' radio net tomorrow morning, see if someone wants to cross over and back. You shouldn't be gone more than a few days," Jan suggested.

"I don't know if that's a good idea. God knows who we'd get, and we need someone who actually knows something about power boats."

"You want a Mexican or a gringo?"

I shrugged. "Guess it doesn't matter."

"We could post something on the marina bulletin board, like, crew wanted for short cruise to Santa Rosalia and back. Must be mechanically inclined, and ugly."

"Ugly?"

"Hetta, you know how you are. You're mad at Jenks, so therefore it might not be a good idea to have a hunk on board."

I gave her a lip curl and snarl. "It's Happy Hour time. Let's listen to the weather report, then make a decision on timing."

"Ya know, Hetta, if you got your *license*, like Jenks *wants* you to, you could actually *ask* for a weather report."

Unwilling to push my luck with the Happy Hour crowd, we didn't get a good weather forecast until eight o'clock the next morning, and it didn't sound so hot. Santa Ana winds were in the works for Southern California, so we had less than a twenty-four hour window to cross over before a predicted norther roared down on the sea. Once the wind started, it could blow stink for a full five days.

"What are we going to do?" Jan whined. "I want to get back to Chino, and I damned well don't want to take that ferry back when it's blowing. Maybe I'll take a plane."

I could see my chances of ditching Trouble going up in smoke. "No, wait. Let me check the chart. Maybe we can leave right now, make the other side before dark. First thing tomorrow, boogie for Santa Rosalia before the blow."

I was already on the move, spreading out the chart and ticking off a mental checklist. Off the top of my head I knew we had plenty of fuel, enough food for an army, and Jenks had checked out the engines, generator and all the other systems before he left.

"See," I tapped the chart, "here. Punta Chivato. It's only sixty-eight miles away, and no tricky entrance to navigate. If we leave by ten, run at ten knots, we're there before dark."

"Is it a safe anchorage?"

I pulled out a Gerry Cunningham cruising guide. "Yep, according to old Ger. In fact, he says it's good in a norther, just in case we get caught by the wind and have to hole up for a few days. And there's even a hotel and a couple of restaurants. What do you think?"

"What the hell, let's go, but what will you do for crew on your return trip?"

I waved my hand. "I'll deal with that later. Prepare to make for sea, matey."

Before we left, I called the Port Captain in Guaymas and told him I'd be gone for a week or so. Captain Reyes said he would alert Santa Rosalia that I was on the way, and would check back, make sure we made it into port the next day. See, nada to worry about.

12

Trouble flew our first hour out, until some pesky seagulls dive-bombed him. For a few exciting minutes we witnessed a Red Baron-like aerial battle, feathers a-flyin'.

Afraid we were witnessing Trouble's imminent demise, we called out, begging him to return, but he held his own in combat until enemy reinforcements arrived,. Out birded, he beat a hasty retreat to the safety of my shoulder, where he boldly screamed taunts at the formation of frustrated gulls.

Sea conditions were ideal. Glassy, in fact. From the bridge, Jan, Trouble and I had a, well, bird's eye view of marine life. The sea teemed with schools of bait fish, hundreds of dolphins, all manner of birds, and even a whale or two. For one heart-stopping instant, when I saw the first whale blow, I was concerned that Lonesome, the blue whale who dogged us down the Pacific coast, had honed in on *Raymond Johnson* once again, but thanks to Chino's tutelage on the whale world, Jan ID'd the critter as a gray. Our most exciting sighting was a twenty-foot giant manta ray, that kept up with us for a few minutes before veering off. If we hadn't been outrunning a weather front, I would have slowed, watched him a while longer, but we were on a mission.

Indoctrinated by Jenks's constant vigilance underway, I descended into the engine room once an hour, checking for water leaks and oil leaks, smoke and other worrisome whatsis.

Not that I knew what to do if we *had* any of those things, other than shutting down the offending engine, but I inspected nonetheless. We also kept a keen eye on gauges.

After an idyllic, uneventful crossing, we dropped anchor at Punta Chivato at dusk. I was feeling mighty full of myself as we retired to the verandah for cocktails, and a weather report. Everyone in the sea was already holed up, hunkering down for the blow to come. No one reported wind. Reassured, Jan and I made plans to leave at first light, pull into Santa Rosalia three hours later. Piece of cake.

Jan scanned the hotel with the binoculars. "Not much going on up there. I can see the bar, but no one in it. What a beautiful setting."

"I looked up the hotel on the Internet. Two-fifty big ones a night. No wonder it's empty."

"Think we can go to the hotel for dinner?"

I shook my head. "Tempting, but I think we'd better leave the dinghy in her chocks and eat on board. Sorry, but our luck has been fantastic so far, and I don't want to tempt Fate."

She grinned. "Hetta Coffey doesn't want to tempt Fate? You usually slap her in the chops. I never thought I'd ever hear that from you. Getting old?"

"Hey, I resemble that remark. Maybe I am. Thing is, I would really, really like for this jaunt to go off without a single hitch so I can rub Jenks's nose in it."

"How romantic. No wonder he's crazy about you. Speaking of, should we call our guys?"

"You go ahead, I think I'll let Jenks stew a little. *He* can call *me*."

Jan tried the Mexican cell phone, but received no signal. I fired up the Satfone system. "Make it short, Jan, this damned thing costs me a fortune. Are you going to tell Chino we're trekking over to Agua Fria by car, dropping in to visit old Grandmaw Yee?"

"I think I'll surprise him."

"Are you even going to tell him we're at Punta Chivato?"

"Actually, I think I'll just leave the impression we're still on the other side. I don't suppose he'd be too pleased at the idea of us running loose all over the Baja."

"Spoken like a true little Mexican fianceé."

"I just don't want him to worry, that's all."

"What's with these men of ours? It isn't as if we're helpless idiots."

"Well, at least not helpless. We do, however, tend toward testing the waters. I guess they want to protect us from ourselves."

"Charming. Okay, go ahead and call Doctor Macho." I left her to her phoning and checked the galley lockers for dinner material. Some of Jan's conversation drifted my way, but for once I didn't snoop. Maybe I *am* getting old.

I fixed another drink and went back out on deck. Fifteen minutes and big bucks worth of phone time later, Jan joined me.

"So, how's the wonderful world of Doctor Chino Yee?" I never tired of the irony of Chino, a Mexican, having the last name, Yee. Turns out he is descended from two shipwreck survivors from the Philippines, one named Camacho and the other, Yee. Any Asian facial features had long ago disappeared, but he was still a Yee, and bore the nickname, Chino.

"He's so excited about starting the dive, maybe even finding the galleon his ancestors arrived on. All those years of hearing the stories passed down through the generations, and he just might find something that belonged to one of them. It *is* pretty exciting, if you think about it."

I nodded. I thought being a ninth-generation Texan was a big deal, but Chino was searching for artifacts that actually belonged to his family in 1600. "I still deserve a reward for finding the astrolabe."

"Forget it."

"So, what else did our marine archeologist extraordinaire have to say?"

"Oh, nothing much."

One thing about being friends with someone for umpteen years is that you know evasive when you hear it. "*Fifteen* minutes worth of 'nothing much'?"

The other thing about having a friend who knows you know them is that they cave in easily because they know their lives will be miserable until they do. "Uh, well, you are not going to believe this, but that jerk, Dickless Richard, the one who tried to kill us? He's out of jail and all charges have been dropped against him."

"What? How can that be?"

"This is Mexico. Chino says there were no witnesses, just our word against his, and we weren't there to accuse him in court. Something in their court system."

"What about his plot to can whales for the Japanese?"

"Evidently the Japanese pleaded guilty, said Ricardo had nothing to do with their operation, which they also claim was hatched by a rogue employee of theirs who is being properly punished in Japan. They paid a big fine, gave their ship to Chino for the duration of the hunt for the galleon, and that's that."

"And?" I knew she was still holding back.

She sighed. "The turd tracked down Chino and apologized for the so-called unfortunate misunderstanding."

"Unfortunate misunderstanding? Ye gads, woman, he not only tried to kill us, he had Chino and Fabio slammed into the slammer. Unfortunate misunderstanding, my ass."

Jan did a quick, properly indignant, head snap. But I still smelled a rat.

"And?"

"Well, uh…okay. Chino has the feeling that Dickless is less than sorry."

I snorted. When Jan and I met the slimeball, it was hate at first sight. And when he said, in his oily way, "Please, call me Ricardo. Or Richard. But please do not call me Dick," we quite naturally nicknamed him Dickless Richard.

"And?"

"Jeez, Hetta, you just never give up, do you? Okay, here's the deal. Chino thought Dickless was not there to apologize at all, but to find out where you went."

My heart did a two-step. I gulped. "What did Chino tell him?"

"That you, and your boyfriend, the FBI agent, went back to California."

"Wow, that Chino is a fast study. We've only known him a short time and already he's a world class fibber. We have taught him well. However, I would have preferred that he tell Dickless Richard that Hetta Coffey, and Guido, her Mafia hit man boyfriend, were in Sicily."

We clinked glasses, finished our drinks while watching a spectacular sunset, then grilled a snapper and hit the hay.

For some reason it didn't occur to me that clouds to the West, thus the vivid sunset, could be less than a good omen.

13

Here's a quick weather lesson, should you someday cruise the Sea of Cortez. No one, and I mean no one, can predict the weather. John Steinbeck had it right when he said this sea is subject to sudden and violent storms.

To make things even more interesting, each anchorage is its own meteorological microcosm, and Punta Chivato, I soon learned, is famously unpredictable. A good shelter from a norther, or even passable in a southeasterly if you hugged up near the hotel, the anchorage, when hit with southwesterlies, is a whole 'nother deal.

Jan and I were rudely awakened just before dawn, when, of course, it is black as pitch. *Raymond Johnson* was sitting quietly at anchor one minute, then suddenly the bow swung toward the southwest and began bucking. By the time I reached the flying bridge, four footers crashed onto the rocks not all that far behind us.

Jan jammed herself in a stairwell and yelled, "Hetta, what's happening?"

"We gotta go, Jan. Come up here. I'll raise the anchor with the remote. If Jenks was here, he'd do it from the foredeck, but you can't do that and neither can I." I started the engines.

I knew, from experience, that I had to ease the tension on the chain and hope like hell the snubber hook would fall off. If not, I could only raise the anchor so far, leaving it to swing freely, possibly even punch a hole in the hull. There was one other, risky, move to free us. If I put even more tension on the chain, swung the boat in a large arc, stern to the wind and waves, I could gain momentary slack on the snubber, make it easier to remove by hand. The problem there is that halfway through the arc we get broadsided, and our stern gets walloped by tons of water while I endeavor to dislodge the anchor.

I opted to move forward, into the waves, and hope for the best, which would be *not* tearing out my bow pulpit and windlass, not losing the anchor, and not putting *Raymond Johnson* on the rocks in front of the hotel. A hotel I wished I was in.

As I struggled to maintain my cool while courting disaster, I recalled Jenks saying, "'You do remember that there is no Coast Guard to bail you out if you two have engine problems, or some other disaster? Which, knowing you, is an inevitability.'" And my answer, "'Oh, come on, Jenks, I'm hardly taking our lives in my hands, you know.'"

But I was. The only one enjoying this mess was Trouble, who sat on my shoulder and sang while I fought the wheel and played with the windlass to gain some ground, only to lose it when forced to release chain when the bow was literally jerked under a wave.

Jan had been through this kind of drill with me before. She dug out the life preservers and was trying to get one on me, but Trouble dug his talons into my shoulder and refused to let go, even when Jan called him a few choice names.

Lights came on at the hotel and we could make out the outlines of several people on the hotel verandah, drawn from their comfortable beds by clanking chains, roaring engines and a bird belting out *The Yellow Rose of Texas*.

"At least if we wash up on shore there'll be someone there to drag us out of the water," Jan shouted above the noise.

"We aren't going to wash up on shore. We're out of here in a jiffy, don't worry," I told her while trying to control the tremor in my voice, sound confident.

"Can I do anything?"

"When was the last time you chatted with a deity?"

"Last time I went anywhere with you."

"Smarty. Start chatting."

Her lips moved and whoever she was talking to must have listened, for I caught a trough just right, dislodged the anchor and brought in enough chain to get it off the bottom, then, ever so slowly, we motored forward while bringing in scope. It was a tricky maneuver; too much chain would let the anchor catch bottom again, not enough could smack the anchor into the hull and hole us.

After what seemed an eternity, but was probably only three minutes, we cleared the breaker line where the swells were no more than two or three feet, and the boat settled out. I had Jan hold us steady while I went out on the bow and brought the anchor into her chocks.

We motored into the wind until first light, then turned around and made for the point, rounded it, and found a safe spot in a small cove to re-anchor just as the sun came over the horizon. On rubbery legs, we went below into what was formerly my beautiful main saloon.

"Holy moly! No wonder Trouble took a powder. Look at his cage." I righted the cage, reinserted his perch and began removing his food dishes. Smashed bananas, shredded hot peppers and bird poop littered my rug. Trouble squawked and flew to inspect his domain, found it unsuitable for his sophisticated tastes, and began shrieking again. Jan, wise to his ways, broke into the chorus from the River City song, and he joined her. It was amazing what a beautiful voice he had. Someone, at sometime in his life, was a talented baritone. I swear, when that bird sings *Danny Boy*, his eyes get misty.

While we straightened up the saloon and scrubbed gunk from the carpet, we took turns prompting Trouble to sing songs we only knew parts of, but he knew in full. His *Havah Nagilah* was as rousing as his *Someday My Prince Will Come* was sentimental. And he had his own rendition of one of my favorites, *How Much is That Birdie in the Window?*

"Ya know, Hetta, maybe you should sell this scow and take Trouble on the road, make a fortune renting him out for black tie dinners, weddings and bar mitzvahs. She'll be coming round the mountain..."

"When she comes," chorused Trouble. Trouble's antics, along with the giddiness one experiences when surviving a crisis, sent Jan and me into hysterics. I wiped away tears and then spotted the clock. It was time for the Sonrisa Net, and I wanted to grouse at someone for being sooo wrong with yesterday's weather call. Northers were predicted, southerlies damned near put us on the rocks. Jan and I listened as boats reported in from all over the sea. Absolutely no one experienced southerlies. In fact, everything was Charlie Charlie, meaning Clear and Calm.

I shrugged and shushed Jan—who began pontificating loudly on how I, Hetta Coffey, was probably the only person on the entire planet who could conjure up her own personal storm—so I could hear the day's forecast. The consensus was that it was going to blow hard from the north and since we had to go north, I started the engines. In less than three hours we'd be in Santa Rosalia, at a dock. Then, let 'er blow.

14

And boy, did she *blow*.

We had barely secured our lines at the Santa Rosalia marina when a blast of wind rocked the harbor, instantly raising little whitecaps. Grateful to be safe, I sent thanks upward for getting me into port by the hair on my chinny chin chin, before the big bad wolf of a norther huffed and puffed and blew me away. Okay, so the hair on my chin has long since been lasered into oblivion, but the metaphor works.

Speaking of, should we call our guys?"

"You go ahead, I think I'll let Jenks stew a little. *He* can call *me*."

Jan tried the Mexican cell phone, but received no signal. I fired up the Satfone system. "Make it short, Jan, this damned thing costs me a fortune. Are you going to tell Chino we're trekking over to Agua Fria by car, dropping in to visit old Grandmaw Yee?"

"I think I'll surprise him."

"Are you even going to tell him we're at Punta Chivato?"

"Actually, I think I'll just leave the impression we're still on the other side. I don't suppose he'd be too pleased at the idea of us running loose all over the Baja."

"Spoken like a true little Mexican fianceé."

"I just don't want him to worry, that's all."

"What's with these men of ours? It isn't as if we're helpless idiots."

We were back in Cellular Land, for my phone, and Trouble, began chirping *La Cucaracha*. "Hola," I said, sticking my finger in my ear to block Trouble.

"Hetta?" said the Trob.

"Who else?"

"Turn down that radio. Where are you? I called the marina when you didn't answer your phone, and they said your boat was gone."

Amazing. Not that he'd learned I was gone, but that he managed such a long, non-cryptic, sentence. He's come a long way in the years I've known him, but is making quantum leaps into basic social skills since marrying my friend Allison.

"Jan and I took her out. Why did you call?"

"Google alert."

Back to cryptic.

"Google alert?"

"Your article."

"My article?" Jan sidled up once she figured I was talking with the Trob. She takes perverse pleasure in listening while I strive to pry basic info from Wontrobski. I rolled my eyes at her and sighed. "Could you tell me *what* article?"

"*Chronicle.*"

"As in, *San Francisco Chronicle*? Again, what article? And what in the hell is a Google alert?" My voice had gone up a couple of octaves and I was knocking my head up against the wall, delighting Jan no end.

"When something I am interested in hits the Internet, Google alerts me."

"And what was your interest?"

"Puerto Nuevo Tucson-Guaymas Corridor."

"Hey, I think I'll sign up for that Google thing. Matter of fact, I was gonna call you today. I can send you a preliminary report with photos in a few minutes, then finish up the end of next week."

"Already have some photos."

How could that be? Jan and I hadn't sent them to anyone except…oh, dear.

"Wontrobski, are you telling me that the article I wrote for some obscure newspaper in some obscure Arizona berg is in the *Chronicle*?"

"Internet. Check it out."

"I will. Bye."

"Bye."

While Jan watched, I pulled up the San Francisco Chronicle and sure as hell, there was my article and Jan's photos, under the caption, **ARIZONA TO DUMP CALIFORNIA PORTS**, with the sub-caption: **Nuevo Puerto de Guyamas and Tucson: Arizona's new deep water port?**

"Hetta, you're famous!" Jan shrieked, then began reading aloud. "'Sierra Vista Dispatch reporter, Hetta Coffey, has uncovered a secret deal being forged between Arizona and the state of Sonora, Mexico—'"

"Secret deal? What in the hell are they talking about? I only took the studies done by others, as well as, I might add, published newspaper articles written about the project, and compiled them. This lead-in makes it seem like I've uncovered some sinister plot to overthrow California."

We read the rest of the article together, which consisted of my byline and the piece just as I wrote it, but then, with dramatic flare, ended with, *Ms. Coffey could not be reached for further comment.*

The phone rang again, and this time it was Jenks.

"Hetta, you're on CNN."

"What?"

"They had a camera crew and reporter on site, in Guaymas, interviewing the port captain. And looking for you. Where are you?"

"Er, on the boat."

"I called the marina when you didn't answer your cell phone. You, and the boat, are not there."

Jeez, did the marina office have to blab to everyone I know? "Well, Jan—"

"Hold on, they are saying something about…you're in Santa Rosalia?"

"How did you know that?"

"Port Captain just said so, on TV."

"Good grief, who in the world gives a damn where I am?"

"Me, for one, and CNN. They make it sound like you've uncovered some big secret scheme. Is your satellite TV working?"

"I don't know. I've never used it."

"Go online, CNN's site, and you can see the report on video. We'll talk about this Santa Rosalia thing later. I'm just glad you're safe. Love you."

"Love you, too. Bye."

An hour later, Jan and I were giggling into our wine, reveling in the brouhaha we'd stirred up. By now I was an "investigative reporter for the award winning Sierra Vista Dispatch," and Jan was an "internationally acclaimed photog." We'd *broken* the story after months of undercover work in both Mexico and Arizona.

"To our fifteen minutes of fame!" I toasted.

"Think we should write something else? Maybe how you single-handedly uncovered the wreck of the Spanish galleon, *San Carlos*?"

I guffawed. "Along with my fellow researcher, that renowned marine archeologist, Doctor Jan Simms?"

Laughter tears rolled as we conjured up wilder and wilder scenarios, until we noticed other boaters eyeing us warily. "Sorry," I waved at them, "we're just…being silly. Hey, do you know if they have TV in this town?"

A tall sailboater, fiftyish, without the prerequisite beard so many sported, sauntered over and leaned on the rail. Peeking shyly from behind him was a sweet-faced white West Highland terrier. Her ears were on alert, and her tail wagged hesitantly. She turned her head quizzically, as if trying to decide whether we were friendly, or just plain nuts. And whether the bird on my head was edible.

The sailor patted the dog's silky back, and she leaned into his leg for reassurance. He gave her ears a rub and said, "Seems to me like you two are having way too much fun. Can we get in on it?"

This sent us into another spate of laughter. The dog looked worried, so when I could control myself I said, "Sorry, you had to be there." We introduced ourselves.

"Nice boat. I'm Smith, and this is Maggie. Our boat is *Taiwan On*."

"Clever. Well, hello Smith and Maggie. Come on aboard and have a cool one."

Jan shot me a frown, which I ignored. She never understands my lack of discrimination when it comes to meeting new people, and even accuses me of lax judgment on occasion. This time though, my friend fell for the charms of Maggie after the dog scampered onto the boat, jumped right into her lap and demanded a tummy rub.

Trouble went airborne and for one horrible instant I thought he was on the attack, but no, he landed daintily on Maggie's head. This gave me a momentary fright as well, for a dog, even one so small and diffident, can do grave bodily damage with a single chomp, but the two became instant friends.

Smith's easy, guileless manner soon convinced Jan he was simply a guy who, when he had a chance, loaded up his dog and set sail. The Sea of Cortez is full of folks who follow their dream of getting down to the twos: two pairs of shorts, two swim suits and two pairs of flip-flops, in case one pair has a blowout. One of my favorite things about the cruisers is their lack of interest over what is happening back home. Except for the occasional case of boat envy, there are no Joneses to keep up with. The main topic of conversation is food, and where to get it. My kind of place.

In that vein, Smith invited us for an *Exquisito* hot dog dinner at a small stand in town. The hot dog vendor's cart is in front of a church designed by the famous French designer, Gustav Eiffel, no less. The Santa Barbara "Cathedral," pre-constructed over a period of two years for display at the World Exposition in Paris in 1889, was later deconstructed and shipped to Santa Rosalia. In 1895 it was erected by the French miners who worked here during the town's hey day as a mining center. Both the church and the hot dogs are truly *exquisito*.

Since Smith had been in town for a week, he was thereby a local expert. He pointed out the quaint mining houses, a bakery that actually makes French baguettes to this day, and the Mahatma Gandhi—go figure—Library. I noticed that many of the people living here had fair skin and blue eyes, no doubt a direct result of former imported miners and sailors.

"Cute town," Jan said as we prepared to hit the sack. While I closed all hatches and doors, she shut down lights, radios, and the like.

"Cute guy."

"One word. Jenks."

"Jeez, Jan, I was just making an observation, not a life changing decision. And don't tell me you weren't entranced by that silky hair and beautiful brown eyes."

"Nope. Nor did I take note of that amazingly rounded, taut butt."

"I was talking about the dog."

"Sure you were."

We chuckled together. "Want a nightcap?"

I burped a little *Exquisito con* relish*, mayonaisa y salsa Mexicana*. "Sure."

We settled on the back deck where we had protection from the wind that still howled, and watched fishing pangas buzz in and out of port, their occupants decked out in yellow slickers against the salt spray and chilly air. "What do you think they're catching?"

"Someone said squid." I sniffed the air. "I detect the stench of a packing plant north of us. Luckily this wind is blowing the stink right past us. When this storm is over, pray for a southerly."

"I'm surprised they're going out fishing on such an ugly night, but I guess they have to earn a living. Tough life, but Chino says many would rather fish than work on someone's payroll and time clock."

"I can relate to that. Speaking of work, ya think we should hire a publicity agent? I mean, now that we're world famous and all."

"Naw, I think our fifteen minutes is up, what with fame being the fickle thing it is."

"I sure hope so. Well, kiddo, I'm plumb tuckered." I stood and stretched. "See you *mañana*."

"I'm turning in, too. Oh, look, the ferry is still trying to dock. Man, oh, man, am I glad I'm not on that sucker. Even with last night's little fire drill, I'm so glad you brought me over."

"Wait'll you get my bill, then see how grateful you are."

"Yeah, well, we can trade invoices. I think I can work up quite a jerky tab for yon critter you're dumping on me."

Touché. We watched as the ferry boat captain gave up on entering the harbor. He went a little off shore, outside the breakwater and either dropped the hook or continued motoring to hold position into the seas. I took one last look out my porthole before drifting off, and could still see his running lights out there, as he waited for the wind to die down, Sometime during the night I was half awakened by loud speakers, so I figured they made it in.

Snuggling my pillow in my warm bed, in the safety of a marina, the windstorm outside didn't seem quite so bad. I stretched and smiled, thinking, *Somewhat like the stupid news storm Jan and I stirred up. No wonder no one takes the news seriously these days if we can make the CNN headlines! What a joke.*

15

"You've got to be joking." Jan's voice, especially the slightly hysterical timbre, half- woke me from a fantasy dream where Jenks, RJ and I were swimming with dolphins. Spending time frolicking with my deceased dog was so special that I fought to recapture the dream, not wake up. But then Jan was bellowing through my open bedroom door—the one I should have locked—"Hetta, dammit! You get up here right this minute. We have company."

My eyes flew open and RJ and the dolphins dissolved. The sun was fairly high in the sky, and the wind had picked up again. I'd slept in my favorite foul weather warmies, a red oversize tee shirt with white stripes on its long sleeves, and even though it covered my knees, I grabbed a pair of sweats from the closet. Company? That called for a splash of cold water on the face, and a smear of Harlot Red across my lips. I slipped on my red plastic clogs, noted the clash with the yellow sweats, didn't really give a damn, and stomped up into the main saloon. It was full of people. People with cameras. Jan cringed in the galley as flash bulbs blinded me.

"What the hell?" was all I could manage. I spun around and headed for the safety of my cabin, but Jan was too fast for me.

She death-gripped my arm and bleated, "Oh, no, you don't. You are *not* leaving me with these…these…*people*."

"Who are these, these, people? And what are they doing on my boat?" And as I said it, I realized, *Hey, wait a minute. This* is *my boat.* I stepped around Jan and commanded, "Okay, everybody off. Now!"

Bright camera lights flooded the cabin as a tangle of questions were thrown our way. With everyone talking at once, it was impossible to make out a single question, but one thing was clear; they were from CNNI and they wanted info on the Tucson Corridor.

"Uh, Hetta," Jan yelled above the questioning, "I sort of told them they could come aboard, but I didn't realize who they were. Sorry."

"Well, then, you can entertain them. Cook them breakfast or something. I'm going back to bed."

"Wait for me."

We scrambled into my master stateroom and slammed and locked the door. Trapped like rats, we were trying to figure out what to do next when there was a loud screech, a bunch of screaming and yelling, and the stomp of feet exiting the boat, fast. When things quieted down, Trouble broke into a hearty rendition of "Hetta, Hetta, she's our gal. If she can't do it, no one shall."

We returned to the emptied main saloon and peered out. On the dock, what had seemed an army of reporters was really only four. One female talking head and three crew camped on our dock. A couple of them plucked feathers from their hair, while the reporter babe from, where else? CNNI, dabbed bird poop from her blouse.

I tickled Trouble's neck feathers and gave him a piece of apple. "What a sweet little press agent you are," I cooed. He blushed and ducked his head for more scratching. I have to admit, I was growing quite fond of him. He flew back outside, where the press dudes and dudette, for lack of anything better to do, filmed him as he loudly demanded, "Oh Boy! Oberto."

With no clever ideas of my own, I called the Trob and told him we had the press on our tails. I thought he'd blow a fuse, or what passes for anger with him, but he sounded pleased.

"You mean you're not upset with me for outing the project?"

"No. Baxters like it."

I've known the Trob many a year, so I knew what he meant. Scary. "I haven't blown the project? I'm not fired? I thought the brothers Baxter would be royally pissed since it seemed they wanted to wrap up my study on the QT before it was universally known this was gonna be a go."

"No."

Jan, who could see I was struggling for aplomb, shoved a cup of coffee in my hand. I shoved it back and she added a splash of Irish Whisky. I took a deep breath and a big glug. "No?"

"Not upset. Glad. Now the politicians are all behind the idea, saying, quote, 'Splendid example of international cooperation in light of our other differences.'"

"Let me guess, those are Republican politicians. What's the other side saying?"

"They're afraid to say anything. Check out the Internet."

"I will. What should I tell these news hounds?"

"The truth?"

"What a novel idea. I will. Thanks, I guess. Bye."

"Bye."

I fired up the computer and read today's headlines. All I wanted to be was *yesterday's* headlines, but it was not in the cards. "Oooh, Jan. As of twenty minutes ago, this is what we looked like." And sure enough, there we were, white faced, hair askew. Caption: *Hetta Coffey and Jan Sims, tracked down on Ms. Coffey's yacht in Santa Rosalia, Mexico, minutes before attacking reporters. CNNI 20 minutes ago.*

"Oh, boy," Jan said, "What's CNNI?"

"It's CNN International. I get it on cable at home. This is going out all over the world."

"I wish I'd had my hair done. And Hetta," she giggled, "is that you, or Ronald McDonald?"

The resemblance was uncanny. With my red striped tee shirt, yellow sweats, fuchsia hair, red clogs, and crimson lips, all I required to complete my Ronald McDonald look was a Big Mac in my hand. We were still howling with glee when Mother called.

"Hetta Honey, stripes? You know they make you look, uh, shorter."

"You mean fatter, don't you? Jan thinks I look like Ronald McDonald."

Mother hiccuped a little chuckle, told Daddy what I'd said, then asked, "What on earth are you doin' on the morning news in your PJ's? You and your father may think it's funny, but knowing you, there is a lot more to this story than they are telling on CNN. Are you in trouble, again?"

"No, Mama, you know how the news blows everything out of proportion. By tomorrow, the world will forget I was ever on the screen. Believe me, there is no secret plot and once these folks do their homework, they'll find out for themselves. This project proposal I'm working on has already been in the works for years. This CNN thing is a tempest in a teapot."

"Well, if you say so. Seems to me you could have put on a dress or somethin'," she drawled. Mother doesn't even leave the bedroom in the morning without combed hair and complete makeup, and she dons Liz Claiborne for breakfast. "Who did you attack?"

"Didn't. It was your bird. Trouble cleared those reporters from my boat in a jiffy. I'm gonna miss him when Jan takes him home with her tomorrow."

"Jan's coming to Texas and bringing the parrot?"

I always forget that "home" means Texas to a Texan. "Her new home, here in Mexico. She'll keep him until we come up with a more permanent solution. I don't suppose you've heard anything more from Aunt Lil?"

"I thought maybe you'd found her by now."

"Mama, she's in Mazatlan and I'm in Santa Rosalia."

"You told me you were in San Carlos."

Uh-oh. It's times like this that require creative prevarication. Mother would pitch a Texas hissy fit if she found out Jan and I had crossed an entire sea by ourselves, so I crossed my fingers. "Not far from there." Not a bald faced lie, as we were located somewhere between *both* San Carloses. Mexico is in dire need of some new saints to name their towns after.

"Well, it *sounds* like everything is all right. I'll call Jan's mother and tell her that, if you like."

"That would be great, thanks."

"You girls have a good time. We miss you."

"We miss you too. Love you."

"Love you, too. Bye now."

"Bye."

"Not far from where?" Jan asked.

"San Carlos. Technically, that's true."

"Technically. Hetta, we're all over the news. What if she tries to find us on a map?"

"She won't. They're on the road. She's calling your mom to let her know this whole thing is bogus."

"Good. Now, what are you going to do about those reporters out there?"

"Hose 'em down?"

"That'll look good on the five o'clock report."

"Okay, okay. Let's get dolled up and hold a press conference. Mother thinks I should wear a dress, but I don't have one on the boat."

"What are we going to say?"

"The truth."

Jan fell on the floor, convulsed with glee. What a cynic.

16

It's amazing how, if you tell the truth, people lose interest, especially when the truth is really boring. So I gave the reporters a very long, tedious, and technical version of the truth, and my part in it. One of the cameramen practically fell asleep, and the poor reporter babe did her best to get in a provocative question or two, but I droned on, and on, and on.

Boring or not, I thought Jan and I presented yachtily intellectual personas for what I hoped was our last interview. Dressed in white slacks, turtlenecks and navy blazers, donning drugstore cheaters for effect, our last fifteen minutes of fame fizzled the second the camera lights went out. Once the reporters learned that I had written the newspaper article based on well-known, documented research that they could check for themselves, their interest fizzled, but they couldn't figure out a way to politely shut me up. The fact that the Guaymas/ Tucson port deal had been in the making for years was, well, old news. Boring engineering stuff. No scandal. No hanky panky. In effect, no news at all.

The rather disheveled reporter gal did comment on the fact that we were two women alone on a yacht, thinking perhaps there was a story there, but we intimated that our husbands were out fishing. I think she at least hoped we were lesbians.

In desperate search of a news lead, she asked to interview Trouble. As I felt a little sorry for this woman who had obviously spent the night on a tossing ferry in search of her big break, I encouraged Trouble to talk, sing his signature song, then wolf whistle and squawk, "Oh boy! Oberto," for a finale. After heavy editing in lieu of bleeps, Trouble earned a thirty second spot on CNN. Jan and I were five second has-beens.

Fame really is a fleeting thing.

Now that we were once again mere mortals instead of international celebs, we fostered a plan to find Granny Yee.

Jan called Chino and casually grilled him if he'd heard anything from his grandmother, and whether he was the only one on the planet who didn't know we were big news. Nothing from Grans Yee, and not a hint he'd seen us on TV. We were golden on that end.

We needed a car, preferably a tank. Our sailboater friend, Smith, volunteered the use of his pickup, which we gratefully accepted, even after seeing the antiquated Ford. Beggers cannot be choosers, they say, and Santa Rosalia was devoid of car rental agencies.

Early the next morning, we loaded up a change of clothes, a roll of toilet paper—we'd learned from experience that public restrooms in Mexico seldom have paper—a couple of gallons of water, a map of Baja, and Trouble. I didn't have the heart to leave him locked up in the boat for who knew how long.

By some miracle, the old Ford truck chugged along just fine. We weren't in a hurry, so we stopped off at Burro Beach in Conception Bay for breakfast at Bertha's, a small café we'd eaten in years before, while on a kayak trip. Conception Bay, like everywhere else in the world, was becoming more populated, but their saving grace was still not having electricity. We even ran into an old friend, Baja Geary, who actually remembered us. Well, he remembered Jan, but who wouldn't. His palapa beach home had undergone some updates, including one of those new composting toilets and satellite Internet service, but little else had changed.

As we drove south, I wondered aloud, "Jan, ya think you could live here, like Geary does, year round?"

"I plan to, with Chino."

"Yeah, but you guys will be on the west coast. Down here it gets really, really hot. No electricity, which means zero air conditioning. It would be like living in Houston with no AC."

"I don't think I could do that."

"Me neither. At least Geary can go sit in the water, but even the bay water is ninety or higher in summer. Remember the year before you got a decent job, and you lived in student housing? No AC, with cockroaches that needed license plates?" I shuddered, recalling a visit I'd paid her one weekend. Ended up checking into a hotel when, in the middle of the night, I flipped on the kitchen lights and hundreds of monstrous roaches scattered, a couple of them running over my feet.

"What a hell hole. Who was that guy you—*tope*

* * *

The nice Mexican family who towed us into Loreto, where we could buy two new tires to replace the oddly bulging ones we dared not drive on after hitting a speed bump at forty miles an hour, seemed totally perplexed that two gringas were wandering around Baja alone. They were terrified of Trouble, even though he made no move to attack. I had revised my thinking on his selective attacks, deciding they had more to do with protecting me than an abiding hatred for Mexican men. Time would tell.

Trouble was having a grand old time. He, Jan, and I settled into the bed of what had to be a 1940s Chevy truck that was in some sort of reincarnated state, reborn with spare parts from other dead vehicles. No two fenders or doors were the same color. Every time we hit a bump, rust rained down in powdery form. I won't even bother describing the tires. We prattled down the road at a breathtaking five miles per hour, with Trouble singing his heart out above the clatter.

From our vantage point in the rotting wooden truck bed, we'd watch cars and SUVs, mostly with US plates, roar up behind us doing eighty or ninety, pass us like we were in reverse, most times on a continuous stripe. There were several close calls when an oncoming bus or semi sent them swerving back within a hair of our rear bumper. To save on nerves, I closed my eyes and kept them that way until, eons later, we were cut lose at *la llanteria*.

The owner of the tire repair shop sold me practically new retreads for thirty bucks apiece, but felt Smith's axel or somesuch was bent, and repairs could take a day or two. Or three. *Mañana*, at any rate. We grabbed a taxi to the airport.

Lucky for us, we just beat a deplaning load of tourists to the Budget desk. Well, I did. After the verbal set-to with the taxi driver over taking Trouble on as a passenger, I felt the car rental folks needn't know about my feathery compadre. I left Jan and the parrot outside while I acquired a nifty little Neon, appropriately named if the iridescent blue paint job was any indication. Iridescence was becoming a way of life, first on my hair, and now my car.

I wondered what this shiny new paint job would look like after we returned from Agua Fria. *If* we made it to Agua Fria.

Forty-five minutes later, we streaked by the turnoff, skidded to a stop, made a U-turn on a particularly nasty curve, narrowly missed getting creamed by a Canadian RV, and read the sign. Agua Fria 41km.

"Forty-one kilometers. Hetta, that's uh…"

"Twenty-five and a half miles, or right at it."

"Twenty-five miles of *bad* road."

"Hey, you're the one who wants to go there. I'd just as soon return to Loreto, check into a hotel, have a Margarita."

Trouble broke into song. Above an earsplitting rendition of "…wastin' away in Margaritaville," Jan yelled, "Put a sock in it, bird. Agua Fria, here we come."

We found the rockslide thirty kidney-jarring minutes, and three miles, later. Checking for a detour around the slide, it was obvious that, with something a tad sturdier than a lunar rover, we might get to the other side. Certainly not in a Neon, even if it was a rental.

"So much for Granny Yee."

"Oh, well, we tried. Chino will be so disappointed."

"Might I remind you that Chino does not know we're here? Where's the disappointment?"

"I wanted to surprise him."

"You wanted to get old Gran's approval of your precious self."

"And that."

"Well, for what it's worth— What's that noise?"

The distinctive boom of subwoofers suddenly filled the desert, followed by the thunder of a fast moving vehicle. Jan screamed and shoved me to the ground just as a jacked up muscle truck literally flew over our heads. Trouble took flight as if to dive bomb the vehicle when he could catch it, which was going to be very soon, as the truck landed smack dab on top of the Neon.

Screeching music, screeching bird, screeching metal, then, except for the whir of tires spinning in the air, and the hiss of escaping steam, all was quiet.

"Holy crappola!"

"I couldn't have said it better. Wonder if they're alive?"

"If they are, Trouble seems set on making them wish they weren't. You grab Trouble before he bites someone. I'll check the truck."

Jan whistled for the parrot, who obediently returned to her shoulder, and the shirt pocket where she kept peanuts.

I walked toward the wreck. Wrecks. "*Hola*. Hello, anybody in there?"

Nothing. I smelled gas.

Now, in Hollyweird, someone rushes to the trapped victim, breaks out the window, hauls the unconscious body to safety, just as the car explodes. In real life, it ain't that easy. For starters, I couldn't even reach the door.

"Hello!" I yelled, louder. "Hey! Wake up."

Nothing.

Jan, who was at a higher vantage point, hollered, "Hetta, there's a guy in the driver's seat, but I don't see anyone else."

"Is he moving?"

"No. Wait, yes, he's trying to open the door. You'd better move—"

I didn't hear the rest of that, because I was too busy

dodging the truck door that fell from its hinges, damned near flattening me. Following the heavy door, the driver landed with a rib-cracking thud that knocked the air from his lungs. He sat up, wild eyed and gasping for breath as I grabbed his shirt collar in an attempt to pull him clear. He fought me, so I let go and snarled, "Okay, you jerk, crawl out of this mess by yourself." If he was in need of Florence damned Nightingale, he'd picked on the wrong dame.

I stomped away until he gasped, "No, please, wait. Help me."

"You won't fight?"

"No. I…can't."

He was a fairly big guy, and dead weight, to boot. Jan scrambled down the hill and, between the two of us and a peck or two of "encouragement" from Trouble, we dragged him fifty feet from the—yep, just like the movies—explosion.

A wave of heat sucked the oxygen out of the air, and the percussion, or rather percussions, knocked us flat. Trouble took to the air and disappeared over a hill.

"Holy shit!" Jan yelled.

"Ditto," I said. Actually, I didn't hear her so much as read her lips. My ears rang like church bells. "Somebody heard that blast, don't you think?" I pointed at the black plume of smoke soaring into the blue sky, "Or at least they'll see the smoke."

"Huh?"

Jan was as deafened as I was. I waved her off. "Never mind." I sat on a rock and waited for my ears to clear. Jan went in search of Trouble, but came back alone.

"Don't you worry," I told her, "he's not that easy to get rid of."

As we hoped, the smoke plume, visible for miles, brought help. Within a half hour, while Jan and I tried to decide on a plan, we heard engines and then two more pickups flew over the slide, barely missing the tangle of smoldering metal. Our luck had changed.

Or had it? With a sinking heart, I recognized the drivers. I mean, who could forget the handsome one?

I sincerely hoped they hadn't taken offense when we threatened them with a gaff and a flare gun at Isla San Francisco. I'd offer them some gas, but mine blew up.

17

"ann-Jay."

"Huh?"

"An-Jay. Isten-lay. E-way ont-day eek-spay nglis-eh." I was never good with words starting in vowels in Pig Latin.

"E-way ont-day?"

"O-nay."

She shrugged, awaiting my lead. If I said we didn't speak English, she probably figured there was a reason.

The guy we dragged out of the wreck was barely conscious by the time his buddies arrived. His friend dumped bottled water over his head, then discussed, with furtive glances in our direction, what to do with Jan and me. Little did they know I possess extrasensory ears, even when they ring a bit.

"It's that redheaded bitch from the yacht."

I need to think about trying a less flamboyant *coiffure*.

"Oh, yeah, I remember *her*. But she ain't got no flare gun, or boyfriend, this time. Just the dish."

Jan heard the dish part and plumped her hair, until she remembered she didn't speak English.

"Think she remembers us?"

Handsome shrugged. "What's it matter? Question is, what's she *doing* here?"

"Let's just off 'em, plant 'em in the desert and be done with it."

I gulped and tried to look nonchalant, but it's hard to do when someone is talking about doing you in and leaving you for buzzard fodder.

"Don't think we oughta do that unless we check with the boss."

"What will he care?"

"What if these two told someone where they were going? Could bring in the heat." I was warming up to the handsome one's sense of reason.

"We own the heat. Hell, we *are* the stinkin' heat."

"But we're dealin' with foreigners here, not a bunch of ignorant fishermen."

I suddenly remembered their names. Nacho and Paco. Nacho of the Calvin Klein look, Paco of the weird druggie persona.

Whatever was going on in Agua Fria was obviously not going to do much for their Chamber of Commerce ads. Visit Beautiful Agua Fria by the Sea, Owned and Operated by goons.

And now that they mentioned it, who *had* we told we were going to Agua Fria? Okay, there was Smith, the sailor back in Santa Rosalia. And Geary, the guy who lives at Conception Bay. He's a ham operator; if we didn't come back, would he put out an alert on us? We told him we'd stop back by, and the way he was eyeing Jan, I figured he'd be looking for us. But then maybe he'd just think we passed by when he was gone. Who else? Certainly not Budget. Far as they knew, we rented a car to pop over to Lopez Mateos, get in some whale time. To paraphrase Leonard Bernstein, why-o, why-o, why-o, did we ever leave the boat-o?

The man we saved was coming around, shooting menacing glares in our direction. He croaked something to his friends, who glanced our way, then they huddled and broke into Spanglish. I couldn't hear it all, but what I picked up was, "Stupid *putas…mi trucke!*"

The ungrateful wretch. We save his life and he calls us whores. *Stupid* whores, at that.

"An-Jay, et-gay eddy-ray oo-tay un-ray."

"Er-why?"

Where to run, indeed? I surveyed the desolation surrounding us. It was miles back to the main road. Jan could probably jog it, but I knew I couldn't. Hell, I probably couldn't *walk* it.

"Damned if I know." It-shay. The at-cay is out of the ag-bay.

Three heads snapped around and six sets of suspicious eyes zeroed in. The one we'd pulled from his wrecked truck growled, "See, I told you they spoke English. I remember them yelling at me."

Jan looked indignant at his obvious lack of gratitude. "Yeah, then we saved your sorry ass in spite of yourself." With her hands planted on her hips and yards of tanned legs showing from under her short shorts, Jan managed, despite scratches, dust and disheveled hair, to look sexy.

From their grins, Paco and Nacho seemed to think so, too. Paco shot a hip forward in what is probably some Latino move designed to look manly and drawled, "I'd say Blondie's got your *numero*, Chingo."

Well, well, well. Paco, Nacho and Chingo. Wonder where

they left Taco? I'd say East LA was certainly well-represented in Agua Fria.

Chingo snarled at Paco, "*Hermano,* you got a chitty attitude."

"Hey, turds for brains, I ain't the one who got us into this mess."

"Me? They's the ones sittin' in the middle of the fuggin' road."

"Would you like my fuggin' insurance card, *hermano?*" I threw in.

Jan sniggered, Paco took a menacing step in my direction, but Nacho broke into a belly laugh and pointed at me. "You got some *cajones* on you, gringa. First you threaten us"—he pronounced it trettin'—"with a flare gun, and now you want to exchange insurance cards? What are you, some kind of nut case?"

Jan shot me a squint and a shrug, as in *what flare gun?*

She'd have to wait for the rest of the story. I pulled a business card from my pocket, where I always keep money, cards and an ID, because you just never know when you'll need it. Them. Like when your car blows up? I offered the card. "Hetta Coffey, *Sierra Vista Dispatch.* And you are just the guys we're looking for."

Paco swaggered my way, snatched the card, and gave his buddies a, *this should be good,* look.

I hurried to make it good. "We're on a special assignment to find the best off-road Baja destinations, and judging by those nifty looking trucks, you guys know your off-road. No sissy-assed dune buggies here, nothing but macho trucks and macho dudes. Well, except for old Chingo there. Don't suppose we should feature him, ya think, Jan?"

"I guess *not*," Jan huffed. "He blew up my camera." Then, picking up my drift, she added, "So, what you got in there?"

She lowered her eyes to Nacho's crotch for a couple of beats, then pointed to his bright yellow pickup, "a four fifty four?"

Good question, but did Jan have any idea what she was talking about. What's a four fifty four, anyway?

Nacho gave her a once-over slowly, then grinned. "Naw, three twenty seven."

I had to remember to give Jan a raise. Hoping the men were uncertain about their next move, I rushed in with, "Perfect, you and your trucks. Just what we're looking for. Only thing is, we have to get back to Loreto, report the accident. You know, what if I just say the car blew up by itself? That way, my rental insurance will take care of the Neon."

"What about *mi trucke*," Chingo whined.

"What about it? After all, you plowed into a parked vehicle. If I were you, I wouldn't push the issue."

He balled his fists. "I'll tell you what I'll push—"

Nacho grabbed his arm. "Easy, *compadre*, the gringa might be right. With the boss gone, I think we'd better just let things go for now. Cool your jets."

Chingo looked for a second as though he was going to challenge Nacho, but he must have thought better of it, because he threw his hands up in a disgusted "whatever" gesture. Now I knew who was in charge.

Nacho walked over to us. "Okay, here's what we'll do. We'll take you to Agua Fria with us, and you can call your rental company."

This is *not* what I wanted to hear. I saw that Oprah show, the one where we learned, in a possible hostage situation, to never, ever, let them take you to a second location. Never.

"That's a great idea," Jan piped up, leading me to believe that the explosion had rattled more than her ears. My mouth must have dropped open, for she pulled her lips in to signal me to shut mine, a code we'd used for years. I reluctantly let her go on. "I mean, we did want to go to Agua Fria, and even though I lost my camera, we can at least do interviews, stuff like that. We'll get the story, take photos later."

They must have thought we didn't hear their earlier discussion—the one where they converted us to carrion— because they seemed to buy Jan's insane agreement.

I was on the verge of throttling my best friend, who smiled sweetly at Nacho while Paco helped Chingo into his truck. Before I could grab her by her swanlike neck, she winked at me, then turned and batted her Betty Boops, wiggled her butt and cooed, "Can we ride with you, Nacho? Your friend," she lowered her voice to a whisper, "well, he sorta stinks of smoke and gasoline."

"Chur. Hey, guys," he yelled, "the ladies are with me. Lead the way."

Still thinking it was a really bad idea, but totally out of my own, I climbed into the jump seat in the extended cab while Jan hoisted herself into the passenger side bucket seat. Even as worried as I was about our chances of surviving another day, I had to admire the interior. It was immaculate, with snazzy black carpeting and leather seats.

Nacho started the truck, waited until Paco's red Jeep disappeared over the hill, then rolled forward. Jan scooched closer to him—no easy task with the gear shifters rising from the floor—put her hand on his arm, managed a delicate cough, and gave his bicep a squeeze. "Can't we wait for their dust to blow away?" she purred, "it makes me all yucky."

"Chur. Don' want you yucky, Blondie."

"And I could use some water. How about you, Hetta?'

"Chur, *Blondie*," I muttered.

Nacho cranked up the sub-woofers to the threshold of pain before hopping out and heading toward the cooler in the truckbed. His feet had barely hit the ground when Jan slid over the gear shifts, into the driver's seat. Catching her movement in his peripheral vision, Nacho whirled around and frowned, but Jan threw those long legs out the door while managing to hike up her shorts. "Hey," she said, "could you make that a beer, if it's not too much Trouble?" She let loose with an earsplitting wolf whistle, which Nacho seemed to think was meant for him..

"No problem," he said with a grin, and managed a half-turn towards the cooler before he was whacked in the forehead with enough force to knock him backward, onto his butt. He cursed and groveled around on the ground, swatting at the blur of gray that continued to pummel his ears and neck.

Jan swiveled back, threw the Toyota into gear, yelled, "Hetta, fasten your seat belt, it's gonna be a bumpy ride," and punched the gas. Rocks and sand spat into Nacho's face as the oversized tires dug in, He stumbled around while Jan executed a sharp U-turn and headed straight for him. In the nick of time, he saw us coming and dove to safety.

I felt like I was riding with Steve McQueen as Jan expertly downshifted, then maneuvered us along the rocky road at death defying speeds. At least, I hoped they were death defying. Leaving old Nacho in a cloud of dust and feathers, she had us back to Mex 1 in minutes. Banking into a sharp left, we hit the blacktop on two wheels, wove dangerously from side to side, then settled out. Blondie McQueen screeched to a halt, ordered me into the front seat, then burned rubber while chanting, "Jan, Jan, she's our gal. If she can't do it, no one shall!"

18

I had to remember to ask Jan where she learned to drive like that, but first, we had more pressing business. "Hey! Loreto's the other way," I yelled over the roar of the big engine and the boom of the woofers.

She didn't hear me. I found the right knob, killed the stereo and repeated myself.

This time she nodded. "I know. That's exactly where they'll look for us. We're headed the other way, to Chino. He'll help us."

"But my boat. What about it?"

"Those guys don't know your boat's in Santa Rosalia. Well," she giggled, "unless they get CNN International. You don't suppose we hurt Nacho too badly, do you?"

"Depends on your definition of hurt. We certainly put one big dent in his overblown ego, but other than that, he'll live. Who cares, anyhow?"

"Oh, I just kinda think he's cute, in a criminal sort of way. Anyhow, since he ain't dead he's gonna be looking for us, and since we mentioned Loreto, my money says that's where he'll start. Maybe that gives us enough time to get to Chino and ditch this truck."

She was right on all counts. Nacho was cute in a criminal sort of way, and we had to get this big yellow SOB off Mex 1 ASAP, find a safe place to ditch it, and get a less conspicuous mode of transport. "Do we know where to turn off?"

"Yep, Chino and I went to Ciudad Constitución one day, so I know the way. I can get us to the dive boat, for sure."

"Do we have enough gas?"

She peered at the gauge. "We have a quarter tank, but don't know what this baby burns. I know there's a gas station in Insurgentes, not too far up the road. You have any money?"

"I have…" I rummaged into my pocket, "two hundred pesos, a couple of bidness cards, some lip-gloss and my driver's license. I left everything else on the boat. How about you?"

"Nada. Everything was in my bag. My burned up bag. Dammit! I don't have anything. No driver's license, passport, Mexican visa, credit card, nada. And to make matters worse, that bag was a Manolo Blahnik."

"Designer bags are overrated for living in a beach hut, anyway. Let's concentrate on our immediate crisis. I have enough pesos for some gas and a couple of tacos, but do we risk pulling into a Pemex station? This truck stands out like a nun in a strip joint."

"Or you, anywhere."

"You can talk. At least I'm short. We need hats." I dug around in the cab and found a handful of baseball caps under the seat, a Baja 1000 sweatshirt, and a Hussong's Cantina tee. After almost running off the road a couple of times trying to dress on the run, Jan pulled over, donned the tee shirt and cap. I was stuck with the sweat shirt, even though the temperature as we crossed the desert was at least eighty. In our new togs, with our red and blonde hair pushed up under caps, I hoped we'd be taken for just another couple of off-roader dudes in a bright yellow wanna-be Baja 1000 knockoff seeking fun and adventure in Baja.

Just as we were ready to get going again, a loud squawk caught our attention, and a very tired and thirsty Trouble landed in my lap. Spreading his wings and panting, he drank the water I offered, then gave us a serious cussing before falling dead asleep. Hot as it was, I nonetheless stuffed him under my sweatshirt, lest he get bounced out. He slept soundly, not even rousing when we stopped for gas. The Pemex gas station attendant cast a wary eye at the lump under my shirt that moved and bird-snored, but I gave him a ten peso tip for cleaning the windows so he smiled and waved as we left.

We stopped again to pick up fish tacos from a roadside stand before speeding towards Chino, and our salvation. Our plans changed abruptly when I spotted a black and white lurking near the left fork in the road, the one that led to Cuidad Constitución, and then on to San Carlos, and the dive boat. "Cop! Stop!" I yelled.

Startled, Jan hit the brakes. "Where?"

"At the intersection, behind the sign." I pointed. "He's probably just sitting there to slow down traffic, but I'd rather we didn't roll by him."

"Okay, then, we'll go to Lopez Mateos. It's only a little over twenty miles, we just take the right turn instead of the left."

"Then what?"

Jan smiled. "Hey, I have family there, remember?"

* * *

Jan's new *familia* in Lopez Mateos included Chino's cousins, about twenty of them, a few aunts and uncles, and some relatives I never quite fit into the family tree. They hid the truck without asking any questions, and agreed to go get Chino via panga. We stayed behind, declining a boat ride into San Carlos; the last thing I needed was for Dickless to spot me on his own turf.

Exhausted, Jan and I headed for garden hammocks, and naps. I crawled into mine, made myself comfortable and drifted off, until some subliminal curiosity roused me. "Jan, you awake?"

"Hmmhmm."

"Where did you learn to drive like that?"

"While you were in Japan, that guy I dated from Vegas? He had a couple of these things he raced in the desert. He let me drive once in awhile."

"You did good."

"I did, didn't I?"

We both conked out for an hour, until Trouble sang us awake. I'd put him in an empty cage Juanita, Chino's second or somesuch cousin, had on her patio. Trouble was less than happy, being treated like any old bird after his heroic attack on Nacho, but since there were Mexican men about, and Jan wanted to keep up good family relations, he just had to suffer. We covered his cage with a towel and he quieted down long enough for us to catch a couple of winks. Truth be known, I think he was as pooped as we were, because his protests were short lived.

Now, after we'd all copped some zees, his dulcet tones brought other family members about, all in awe of his singing and talking abilities. One cousin offered me fifty bucks for

Trouble, and I have to admit I was tempted. We were flat broke and without transportation. With fifty bucks, I could catch a bus back to Santa Rosalia.

"Hetta, you aren't really considering that offer, are you?" Jan asked, her voice dripping disapproval.

"You think I can get more?"

She gave me a look of disgust.

"Okay, okay, just kidding, but if he ups it to a hundred…" I waggled my hand. "Or even better, I could pull a *Skin Game*."

"What's that?"

"There is this old movie, one of my dad's favorites, with James Garner and Lou Gossett. Garner and Gossett play con men who hit on the perfect con. They ride into town, Garner sells Gosset off as his slave for big bucks, then Gossett either escapes or Garner springs him, and they go to the next town. Trouble could easily spring himself."

"That's brilliant, but I won't let you do it to these nice folks. However, it's an idea if we get stuck and need dough."

"We are stuck and we do need dough."

"Chino'll be here soon. He'll come up with something."

"Meanwhile, we need to consider our options."

"What options?"

"Dunno. Let's see if there's a map in that yellow bomb."

There was, a good one which showed back roads, like the one to Agua Fria. "Look Jan, at all these roads. Well, some of them are marked as paths but, with the right vehicle, we could get all the way back to Santa Rosalia without taking Mex 1."

"And we sure do have the right vehicle."

"All we need is gas, food, and—"

"—a miracle. What if we blow a tire, or break down?"

"Call Triple A?"

"My point, exactly."

"I didn't say it was a *good* option."

"I'll take my chances with Chino. He'll know what to do."

19

So there we were in Lopez Mateos with a stolen truck, no money, and on the lam from some very nasty characters. I sincerely hoped Jan was right, and Chino would know what we should do next.

But when he showed up, and we told him our story, he shook his head. "I have absolutely no idea what to do next. You *stole* the guy's truck?"

Jan huffed, "*Stole* is such a harsh word, Chino. And I would expect that you would be more concerned as to why we had to escape him."

"What I meant was that stealing a truck could earn you a one-way pass into a Mexican jail."

"Hey, he tried to kidnap us." Jan's lower lip quivered, which had the desired effect.

Chino patted her hand. "Oh, *mi corazon*, of course you had to take his truck. I'm just having trouble adjusting to the fact that while I thought you were safe and sound on the other side of the Sea of Cortez, you were not only taking a boat ride to Santa Rosalia in the middle of a storm, but then you had to go *looking* for trouble." He gave me a meaningful glance. Meaning it was all my fault.

"Ya know," I said, "speaking of Trouble, I think I'll just let the little bugger out of his cage."

"No!" Jan squealed, evidently not wishing grave bodily trauma upon her fiancé, even if he was being less than understanding.

Chino, startled by her outburst, put his arm around her and babytalked. "My poor darling. You've had a terrible day and here I am being an old meanie."

His little darling, all five feet eleven of her, leaned into him and shot me the evil eye before I could gag. She did that lip-quiver thing again. "I *have* had a horrible day."

"Oh, not me," I said. "I've had a grand old time. Wrecked a friend's car, blew up another, stole a third and now have a bunch of thugs hunting for me. Gosh, *darling*, it's been a blast."

Jan, unable to hold the pouty pose any longer, broke out laughing. "It did have to be up there in our top ten, huh?"

Chino was not amused. "I appreciate that you tried to find my grandmother, but now I am more worried about her than ever. Tell me about these chaps you encountered."

I grinned at his choice of words. Once in awhile his British education surfaced. Deeply tanned from his work as a whale specialist, Chino was over six feet tall, and very handsome. If there was any Yee left in him, it was his beautiful coal-black hair that he wore slightly longer than I like on *my* men, but for him, it worked. For living on the beach, a ponytail is infinitely practical. To his credit, he shaved daily even if he had to use sea water, and his clothes, although wrinkled, were always clean. And let's face it, he and Jan made a very attractive couple, in a primitive sort of way. I wondered, though, how they'd fare together in Jan's world.

Jan launched into a description of Nacho, Chingo and Paco, with me filling in details as I remembered them, then Chino went out to check our steal of the day. He whistled when he saw the yellow truck.

"This is some vehicle. You know what you have here?"

"Uh, a fancy yellow truck?"

"This is a Toyota four by four, all fixed up for off-road, like the kind they race in the Baja 1000. This thing can take on just about anything the Baja roads throw at them. Man, would I love to have one like it."

"Consider it done. It's all yours," I said. "Heck, by tomorrow morning I'll bet some mechanic cousin of yours could have this thing repainted, the identification number removed, new Mexican plates on that fancy bumper, and if need be, I have friends in low places who can have it registered in your name."

I could tell, by Chino's hesitation, that he was sorely tempted. On his salary, he could never afford such a vehicle. "I do have this cousin…" he started, then shook his head, "but, no, that would be wrong."

"What do you bet, if I ran the VIN on this baby, it would come up missing in Los Angeles? If it is, why shouldn't you keep it?"

"The vehicle identification number? You could find out if it is stolen? How?"

"I there an Internet Café in this berg?"

"Better than that. My cousin, Juan Yee, has high speed service at his house." He shook his head and looked sad. "That is, unfortunately, how we lost my grandmother."

Jan and I exchanged looks. I shrugged, but she asked, "Would you like to elaborate on that?"

"My grandmother, Abuela Yee, met someone on the Internet. A *young*er man from Agua Fria. Next thing you know, she ups and goes walkabout. Needless to say, the family is upset, but what can we do? After she left, she wrote that she was so happy with Arturo, we didn't try to interfere any longer."

The look on Jan's face was priceless. Somewhere between moronic and stunned. She struggled to speak, but failed, so I stepped in.

"Let me get this straight. Granny Yee hooked up with some guy on the Internet, then upped and took off to live with him?"

"Yes."

My preconceived vision of Grandmother Yee—a tiny gray haired lady dressed in black—went up in smoke. I broke out in a guffaw, Jan joined in, until we both came close to peeing in our pants. When she could finally speak, Jan asked, "How old is your grandmother, for pity's sake?"

"Let me see," Chino paused as he calculated, "she had my mother when she was fourteen, my mother was fifteen when I was born, and I am now twenty-six, so my grandmother is fifty-eight."

Well, well, well. I shot Jan an evil grin. "Gee, Chino, how old is this Arturo, her *younger* boyfriend, do you figure?"

Chino drew to his full height and snorted indignantly, "At least *ten* years younger."

Well, well, well*, well*. "Ten whole years? An abomination, don't you think, Jan?"

Jan somehow managed to close her mouth before a large fly landed on her tongue. Her expression went from stunned to venomous, with the venom aimed in my direction. No doubt, should I pursue this age difference thing for one more second, she would spit in my eyes and blind me. Judging by her reaction, I surmised she had no freaking idea she was ten years older than her dearly betrothed. Was I gonna have fun with this or what?

"We can run a trace for under thirty bucks," Jan stammered.

The fast change of subject confused Chino. "On my grandmother?"

"No, silly," she said, "the Vehicle Identification Number on the truck. We go online, put in the VIN and see what pops up on CARFAX. Problem is, I don't have a credit card. Mine was burned up."

"And I do not own one," Chino said.

Jan Sims, of the I-shop-exclusively-at-Niemans-Sims, has a boy toy without a credit card? This was getting better and better. "Not to worry," I said with a happy grin, "I have several."

Jan frowned. "I thought you left everything on the boat. You used my card to rent the car."

"I didn't say they were *mine*." I reached in my pocket, pulled out a wallet and flipped it open with flair. Several credit cards and a California driver's license showed through the plastic pockets. "Courtesy of Lamont Cranston, AKA, Nacho. AKA, The Shadow. Oh, this is rich. Not only is Nacho cute, he's funny, in a criminal sort of way."

"Shadow?" Chino asked.

"Only the Shadow knows. He was a character in a very, very, old radio show starring a rich playboy, Lamont Cranston, with an alter ego, The Shadow. I'm *sure* Jan can tell you all about him."

"Oh. As far as using his credit card, I do not think—"

"Not to worry, Chino. Jan and I are experts at this sort of thing, what with all our *years*, and years, and *years* of experience." As I said that last *years*, Jan reached over and viciously yanked my hair.

"Ouch!"

"Just plucking out a gray hair, Hetta dear. All gone now. Okay, Chino, lead us to Juan's computer."

20

Nacho's truck was not on record as stolen, and the VIN number actually matched the vehicle description. Go figure.

"So, now what, Sherlock Coffey?" Jan wanted to know.

Chino looked a little down in the mouth. I think he had warmed to the idea of owning the Toyota, if in fact it was stolen by someone other than Jan and me. Traceable, it lost its allure.

We sat glumly around the table until a young boy, breathless from running, rushed in and whispered something in Chino's ear. Chino, obviously alarmed, stood and followed the boy outside. In five minutes, he was back.

"I have learned," he told us with a frown, "that the man who threw me in jail, and tried to murder you when you were here with your yacht—"

"Dickless Richard?" I cut him off. "What now? I heard the SOB was out of jail."

"He has evidently learned that you are here, in Lopez Mateos. He holds no grudge against my Jan, for she is part of my dive team, but I fear he will harm you if he catches you alone."

"Why? He's not in jail anymore because I didn't return to testify against him. The creepy little bastard should be grateful."

Jan couldn't resist. "Gee, Hetta, let me think why he might be upset. All you did was blow up his panga, set him adrift at sea in a leaky boat, and then get him arrested for attempted murder."

"He deserved worse."

"I know that, and you know that, but looks like he thinks he has a score to even. Right, Chino?"

"I think so. He told me he did not wish Hetta harm, but we all know he is not to be trusted."

"I do believe it is time for me to ditch this joint and head for the hills." I picked up a map. I couldn't go back to the boat via Mex 1, the road Jan and I traveled with Nacho's truck, because he and his thugs were without a doubt looking for me. It's that old rock and hard place syndrome come to rest.

"Where will you go, Hetta?"

"Into Hell."

"Huh?"

I stood and drew myself to full height, then quoted grandly from Alfred, Lord Tennyson's *Charge of the Light Brigade*: " '*Cannon to right of them, Cannon to left of them, Cannon in front of them Volley'd and thunder'd; Storm'd at with shot and shell, Boldly they rode and well, Into the jaws of Death, Into the mouth of Hell.*' In short, I am taking this fancy yeller truck and heading for the hills. Literally. Since I don't dare return via Mex 1 past Agua Fria, I intend to take back roads most of the way to Santa Rosalia."

Chino shrugged. "It can be done. It is done, all the time. Many ranchers, even in old vehicles, traverse these roads."

"Are there any cop stops that you know of?"

He shrugged. "The military stops change, and the roads? They are dirt, gravel and sand, but no problem for *that* truck. My only concern is that since the hurricane last fall, there are massive washouts and the road is not clearly marked. Perhaps I should drive you."

"Ab-so-lut-a-mente not. There is no reason to involve you any further in this mess."

Jan grabbed my arm. "Chino, I need a word with Hetta." She pulled me out into the garden and whispered, "Surely you aren't planning on going alone?"

"Don't call me Shirley," I countered, using the old saw from the Airplane movies, hoping to get a laugh. Didn't work.

"No way. No how. It's too dangerous. I won't let you do it alone."

"And how do you propose to stop me?"

"I'll…I'll…call your mama!"

"She's on the road in the RV. No cell phone."

"Then I'll call Jenks."

"And tell him what? Look, no sense worrying him. He's halfway around the world. What can he do? By this time tomorrow, I'll be safely back on the boat."

"What about those thugs from Agua Fria?"

"Jan, they have no way of connecting me, or you, to a boat in Santa Rosalia. Anything that can ID us is toast. Even if they trace the burned up Neon to the rental agency in Loreto, there is nothing on the Budget paperwork that mentions the boat. As far as the rental folks are concerned, we flew into Loreto, then rented a car for a few days of touring. Hell, the car isn't even overdue yet."

She was waffling, I could tell by the softening in her stance. I went in for the kill. "Besides, you need to spend some time with Chino. I think you might have some 'splaining to do."

She deflated like yesterday's balloon. "How the hell was I to know he was only twenty-six?"

"Exactly. That's why people get to *know* each other before they jump before a preacher. Although, I would have thought that after living with a man for several weeks you'd at least know his age. What else don't you know, for cryin' out loud."

"He looks older. And he's a *doctor*."

"So was Doogie Howser."

"That was TV."

"Jan, Chino has doctorates, he's not a brain surgeon. Maybe he graduated from college when he was fifteen. Bottom line is, the age difference shouldn't matter, but the way he was talking, it does to him. You need to stay here and get this thing resolved. Now." I've always found that getting someone to focus on themselves gets the heat off my precious self. My redirect seemed to be working just fine.

"You're right. I do. What a muck up."

"Yes, for the moment things look a little grim, but you'll work something out if you stay here. Meanwhile I can get back to my boat, head for the mainland, tie up *Raymond Johnson,* go to California, and the new project I've scheduled."

Jan looked as though she would argue, then shrugged and we rejoined Chino, who was studying the map. "So, how long will this little trek across the Baja peninsula take me?"

"Oh, not so long." Chino traced a line on the map we'd unfolded. "According to the GPS waypoints I entered, here," he circled a spot on the map with a ballpoint pen, "here, and here, your driving time should be less than six hours. That is, of course, without a flat tire, a breakdown or a block from hurricane damage. The roads are unmarked. You should always follow the deepest tire tracks. When you hit a fork, and are unsure which way to go, check the next GPS waypoint. Also, over the years, it has become customary to place a row of rocks in the road when a choice is to be made so that the driver will not wander off onto someone's ranch, but the rule is not solid.

"From Lopez Mateos," he ran his finger along a road, "one must backtrack, along the main paved road, then turn north here, toward La Purisima. This will take less than an hour, for it is asphalt, but then the pavement ends and the fun starts." He continued to calculate driving times, using a kilometer per hour figure of forty, or twenty-five miles per hour. According to his estimate, I could be in Mulege within a few hours of leaving the pavement, then, once back on Mex 1, it was only minutes to Santa Rosalia.

So far, so good. Searching my memory banks, I said, "I don't recall seeing a military stop between Mulege and Santa Rosalia."

"There has never been one, so far as I know."

"Then that's that."

"SQUATAll's well that ends well, right?"

Okay, so there were still a couple of loose ends, like Chino's grandma was still missing and I had thugs from two different camps looking for me. Grams was on her own as far as I was concerned, so my agenda was to navigate a hot off-road truck over treacherous Baja back roads, find my boat, report a burned-up Budget, somehow get to Loreto to pick up Smith's pickup from the *mecánico*, and then singlehand *Raymond Johnson* across the Sea of Cortez. First and foremost, however, I had to get out of Lopez Mateos before Dickless Richard found me.

Although the Toyota was equipped with a bank of lights with enough clout to light up the desert for a quarter of a mile, I had no intention of driving after dark. I still had a couple of hours before sunset to get on down the road, find a place to hide.

Chino rummaged through a storage locker in his cousin's back yard, dragged out a sleeping bag and threw it into the truck bed. He also gathered some warm clothes, a flashlight, two gallon jugs of water, and topped off my tanks with jericanned gas.

"I believe you are ready to roll. However, you will need this." He shoved a handheld Global Positioning System receiver into my hand.

I shoved it back. "No need. The Toyota's got a GPS."

"Do not use it. It might contain a tracking device. Many of these off-road vehicle GPS's do, in case the trekkers get lost."

"Good thinking, Chino, you're a rock. Please, give my heartfelt thanks to all the Camachos and Yees for their help, as well.

I gave him and Jan a hug, then scratched Trouble's neck feathers through his cage. I'd miss them all, especially my fine feathered friend, but Trouble would be better off living with Chino and Jan. I double-checked the little escape artist's cage lock, and set off into Hell.

Next time, I think I'll try something simple. Like bungee jumping off Mount Everest.

21

Did I mention that my idea of camping out is a hotel without twenty-four hour room service?

I found a side road and drove the Toyota behind the cover of a little hill just as the sun set and—there is a God—an enormous full moon rose.

I stepped from the truck to stretch, and was hit by such a profound silence that a rush of fear coursed through me. Any idea I had of sleeping in the truck bed was chased away by my own fear of being so alone, so...vulnerable.

Heart thumping, I grabbed the sleeping bag from the truck bed, jumped back inside and slammed the door locks shut. Still frightened to the point of almost panic, I considered continuing the drive, maybe finding a hotel room at La Purisima. If they had one. Which they probably didn't, but it was my experience that Mexicans generally let you park anywhere. I could park in front of the police station. If they had one.

Indecision finally calmed me. I climbed into the jump

seat in a futile attempt to find a place to sleep, but it was well nigh impossible. Even moving from the front to the back required a contortion more likely found at the Circe du Soliel.

Fearful of opening a door to change places the easy way, and sweating from effort and residual fright, I maneuvered myself into the passenger seat and found a lever that tilted the seat back to almost horizontal. The only thing preventing it from going flat out was the jump seat in the rear, so I raised it, *et voila*, I had a bed. Within minutes, though, a chill settled into my bones though my damp clothes and I knew, despite my deep fatigue, that I had to fight my way into that moldy old sleeping bag. Using what I was sure were my last reserves, and trying not to think what might have been using that bag for a home back in Chino's shed, I struggled in, zipped it up and, against all odds, fell into a deep sleep.

My own snoring woke me up sometime in the wee hours. The moon had traversed three quarters across the sky, which told me I'd slept for quite a few hours. Stiff from sleeping in one position for so long, I tried to sit up, but snored again.

Snored? No, I was awake, so what was that sound?

I peered out the window and saw nothing but a desert lit by moonshine bright enough to read by, but with colors faded to an almost uniform gray. Green cactus and brown rocks seemed to blend, only discernable by their shadows and shapes. I rolled down the window and listened, but quickly rolled it back up when I heard a snuffling sound, then saw something move. Several somethings.

Shocked, I screamed, and slammed my hand down on the door lock, then remembered they were already secure. Every hair on my body was standing on end as I reached over, turned on the key and hit the desert lights.

The coyotes, startled by the suddenly lit desert, scampered back a bit, but then stopped and stared with evil yellow eyes.

The pack, probably thirty of them, surrounded the Toyota. A frisson of unreasonable fear ran through me. Unreasonable, because what could a few coyotes do to me? I was inside a vehicle, doors locked, windows up. Coyotes slink and hide, they do not break windows and gnaw one's bones.

One of them, however, didn't believe his own PR. Advancing on stiff legs into the circle of light, he snarled, walked insolently to the truck, and lifted his leg.

I hit the stereo button, and the pissing contest was over in an instant.

Tucking tail and yelping away into the night, he left a trail of pee in his wake.

My woofers are bigger than his woofers.

I rolled down the window and let loose with a primal howl, reveling in my triumph, even if it was over some wretched desert creature. From somewhere far off, the howl was returned, no doubt a hosanna for Hetta, Queen of the Desert, from one of her subjects.

Flushed with victory, and with only Freddie Fender singing *Hey Baby Que Paso* for company, I gave up any idea of more sleep and set out to single-handedly conquer the Sonoran desert. Okay, so I had a truck that could probably climb Mount Everest, a GPS, and a pile of burritos to aide my progress, but I was still on my own. I turned up Freddie.

Nacho, as well as being handsome in a criminal sort of way, had a great music selection.

La Purisima at dawn is quiet to the point of dead.

I killed the music to keep it that way.

With the exception of a few dog barks, a donkey bray and a rooster crow or two, I was the noisiest thing in town, even with the stereo turned off. The biggest surprise about this desert town was its placidly flowing river flanked by reeds, palm trees and orchards. Downtown consisted of several Colonial style buildings, white, square, and squat, lining a semi-paved main street.

Typical of Mexican architecture in many small Baja pueblos, the buildings' doors open onto the street, with only a narrow sidewalk serving as a curb. Quaint and quiet, La Purisima was the kind of place I'd like to further explore, but with the Hounds of Hell on my tail, I thought it best to boogie on through.

My heart skipped a little beat when I spotted a dusty black and white on the edge of town, but to my relief, it was not only unoccupied, it had probably quit running sometime around 1979. As far as I knew, except for the dog that gave me a half-hearted bark or two, I passed through the village unnoticed, which is a miracle considering I drove a canary yellow Toyota boasting straight pipes with the decibel level just under that of a C-5 transport plane on takeoff.

I had, between yesterday and today, mastered the rhythm of the Toyota's gears. Although on a two-track dirt road, I had a handle on the vehicle and was enjoying the ride. The slow ride. Chino figured it would take me only a few hours to make my way to the other side of the Baja Peninsula, barring mechanical problems, banditos or rolling over in the desert and ending up as a mummy. I pushed such pleasant thoughts aside and concentrated on the road, which wasn't all that bad at slow speeds. I was averaging about five miles an hour. Every time I was emboldened to go faster, I'd hit a ravine, gravel, a rock, or something that scared the speed right out of me.

Several hours, and only several miles out of La Purisima, I crested a ridge and the low morning sun blinded me to the point of jamming my foot down on the brake pedal. Creeping along even slower than usual, trying to make sure I didn't drive off the so-called road, I was suddenly surrounded by a deafening cadre of motorcycles—dirt bikes, actually. Blinded further by choking dust as they shot past me, I came to a full stop and pulled my tee shirt collar up over my nose and mouth. Several more bikes roared by and, ticked off, I shot them a single digit complaint. I was waiting for the dust to settle when one of the bikers stopped, turned around, and headed straight for me. Do I never learn?

My mind raced. Options? Put old yeller in gear and run him down like a dog, or maybe smile and explain that a raised finger in my native country of Lower Slobovia is a gesture of affection, or…I was out of ideas.

The biker blocked the road in front of me, climbed off his bike and sauntered my way. With his helmet facemask on, I couldn't read his expression, but the walk had a decidedly unfriendly gait to it. Either that, or he had a major wedgie.

I waggled my fingers feebly and pasted a stupid grin on my face. Then, over my motor noise, I realized the biker was trying to talk to me. I cut the engine. Blessed desert quiet descended, with only the crunch of boots to break the silence. Well, that and my hammering heart.

"Hi," I said, forgetting I was Lower Slobovian.

"Hi, yourself." The voice was muffled as the biker leaned over and began removing his helmet. A tumble of shiny black curls covered his face, then he tossed his head. He was a she. "You got trouble?"

Nope, he's back in Lopez Mateos. "I'm fine. Sun hit me in the eyes. I didn't hear you guys behind me, so you gave me a fright."

She grinned. "So I noticed. You American?"

"Yep. You?"

"Yeh. California. You?"

"Texan. I'm Hetta Coffey."

She stuck out a gloved hand. "Victoria Antoinette. So, what are you doin' out here by yourself?"

"I might ask you the same."

"I ain't by myself."

"Oh, yeah, there's that. I'm going to, uh, Loreto. Where are you headed?"

"San Ignacio tonight, we hope. We'll pick up Baja 1 just below Conception Bay, then ride hard for Ignacio, hope to get there by late afternoon. Last thing we want is to be on the road after dark. Then tomorrow we have..." the sound of more bikes caught her attention. "Hey, here comes the rest of the gang."

I didn't like that "gang" part. Motorcycle gangs have a shaky reputation in most parts of the world, and here I was in, like, nowhere Baja, surrounded by one.

"Problems?" the lead biker yelled as he came to a dusty skid that ended within inches of my fender.

"Nah, Mad Dog. The first group just startled her 'cause she was doing about three miles an hour when we overtook her, and she didn't hear us coming up behind her."

Mad Dog?

"What's she doing out here by herself?"

"Hel-lo," I said with a wave, "the *she* of whom you are talking is right *hee*-er."

White teeth gleamed in a dusty, whiskery face. "Okay, then," he drawled, "what *are* you doing here by yourself? And why so slow? Mechanical problems?"

I wasn't about to admit I was creeping along because I was scared to drive faster. "No, my rig's running just fine, thank you. I'm just not in a big hurry, unlike others I could mention. And I'm alone because my boyfriend pissed me off, so I offed the bastard, buried his body back there in the desert and stole his fancy yeller truck."

There was an ominous silence until Mad Dog guffawed, gave me a thumbs up, and was joined in laughter by his buddies. I relaxed. Most times, if people plan to slit one's throat, they don't take such delight in one's small witticisms.

Mad Dog—no doubt named that by his mama— dismounted his dirty bike and leaned against my dirtier Toyota. "Where you headed?"

"Paris."

"Before that."

"Uh, Loreto?" No use telling this guy I wanted to get to Santa Rosalia as fast as my stolen vehicle could take me.

"Did, by any chance, your old man show you anything resembling a map before you offed him?"

"Huh?"

"Map? You know, a piece of paper that shows those who know how to read one how to get from point A to point B?"

This guy was growing on me. Sarcasm and tight leather'll do that to a girl.

"I *know* where I'm going," I insisted, even though I didn't.

"Yeah, but do you know how to get there?"

"Duh, I follow the road."

"No, Honey, you follow us. If you want to get to Loreto before dark, that is. At the rate you're movin' you'll be out here all day and night."

Dark? Dark? The idea of spending another night alone on what served as a road sent a shiver up my spine. What was I thinking, running off into the desert without Chino and Jan? I could end up as coyote food and no one would ever know where to look for me. The enormity of my situation suddenly hit me. I had a bag of *chicharones*, one burrito, and a gallon of water left, no weapons. Munching on pork skins without a beer to wash them down, crammed into the Toyota with no way to defend myself against dangerous critters, suddenly seemed like a really bad idea.

My answer came out whiney. "I can't keep up with you guys."

"Sure you can. This rig was made for off-road. If we can do it on dirt bikes, you can definitely keep pace in such a fine vehicle. That is, if you know how to drive it. You do, don't you?" he challenged.

"Of course, I do. Get on that puny little bike of yours and lead the way, big boy."

Pride goeth before destruction, and an haughty spirit before a fall. Proverbs 16:18.

22

Two hours, and what felt like several broken ribs and a need for an emergency kidney transplant later, we roared out of the desert, onto the blessed pavement of Baja 1. Evidently Mad Dog never heard of such things as death, or dire bodily injury.

Five minutes after we hit the pavement, the entire gang, who moved like a flock of birds as a unit, swooped to a dusty halt in front of a truck stop. I followed. We all looked like photos I'd seen of mud men in New Guinea. Crawling from the driver's seat, I made the mistake of shaking my head. Dirt rained like red flour all around me. Two little kids came out of the truck stop café to ogle and giggle. I was bent over, knocking more debris from my hair when I sensed someone standing behind me. Very, very close behind me. I whirled up, ready to do battle, and found myself face-to-face with Mad Dog.

"Here," he said, handing me a gallon water jug. "Try

this." From the looks of his relatively clean, damp, face and hair, it had worked for him.

"Thanks." Leaning my head back, I let the heavenly, if chilly, water roll down my face and over my hair. Shaking like a dog, I opened my eyes. Mad Dog was grinning.

"You have red hair."

"It was this morning."

"I like redheads. Especially those with balls. Since you offed your old man this morning, buried him in the desert, I guess that makes you, like, available?"

"I guess that makes you, like, wrong?"

"Too bad. Oh, well, since you put it that way, can I share a small secret with you?"

There's something about a man in leather, especially one with beautiful white teeth, green eyes and coal black hair. "Please do."

He reached over and gently tugged my chin, turning my head back towards where we'd just come from. "That," he purred, "is the way to Loreto."

I jerked my head away. "I knew that. I was just following you until we…uh, got to this truck stop."

"Sure you were. Wanna beer before you head back?"

"I thought you had to rush off to San Ignacio."

He leaned forward and whispered in my ear. "I could be detoured."

My ears and whiskers, was this guy sexy or what? A little devil whispered in my other ear, "*Who will ever know if you have an unscheduled tryst in the desert? Invite this beautiful man back to your boat. A hot shower, a drop of champagne, and…*whack! The devilish voice was gone and another, annoying one, yelled, "*Hetta, get a grip! J-e-n-k-s!*"

How I hate the voice of reason. It never lets me have any fun.

I bought the whole gang a beer and we went our separate ways. Mad Dog, whose real name turned out to be Russ Madden, gave me his card before riding out of my life. A dentist; who knew? Maybe I'd go in for a cleaning.

I drove a couple of miles south, contemplating what had just happened. Old habits die hard, it would seem. I had been with Jenks in a m-m-m-m-monogamous—there, I said it— relationship for months. What was I thinking back there? That Jenks was always gone? That I was eating more meals alone now than when I was celibate? That this long distance romance was getting a lit-tle old?

I shook off my little pity party and headed for Santa Rosalia, but to give my entourage, and the dentist, a considerable head start, I dropped in on Geary at Burro Beach, had a snack at Bertha's Restaurant next door, stopped in Mulege for a few provisions, and made my way toward home, sweet boat.

Rolling into Santa Rosalia late in the afternoon, I parked the flashy yellow Toyota on a back street, left the keys in the ignition, and managed to wearily trudge the three long blocks to the marina. With any luck, by this time tomorrow, Nacho's pride and joy would be in a chop shop, and I'd be back in my slip on the other side of the sea.

As I entered the Santa Rosalia Marina's gate, I saw a group of yachties sitting around on the dock, having cocktails as they did every afternoon. And some mornings. There was no way to sneak past them, so I plopped into a plastic Pacifico Beer chair.

"Hey, there, Hetta, welcome back. We knew you were on your way."

"How did you—"

"Oh Boy! Oberto!"

"He flew in about noon," Smith told me. "I let him in

his cage, gave him fresh water and some jerky. Poor little bugger was worn out."

"That makes two of us."

"Want me to get your stuff out of my truck?"

Oh, crap. "Ya know, Smith, I think I'll just take a shower and crash. Let's deal with the truck tomorrow, okay?"

"Okay by me. I have to hustle, myself. I'm getting ready to cross over, you know. Tomorrow I have to find a place over here to leave my truck until I get back."

How about la llanteria *in Loreto*? "I may have some ideas on that. Later."

"Later."

I headed for my fridge and an ice cold Tecate. Trouble latched onto my shoulder and began gnawing on my hair the minute I sank down onto the settee. I was bone weary, but elated to be back home safe and sound. "Ya know, Trouble, if you'da given me a ride, I'd be more inclined to forgive you. What part of, 'you cannot live with me' is it that you do not understand?"

He made cooing noise and nibbled my cheek.

"Flatterer." I gave him a sip of beer, then pushed myself up and to the sat phone.

Jan picked up on the first ring. "Hetta?"

"That would be me."

"Thank God. Where are you?"

"On the boat, tucked in safely for the night."

"Where did you leave, uh, the, uh…evidence."

"On a back street in Santa Rosalia, keys in ignition."

"Good. Hetta?"

"Yes, Jan."

"I have some bad news for you."

"Oh, really?" I gave Trouble a neck scratch. "What would that be?"

"Well, I've sorta misplaced Trouble."

"Misplaced?" I was annoyed enough to let her squirm a mite.

"You know that old cage we put him in at Chino's cousin's house? Trouble picked the lock and is gone. I'm really, really sorry."

She sounded so pitiful I decided to let her off the hook. "He's here."

"What?"

"They always say bad news travels fast, and the little bugger beat me back to the boat by hours. I don't suppose you want to come over and pick him up?"

Silence.

"That's what I thought. Oh, well, I'll just take him back across to Sonora with me and try to figure out what to do with him when I have to head up to Oakland. Maybe the port captain will bird sit. At any rate, I'm too tired to worry about it right now."

"Did you tell Smith about his truck?"

"Not yet. I'll take the bus to Loreto tomorrow, pick up Smith's truck, and as soon as I get back here, I'll leave for Sonora."

"At night?"

"Probably not. I'll probably wait until dawn. That way I'll be back in my slip for Happy Hour."

"Hetta, I really don't like the idea of you crossing alone. I know it's only a little over seventy miles, but it *is* a sea."

"Oh, come on, I'll be fine. Hell, I'll be within radio contact of both sides all the way over. If something goes wrong, I'll just yell for help."

"How about weather?"

"I'll listen to the early ham nets. If there's a problem, I won't go."

"Promise?"

"Promise."

"Well, okay then. I guess I'll turn in now. Chino's already sawing logs."

"Did you remember to burp him?"

"Bitch."

23

"Ahoy, *Raymond Johnson*. You up, Hetta?"

I took a sip of coffee and yelled for Smith and Maggie to come on in. I had the Sonrisa Net on, getting the dope on the weather in the sea for the next day's crossing.

"Hetta!"

"Shush, Smith, I wanna hear this."

"But, Hetta, my truck. Someone stole it!"

"Hush. No they didn't. I know where it is. Get some coffee and settle down."

Smith slunk to the galley and came back with a steaming mug of coffee and a pouty look on his normally cheerful face. I listened to the weather guessers long enough to satisfy myself that leaving at oh-dark-thirty the next morning would be a good idea. Santa Ana's were predicted in California soon, so I had to scoot before a norther blew in and trapped me in the harbor for several days. As soon as I turned off the ham radio, Smith jumped to his feet, dumping poor Maggie onto the carpet.

"My truck?"

"Long story. I'm going down to Loreto to retrieve it this morning. The bad news is that we had a little mishap. The good news is that you're gonna have a brand new axel and two new tires."

"You broke my axel?"

"Not me, exactly. A pesky *tope*. But not to worry. All fixed."

"I'm going with you."

"As you wish. Do you know what time the first bus heads that way."

"Last time I checked, not until after noon."

"Well, fooey. I wanted to get down there, pick up your pickup and be back here fairly early. I plan to leave at first light tomorrow morning."

"Really? Me, too. We can buddy boat."

Oh, great. The last thing I wanted was to cross at a snail's pace with his Taiwanese-made boat, which he quite appropriately dubbed *Taiwan On*. "You know, there isn't gonna be any wind tomorrow and you *are* a sailor."

"Not tomorrow. I plan to motor."

"How fast can you motor?"

"Four, five knots."

"I'll do ten, twelve."

"Oh. Okay, I'll leave tonight, you can cover my back."

Sigh. "Fine. Let's go get your truck."

"How are we gonna get there? Hitchhike?"

"With a little luck, I think I can find us some wheels."

Old Yeller was right where I left her, doors unlocked, keys in the ignition. Are there no self-respecting car thieves left in Mexico? Have they *all* moved to the States?

"Hop in."

Smith hesitated. "You sure?"

"Absolutely." I fired up the Toyota and we were in Loreto in record time. I have to say, though, traveling Baja One in broad daylight in a stolen, bright yellow off-roader that belongs to a murderous drug dealer gave me a moment or two of worry, but what the hell? Beats the bus.

Not wishing to push my heretofore good luck, though, we dumped Nacho's rig in downtown Loreto. Just for fun I turned on the GPS before locking the keys inside. Maybe Nacho would be able to track down his truck and be so grateful that he wouldn't try to hunt me down and off me in some very unpleasant fashion.

Much to my relief, and Smith's, his old pickup was still at the *llanteria* in Loreto, and all fixed up, ready to roll. Seventy bucks later, we were driving north.

Finally, something was going my way.

To keep it that way, I decided I'd notify Budget of the demise of their Neon only after I was far from the long arm of the Loreto law.

By the time we dropped off Smith's pickup with the family he'd found to store it with, it was getting dark.

As we walked back down the dock, we heard laughter from the boats, and the sounds of their owners making dinner, playing cards, watching movies and all the regular stuff cruisers do before turning in at Baja midnight, which is about eight-thirty.

"Smith, you must be as exhausted as I am. Maybe you shouldn't cross tonight. I can wait another day, I guess. Only thing is, we're expecting nasty weather ."

"I'll be all right. I got all the way down here alone. Once I clear the harbor and get a few miles out, I'll set the autopilot and my radar alarm. To be on the safe side, I have my alarm clock set to go off every hour so I can check things out for myself. I stay in the cockpit, not below, and as you know, there's almost no traffic between here and the other side, once I clear Tortuga Island."

"Every hour, huh? Let's see, if your deck is three feet from the surface and you are over six feet tall, let's say your eye level is nine feet from sea level. You are traveling four knots—"

"Sometimes five," he corrected proudly.

"Bear with me. Let's use four. Anyhow, from nine feet, you can see about three and a half miles. Do the math. Once an hour ain't so good, especially if, like you say, you sometimes average five knots. Hell, at only four knots an hour, you'd run over someone in fifty-two or so minutes."

Smith's mouth had dropped open somewhere in the middle of my little calculation session. "Jeez, Hetta, what are you, some kind of brain?"

I hadn't heard that term used in a very long time. I laughed. "Nope, I just have a good memory for formulas. One point seventeen times the square root of your eye height equals the distance to the horizon in nautical miles. So three times one point one seven equals three point five one miles. I could be a little off, depending on you deck height, but I'd rethink that alarm clock timing if I were you."

"Like I said, I got down here." He sounded pretty defensive, which is the reaction I get from most men, right before they start avoiding me. Only Jenks appreciates stuff like this, but I think that's because he can figure circles around me, could have had that calculation down to the last decimal point before I started. Oh, and he doesn't feel threatened by a woman who actually knows what six inches is.

"But like you said," I said in an attempt to pat down Smith's ruffled ego, "you do it all the time. It's just that the idea of some guy underway, asleep, at night, and on autopilot, isn't all that reassuring for the rest of us."

"You power boaters worry too much. If I get really tired, I just heave to, put on my strobe light, go to bed and drift."

"We've done something similar. Kill the engines, turn on the strobe and drift. Even then, though, we have someone on watch. Are you banking some shrimper's gonna post a watch?"

"So we do a little bump in the night."

"It's you boat," I said, parroting a former boat captain of mine. "What radio channel will you be on?"

"I'll monitor sixteen and seventy-two. I'm all set to leave, wanna help me with my lines?"

He started *Taiwan On's* engine, and several other boaters sauntered over to help him on his way. As I watched him pull out of the harbor, it made me feel pretty wimpy that I was worried about crossing a little patch of sea by myself in broad daylight.

Trouble, who had been perched on my shoulder since we left the pickup, flew ahead of me as I headed for *Raymond Johnson*. I followed, but another boater came out on the dock.

"Hey, Hetta, what time you leaving?"

"Four, four-thirty."

"Need me to help with the lines?"

"Naw, I'll be fine. I just hope I don't wake everyone up."

"Well, if you—"

A raucous squawk and a scream cut the night air. I ran for the boat, only to find a man face down on my deck, with Trouble sitting on his back. Every time the man moved, Trouble bit his ear.

"Good bird! Hey, who are you and what are you doing on my damned boat?"

"*Por favor*. Can you to remove him from me?"

"I'll think about it. Why are you on my boat?"

"I am from Arturo." He tried to reach in his pocket, but was nailed for his trouble.

"Arturo? Arturo who?"

"Señor Arturo Oberto. He sees this animal on television and wish to purchase him."

"As in, Oh Boy! Oberto, Oberto?"

"*Si*. I have the letter."

"Trouble, get over here and leave the man alone." I turned to the crowd that gathered on the dock. "Everything's all right. Sorry for all the racket." People began to drift off as I helped the man up. He eyed Trouble warily, dug in his front pocket and produced a piece of paper. Stretching his arm as far as it would go while leaning away, he handed me a note and snatched his hand from harm's way. Just for fun, Trouble made a little feint in his direction, which made the man jump back.

"Quit it, Trouble. This man is your dream come true. Your ship has come in. Seems Mr. Art Oberto, who obviously saw your television debut on CNN, has a place near here and he sent this nice man to buy you. Think of it. Unlimited jerky for-ever."

I turned to the cringing man. "Mr. Oberto doesn't care to buy me as well, by any chance?"

"*¿Mande?*"

"Never mind. Please, sit down, I'll be right back."

I felt a little guilty when Trouble went passively into his cage, never guessing that I was, quite literally, selling him down the river. "It's for your own good, honest," I said, but I wasn't sure who I was trying to convince, him or me. I gathered up some goodies for his road trip, covered his cage, and took it outside. Quickly jotting down Trouble's idiosyncratic eating habits, his desire for a daily warm shower, and a warning as to his racist tendencies, I handed the man the list.

"Here you go. Whatever you do, do not open this cage, *intiendes*?"

He didn't need any convincing there. "Oh, *sí*, do not worry, I will not to open the cage. How much?"

"At least a few days."

"*¿Mande?*"

"Keep him in cage. *Tres, cinco dias.*" I figured three to five days would give me time to get the hell out of Mexico.

"*Sí*, I understand. How much pesos?"

I could hear Trouble mumbling contentedly, as he always did before he went to sleep. "Thirty pieces of silver?"

"*¿Mande?*"

"Just joking. No money. Here," I turned the letter over and scribbled on the back, "give this to Señor Oberto."

"*Gracias. Muchas gracias, señora, y que vaya bein.*"

"Same to you. I guess."

As I watched them leave, I teared up a little, but this is what I wanted, right? Trouble has a good home with lots of jerky, and I'm as free as, well, a bird.

Twice during the night I awakened to the flutter of wings, but it turned out to be a great blue heron instead of the great gray Trouble.

I missed him.

To my complete and utter surprise, I crossed the sea without a single incident.

After oversleeping, I was underway by seven, overtook Smith around noon. I waived gaily as I passed, noting that he looked grouchy and tired, and I figured he still had a good thirteen miles to go. So much for his hoped for five knots; he was barely making four.

I was back in my slip by one, and helped Smith with his lines much later. He and Maggie joined me for a rum and coke—she takes hers with ice, hold the rum, hold the coke—then, worn out, the sailor headed for his bunk. I didn't ask how often he'd set his alarm the night before, but it was obvious that only one of us had a restful night.

Feeling mightily pleased with myself for my uneventful crossing, I deigned to call Jenks and brag a little, but his cool reception led to a strained conversation that I was in no mood to lighten up. It was only after I hung up that I wished I'd been less defensive when he expressed relief that I was back in my slip.

How dare he worry about me.

$$24$$

I wrote a wrap-up report for the Trob, to which I planned to attach a grossly inflated invoice. Knowing he would question it line by line, it was a padding game we played, even though we both knew where we'd end up.

Trouble, safe and sound at Rancho Oberto, was no longer a reason to linger in Mexico, and with my silly self the possible subject of a search by at least three bad guys and the Budget rental police, my host country was growing a mite unwelcoming.

And I was lonely. Yes, there were cruiser parties almost every night, and yes, I did lots of busy boat work and supervised even more, and yes, I spent hours on the computer working, but I was still alone. Jan was diving for treasure with Chino, Jenks was in Kuwait with his brother, Trouble was, according to phoned-in progress reports from Rancho Oberto, in Baja, happily munching unlimited jerky, and Mom and Dad were RV-ing somewhere in Canada.

My stateside project wasn't due to get started until after

the first of the year, so what I needed was a new project— somewhere besides Mexico, and preferably *muy pronto*— before I reverted to type and slid into a Tequila stupor. Jimmy Buffett knows of what he sings when he talks about wasting away in Margaritaville.

Before I fell into a permanent blue funk, I picked up the phone. "Yo Trob, I need a job."

"I gave you a job."

"I need another."

"Finish the one you have."

"You'll have the whole enchilada tomorrow."

"I thought you had another deal lined up."

"I do, but not until after Christmas."

"I'll put feelers out. When will you be back up here."

"Soon. Say, has Allison mentioned my car lately?"

"You better talk to her, she's your so-called lawyer."

"I was afraid you'd say that."

My so-called lawyer, Allison, barely gave me a chance to say hello before launching into a quite un-lawyerly diatribe. "Hetta, you can't hide out south of the border forever. If you don't start returning my damned calls, I'm going to come down there and drag your skanky self back here myself. One more call from the OPD and I'm telling them you are no longer my client. They only want to talk to you, not arrest you. They know you had nothing to do with that body in your car."

"Okay, okay. I've been a little busy. And I am coming home. I did call them and they said they would release the car to you."

"Not exactly."

"What exactly?"

"They let me take it to the mechanic, but he won't release it onto the street until he gets an okay from Norquist. And Norquist wants to talk to you again."

"What now? Doesn't he have better things to do?"

"His life is full of boring stuff, like murders and mayhem. He needs a little excitement."

"Har har. He'd be bored with what I've been up to."

"Liar. Jan called."

"Oh."

"Car theft? Consorting with drug runners? Attempted vehicular manslaughter? Have I missed anything?"

"I sold my bird down the tubes."

"Save that one for when you get home. And when will that be?"

"Real soon, I promise."

"They running you out of the country?"

"Something like that. How much for my car?"

"Three grand."

"What? The whole car isn't worth that much."

"You said to fix it, I had it fixed."

"I'm going to revise my invoice to your hubby. Looks like I'm going to need a cash influx."

"Plus two more grand for the deductible on that rental car you blew up in Baja."

"Uh, car?"

"Yes, car. As in a Budget rental, wrecked, burned and abandoned in the Baja?"

"Oh, *that* rental car. How does Jan know how much the deductible is?"

"She may not know yet. Police in Baja called POD since your address of record is in Oakland. And believe me, when your name crops up, the local cops listen. Especially Norquist."

Damn. I knew I should have called Budget and reported the car fire. Evidently they found out on their own.

"Not only that, the cops in Baja thought maybe you two had died in the fire, and that caused quite a stir. When they found no bones, they searched the desert. In other words, your crass irresponsibility caused everyone a great deal of time and expense."

"Sorry, but I—"

"Too late. Jan explained how the car overheated and caught on fire, so what was the big deal reporting the loss?"

Bless Jan's little lying heart; I've taught her well. "Okay, go ahead and give Norquist my Mexican cell number. I'll explain about the amnesia."

"Amnesia?"

"Until this very minute, I had completely forgotten about that rental car. Must have been the shock. Now it's suddenly all coming back to me."

"Well, then, Miz Hetta, you'd best suddenly call Budget, for they are on the very verge of issuing an arrest warrant for your amnesiac self. And you would not like the inside of a Mexican jail. Plus, I will *not* be coming to get you out this time."

"I'll take care of it. I promise."

"Now?"

"Yes, now. Do you have, like, a contact number for Budget? My rental papers were sort of blow…burned up."

"Along with your memory? Or could it have been a recurrence of your brain cancer."

Jeez, that Jan has a big mouth. "Just give me the damned number."

She did. I called, told them how, right after the car caught on fire, we were set upon by banditos who attacked me, hit me on the head, and I had been recovering ever since in a San

Diego hospital. They agreed to charge the deductible to Jan's burned up Master Card.

I plumb forgot to notify Jan of the charge.

That amnesia is a bitch.

In a surge of contrition, I set out to ameliorate the swath of crap I'd managed to leave in my wake the past couple of weeks.

I called Jenks, apologized for acting like a jerk and not listening to his advice. After all, I needed to stay at his apartment in Oakland. He graciously accepted my apology and our conversation ended on much friendlier terms than the last.

I'd already handled Budget.

After a visit to the Port Captain, I found I wasn't in hot water with Capitan Reyes, and that in fact he was basking in the light of being somewhat of a local celebrity after his interview on CNN International. I asked him to recommend a boat watcher and when he found out I was willing to pay two hundred a month, he jumped on the job himself. He was free on weekends and, if I gave him a maintenance checklist, he'd be more than happy to make sure she didn't sink in her slip. I figured he didn't make a lot of money, and that my contribution would be a huge addition to his Christmas budget.

Lucky for me, my own credit cards were in my boat safe, as was my debit card, so I was set for moola for the time being. I polished up and sent my final report to the Trob, and topped off *Raymond Johnson's* tanks like Daddy always told me to do.

Now all I had to do was arrange to get myself back to the Bay Area with my entire working wardrobe, which I figured would fill at least three suitcases. Everything I owned was on the boat. I would have to attend meetings up north, and set up a working office in Jenks's apartment in Oakland. That meant I'd need my computer, printer, and fax machine. The list of stuff I had to haul was huge, prompting me to consider renting a car and driving back.

A couple of calls told me that Budget, as well as every other rental agency in Mexico, had me at the top of their S list, and I couldn't quite picture driving the Thing all the way to the Bay Area, even if I could get it across the border with Mexican plates.

The solution came to me in a flash of red and yellow.

"Day-ache-elle!"

I stuck my head out the teak slider and was greeted by my old pals who'd brought me Trouble. I waved them on board and they headed straight for my replenished beer supply.

"So what is it today, guys? Got an *elefante* in your truck?"

One of them grinned and handed me an envelope, this one from the Trob. I quickly tore it open and saw a fat check attached to a disclaimer that Baxter Brothers was not responsible for my actions, and that by cashing said check, we were no longer affiliated. I also noted that for some strange reason, he gave me full invoice amount. Damn, I'd shorted myself if he agreed to all my demands.

I was free to head north, and I had a solution to my move at hand.

Two hours and a case of beer later, my clothes and office paraphernalia were packed into collapsible storage boxes I had stashed away, and loaded into the DHL van. I gave my stuff a fifty-fifty chance of arriving in Oakland, so I held on to my laptop, but it was the best I could come up with on short notice.

I was getting ready to call the airlines for a reservation on the next flight out when the phone rang in my hand.

"Hetta," Jan wailed, "I need help."

A friend in need is a pest.

25

"What's wrong, Jan?"

"I've broken up with Chino."

"Did he doo doo in his diaper?"

"Just stop it, right now—"

"Okay, okay. Sorry."

"You should be. I need help, and, after all, you got me into this mess."

"I forced you to jump ship and take up with a beach bum?" Calling Chino a bum was pushing the envelope, but maybe that's what she needed, a little negative reinforcement.

"There's that, but what you really did was blow up my passport, Mexican visa, and credit cards. Now I'm stuck in Mexico and can't get home."

I didn't bother to argue that it wasn't me who blew up the rental, but a wild and crazy drug dealer, and we wouldn't have been there in the first place if she wasn't looking for Granny Yee. She wouldn't listen anyhow. "What do you want me to do?"

"I want you to come get me. I can't get on the ferry without my visa, and I don't have my passport to get a new one. And I'm broke because I don't have a debit card to get money."

"You could ask Chino to reimburse you for his allowance, or maybe raid his piggy bank."

"Het-ta, give it a rest."

She was getting testy. "Where are you?"

"The bus station in Santa Rosalia. I do have enough pesos for a room tonight, but that's about it."

"Seriously, Chino let you leave with no money and no way to get back to the States?"

"Well, I sort of didn't tell him I was leaving. I left a note."

"Did that note mention your age?"

"Just shut up and come get me."

"I need to think. Call me back in thirty minutes. Do you still have minutes left on your Ladatel card?"

"Not much."

"Okay, then, go down to the marina office at Santa Rosalia. I'll call you there. If no one is around the office, find a ham operator on one of the boats. I'll be on Happy Hour. Got that?"

"Oh, Hetta, bless you. I was so afraid I wouldn't be able to reach you, and…" she began to whimper.

"Jan, pull in that bottom lip and go to the marina. Everything will be okay, I promise. I think there's an American Consulate in Hermosillo, but right now we have to get you over to this side. I have a plan."

"You do? Fantastic, bye."

"Bye."

I needed a plan.

* * *

Double crappola. Here's what my Google search told me about getting Jan legal:

In the event that your passport is lost or stolen while in Mexico please come in person to the Passport & Citizenship Unit (Working Hours). Depending on your personal circumstances, the Passport office will process your application for a new full-validity or emergency (limited-validity) passport. Application requirements, including fees, for emergency passports are the same as those for full-validity passports. You will need proof of citizenship and a photo ID, such as a driver's license or school ID. The cost of the passport is $97 USD for adults and $82 USD for minors under age 16.

The Passport & Citizenship Office will only issue emergency passports that are needed for urgent travel. Applicants requesting an emergency passport will be required to provide proof of immediate travel plans such as a valid itinerary or airline tickets, as well as an explanation for why the travel plans cannot be changed to allow sufficient time for the processing of a full-validity passport (usually about two weeks). In most cases, same-day issuance is possible for emergency passports. However, some cases require approval from the Department of State prior to issuance.

Hello? Hetta to the US Passport and Citizenship Unit, who in the hell carries proof of citizenship when you have a passport, which *is* proof of citizenship?

Jan didn't have proof of citizenship *or* a photo ID. We'd have to call her mother, have her send a certified copy of her birth certificate to her in San Carlos, call California for a duplicate driver's license, and after all that finally arrived, apply for a passport. I doubted the Department of State would deem breaking up with your boyfriend enough of an emergency to issue an emergency passport, so we could be stuck in Mexico for another month. Not that I would normally mind, but like I said, I felt the welcome mat was a little worn.

Maybe I should call my DHL guys. Hell, they shipped an illegal parrot, what's a blonde to them? Once DHL landed Jan in San Carlos, and I uncrated her, we could make a run for the border. My experience so far was that the Mexican military rarely asked to see Mexican visas at their inspection stations, or any other ID, for that matter. Once we made it to the US border, they might not ask for ID at all. We were a year away before the law went into effect of having to produce a passport if crossing into the US by land. Even if they did want paperwork, Jan could start crying, tell her sad tale of woe, and they'd probably let her in.

But back to reality.

I really, really, didn't want to press my luck and take *Raymond Johnson* across the sea alone again, and I didn't want to take a week to do it. I was wracking my already overloaded brain when the phone rang again.

"Jan?"

"No, Jenks."

"Oh."

"Gee, your response makes me feel all warm and fuzzy."

"I'm sorry, sweetie. Jan called and she's left Chino and needs to get over here, but she doesn't have a passport or Mexican visa."

"What happened to her papers?"

"They were burn…uh, burgled." I didn't think Jenks needed the ugly details, especially since it would only reinforce his silly idea that I'm a disaster looking for a place to happen.

"Burgled?"

"Her purse."

"Ah. And Chino? He was burgled, too?"

"No, he was dumped. If he calls you, tell him Jan's all right, and on her way here."

"You think he'll call me?"

"He might. I guess she just kinda left him a Dear Chino note."

"At least she called my brother, Lars, to dump him for Chino. Do I detect a pattern here?"

I laughed and it felt good. It also felt good to know I had Jenks to confide in, laugh with. It wasn't what I was used to.

Being a single, professionally successful, highly independent female of a certain age has many pitfalls, the most dangerous of which is being stubbornly single, sovereign, and solo. I won't even address the certain age part.

As the years roll by, insecurity builds, despite one's secure facade. Ever more on the defensive, even the slightest hint that your life is not absolute perfection sends you into an increasingly defensive mode to protect your dirty little secret, which is that you would rather be helplessly dependant on a significant other, but you don't know how.

It is just this conundrum that led Gloria Steinem to quip, "I have yet to hear a man ask for advice on how to combine marriage and a career." It's women like me who keep the Dr. Phils and Lauras of the world in bidness.

My personal defense mechanism is flamboyancy in the extreme, which is a great attribute when amusing your friends, but a risky trait when attempting to attract and keep a soul mate, or whatever they call them these days.

Right now, my defenses were down. "Jenks, I miss you. Can't you come home?"

"Sure, in a month."

"I mean now," I whined. I hate whining.

"Hetta, are you in trouble again?"

"Why do you think that?"

"You whined."

"I did not. I do not whine."

"That's what I mean."

This conversation was destined for derail. There were a couple of ways to handle the situation, one of which was sweetness and diplomacy, perhaps exercising a little non-defensive self-control for a change? It could happen, but where's the fun in that?

"Screw you, Jenks, and the camel you rode in on."

"That's more like it. Gotta run. Love you."

"Yeah? Well come home, then."

"Bye."

26

The afternoon rolled by with no call from Jan, and my calls to the marina office at Santa Rosalia went unanswered, so I put myself to work, decorating *Raymond Johnson* for Christmas, just in case I stayed longer than I should. It gave me something to do instead of fretting and waiting for Jan's call. Smith came by and gave me a hand with the lights, said he'd turn them on for me if I wasn't here, and even volunteered to take them down after the season.

Satisfied that both the strings of white lights lacing the rails and a wreath gracing the bow pulpit passed muster, I tuned up the ham radio, poured myself a glass of wine and waited. On the dot of five, familiar voices started chattering about boat parts, weather, the price of diesel, and the latest gossip. After ten minutes with no call from Jan, I grabbed the mike. "Edgewise," I yelled.

"That sounded like Hetta. That you, Hetta? Did you finally get a license, or is this another emergency?"

"This really is an emergency."

"Okay, everyone stand by while I get formal. Station calling, what is the nature of your emergency?"

Why hadn't I thought this through? Think, think. "*I* don't have an emergency per se, but I do have a sort of important message for a friend who may be on a boat in Santa Rosalia, listening in and waiting for this, uh, traffic."

The net manager, Gene, sighed. "Name of person you are trying to contact?"

"Jan Sims."

"Boat name?"

"*Raymond Johnson.*"

"Not *your* boat name, Hetta. Jan's."

"Oh. I don't know. She was supposed to look for a boat with a ham radio."

"Okay, then, standby. CQ, CQ, CQ, Santa Rosalia."

Silence.

"CQ, CQ, CQ, Santa Rosalia."

A booming voice straight out of a Grade B WWII war movies answered, "Tango Lima, Santa Rosalia. Ist Herbert here."

"Herbert. Haven't heard from you in a dog's age."

"I listen. You haf need of Santa Rosalia?"

"Roger. Okay, Herbert, finish your call sign, and Hetta, stand by until he finishes, then talk to him."

I jotted Herbert's call down as he checked in, then raised the mike. "Tango Lima, Santa Rosalia, have you seen a tall blonde wandering around the docks there?"

"No."

"Oh. Well, can you ask around, or put out a VHF call for someone who may have seen Jan Sims? It's real important."

"I vill look."

"Thanks. Back to you, Gene."

There was a cacophony of voices, all trying to talk at

once. Gene finally regained control by virtue of his signal strength. "Okay, everyone who *isn't* a singlehander wanting to find the blonde, don't talk."

Dead silence. "I thought so. Now, where were we?"

The net went on in normal fashion for what seemed like hours until I heard the Santa Rosalia station break in. I hunched closer to the radio and held my breath.

"I haf your friends here. Vee vill arrive in San Carlos tomorrow morning."

"Wow! Thanks."

"Ist not problem. Out."

Gene cleared him, then quipped, "Gee, Hetta, that must be some blonde. Herbert hasn't left port in a year."

"Jan has that affect on the male populous. Thank you all so much. And I am studying for my test, really. I'll be uh, QRT."

The net went on, but I was pulled away by a call on VHF. "*Raymond Johnson, Raymond Johnson, Taiwan On.*"

"*Raymond Johnson*, here."

"Switch seven-two

"Seven-two."

I switched the channel, as most likely did the entire boating population within range. "Reading the mail," as we call it, is what folks do for fun, especially during happy hour. There are no secrets in the Sea of Cortez.

"You there, Hetta?"

"Yep, how you doin' Smith?"

"I'm fine, but are you going to be on the boat for awhile?"

"Sure. Why?"

"Need to talk. I'm walking your way right now. I'm on my handheld. See you in two seconds."

"Okay." I switched back to channel sixteen, wondering what this was all about, as were, I'm sure, the rest of the mail readers. The boat dipped, so I walked to the door to meet Smith and Maggie. He had an almost empty beer in his hand, so I got him a fresh one, another glass of wine for myself, a dog cookie for Maggie, and we settled into deck chairs.

"Your Christmas lights look great, Hetta."

"So do yours. Doesn't the marina look festive with all the boats lit up?"

"You gonna be in the lighted boat parade?"

"Don't know. Depends on when Jan gets here, and when we head north. So, what's up? You called me."

"Well, uh, I really don't know how to…uh, well, I…"

"Spit it out, sailor boy. Can't be that bad."

"I hope not. Okay, here's the deal. That guy you were just talking to on ham radio, Herbert?"

"Yes."

"Well, I know Jan's a big girl and can handle herself pretty well, but I'm not sure she should be alone at sea with this guy."

"What is he? A serial rapist?" I quipped.

"Actually, I've heard rumors something like that."

I almost spit out my wine. "You're kidding. What kind of rumors, exactly?"

"Several women have answered his ads for crew, and everyone of them left the boat the day they arrived. One of them, one I actually met, had a black eye. She didn't want to get into details, but evidently this skoady toad has a seriously twisted porno library on board."

"How old is this guy?"

"Gotta be pushing seventy, and makes no bones about being an ex-Nazi. And that ex-part? Some say not so. God only knows what he did in the war."

"Oh, that's just great. The net is over, and we have no way to contact them. Too late now for a warning, I guess."

My apparent lack of concern had him looking at me like I was a bug. "I thought Jan was your best friend. This could be really serious."

"I know. Poor guy doesn't know what he's in for. I just hope Jan doesn't kill him *before* she gets within VHF radio range. She can't sail, you know."

It was Smith's turn to spit beer. Actually, some bubbled from his nose. I've never seen anyone laugh so hard in my whole life, and I come from a long line of serious laughers. When he finally gained control, he managed to gasp, "My god, but you two are a pair to draw to."

After Smith left to take Maggie for her evening walk, I found salad makings, added a chopped boiled egg and ham, the last of my hard to come by feta cheese, and went out on the back deck to watch the lights glow ever brighter in the fading light.

Despite my joking with Smith, I was very concerned for Jan's safety, but like he said, she's a big girl. She would arrive safe and sound, but we still had to get out of Mexico. I was mulling over our avenues of escape when something from my conversation with the alleged deviant popped into my head. Did he, or didn't he say, "friends"? Racking my brain, I recalled what he said. He *did* say, "friends." In fact, he said, "'I haf your friends here. Vee vill arrive in San Carlos tomorrow morning." Just bad English?

I finished my wine, did some boat chores and went to bed early with Carl Hiaasen. I love a funny guy. Sometime during the night I woke to a howling wind. Jan was not only out to sea with some kind of sexual deviant, she was out in a storm, in a boat that hadn't left the dock in a year. I said a little prayer that she didn't have to kill Herbert until they were on this side of the sea.

Wide awake and worrying, I decided to go on line, search

for options to get us to the border. Without a passport, air travel was out of the question. Without a Mexican visa, the bus was iffy. That left hitchhiking or driving, and hitchhiking is not my cup of tea. Since a real rental car was out, the only thing left was the VW Thing I'd been driving. Impractical or not, it seemed the only way. We'd have to make the two-hundred or so mile trip north in it, ditch it at the border, then walk across, and hope no one asks for ID.

I've walked across the border a few times and I know the customs guy generally asks if you are a US citizen, you say yes, he asks what you are bringing back from Mexico, you say rum, and across you go. Easy as pie.

Worst case? They won't let Jan in, I go across, get her birth certificate and driver's license sent to me, then come back and get her. Who knows, maybe Jan would enjoy a month or so in Nogales. Or a Mexican jail? What if she's turned back, and then the Mexicans demand ID? I decided not to bring that scenario up. Why worry her?

I looked for car storage in Nogales. No luck. I'd just have to find a car repair place, pay them to store the Thing until someone picked it up.

I crawled back into bed, but not before sticking my head outside. It was blowing at least thirty knots from the northwest. Poor Jan was having a seriously bumpy ride, but that might be a good thing. If Herbert was busy steering the boat, he'd keep his hands to himself and Jan might not have to kill him. It could happen, but I feared that sooner or later I'd be forced out into the gale on a search and rescue mission.

I left the VHF radio on, just in case Jan had to put out that dreaded May Day.

I hoped she'd remember to weight the body before dumping it overboard.

27

"Raymond Johnson, Raymond Johnson, *Manga Manga* here," Jan's voice warbled through the cabin.

I jumped up, almost overturning my morning coffee into my keyboard, and dove for the mike.

"*Manga Manga*, go channel eighty-eight." I chose eighty-eight because it was seldom used, and unwelcome listeners wouldn't have it readily programmed into their radios, giving me a few seconds to speak with Jan in privacy.

"Hetta, you there?"

"Yes. Don't say anything that can be used in court."

"Huh?"

"Let me rephrase that. Is everyone all right?"

"Yes. *All* of us," she said in a deliberate fashion that told me something was amiss.

All of them. Who is all? I thought this Herbert character was a singlehander.

"And," I drawled, "where're all y'all at?" Texan grammar, granted, but only in Texas does one get away with working two all's into one short sentence, ending in a preposition that has no object, and still be clear. Jan would know immediately that I'd caught the extra *all*, meaning more than two. But who?

"We should be arriving at your marina in a couple of hours. We made fantastic time. Can you arrange a spot near you? Like, right next to you, if possible?"

I looked out and saw the slip across from me remained vacant. "I think so. I'll call the marina office when they open and get back to you. We'll be waiting to catch your lines." I caught her *all*, she'd catch my *we'll*.

"Great. Ice down a Corona for me, will ya?"

Corona? Jan hates Corona. She says it tastes like a skunk smells. Something was definitely wrong, but I'd have to wait a couple of hours to find out what. Perhaps I should try to find a body bag, just in case the all in y'all got offed?

The wind dropped to nothing, so I took my coffee on deck to contemplate my next move. Smith sauntered up, laughing softly. "Good one, Hetta."

Huh? "Glad I'm so amusing. What did I do to put you in such good spirits this morning?"

"You're kidding, right?"

I shook my head.

"Eighty-eight?"

I must have looked as bewildered as I felt, so Smith explained. "It's an inside joke down here. Lots of Germans emigrated to Mexico after the war, and in La Paz they use channel eighty- eight to chat in their mother tongue. One year, this very clever boater who was some kind of radio broadcaster was down here for a season and came to the conclusion that the Germans used eighty-eight, *achtundachtzig*, because H is the eighth letter in the alphabet. HH. Heil Hitler. You just called Herbert, the Nazi, on the Hitler channel. You're the dock hero. "

I chuckled in spite of my worry over Jan's plight. Boaters evidently have *way* too much time on their hands. All they really worry about is food, and where—

"Hey, Smith, how'd you like to help me host a little brunch this morning?"

"Sure. I picked up two dozen eggs yesterday."

"And I have plenty of frozen English muffins. I'll even throw in some Bloody Marys. You alert the troops...say brunch on the dock in about two hours?"

By the time *Manga Manga* motored into her slip and Jan threw me a line, there were a dozen people milling around the dock, munching on free brunch.

Smith grabbed the stern line while I tied off the bow. Jan stood woodenly on deck, twitching her eyebrows and rolling her eyes to the right. Herbert, stone-faced, cut the engine and went below, then Jan turned and, zombie-like, followed. What were these folks on?

I walked to the back of the boat, leaned over the lifeline, and spoke to the black hole that was the open cockpit hatch. "Jan? Y'all want some breakfast? And I have that Corona good and cold for you."

"Oh, good. Uh, could you bring it to me?"

What the hell? "Ooo-kay." I looked around at the disappointingly empty dock, hoping for backup, but with *Manga Manga* safely in her slip, and the majority of my McHetta muffins and bloody Marys scarfed down, my welcoming committee had vanished. Only the dock dog, Marina, remained to pick off the scraps. Dammit, I should have told Smith of my suspicions that all was not well aboard the German's boat, but typical of me, I didn't. Now I sensed it wouldn't be a great idea to call in the troops, either in person, or on the radio. I'd just have to wing it.

Trying to sound cheerfully nonchalant, and not the least

bit suspicious, I called to Jan, "I'll be right back with your brekkies and beer." I headed across to *Raymond Johnson* for food. And ammo.

Shrugging on a lightweight jacket in spite of midmorning warmth, I slipped a loaded flare pistol into a deep inside pocket. Rummaging in a locker, I pulled out a roll of duct tape, known to the boating bunch as "hundred mile an hour tape," and grabbed my handheld VHF radio.

My next move had to be really fast. I wrapped the tape around the radio, but not so it would hold down the transmit button…yet. Then I opened the door, stepped out onto the deck and reached back in for the fixed radio mike.

"*Manga Manga, Raymond Johnson.*"

I waited. Finally, Jan answered, "*Raymond Johnson, Manga Manga here.*"

"Switch to eighty-eight?"

"Eighty-eight."

"How many beers?"

There was a delay, as if she were asking for a beer count. "Just one."

If I'd hoped for a clue, that wasn't it. "Okay, uh, stand by on eighty-eight." By now, surely we had radio lurkers galore. Sunday's a slow news day.

I threw the mike back in the door, pulled the tape over the transmit button on my handheld, scurried to the dock, dashed across, and leapt aboard *Manga Manga*. The sailboat rocked violently while I, hoping for an element of surprise, launched myself down the stairs, into the saloon. As my eyes adjusted to the gloom, I saw a pale-faced Jan seated at the nav station, radio mike still in hand. Scoady Toad perched on the edge of his settee, blotchy faced and rather green. Unhappy, I'd guess, but then maybe he always looked that way. I took two steps in. "Now, what…?"

The cold steel of a muzzle nuzzled my neck, and a hand slid around to muzzle me. I was twice muzzled, and not feeling all warm and nuzzled. Pushing me forward, my attacker shoved me rudely into Jan, then reached down and turned the VHF radio volume up. I was standing practically nose to nose with Jan, whose eyes were like saucers. I mouthed, "Who?"

Her bottom lip quivered, but she didn't answer.

Behind me, a familiar, gruff voice said, quite loudly, "Yes, we had a great crossing, Hetta. Good to be back in San Carlos again. Hey, thanks for the beer."

His seemingly innocent statement boomed from my pocket. Whirling me around, he motioned a gimme sign, and put his finger to his lips to make sure I didn't yell for help. I reluctantly handed over the radio, which he turned off. He then turned off *Manga Manga's* radio. "There, that's better, a little privacy. So, Red, did you miss me?"

I gaped at Nacho, who was probably the last person on earth I missed, or wanted, to see ever again. "*Merde.*"

28

Nacho grinned. "You gonna hurt my feelings, *chica*. Here I come all this way, and that's all you got to say? '*Merde*?' How 'bout somethin' like, 'Nacho, I been keepin' your wallet for you?'"

"What wallet?" I can be so clever in a pinch.

"The stinkin' wallet that you took from my stinkin' truck." He pulled Jan next to him and nudged her ribs with what looked like a Glock, for cryin' out loud.

"Oh, *that* wallet. It's in a safe place. If I give it to you, will you get lost?"

"It ain't that easy, Red. You gotta pay."

"Hey," Scoady Toad piped up, "if you're gonna do something kinky, can I watch?"

Nacho gave Scoady a look of disgust. "Shut the hell up. I shoulda dumped your scrawny ass overboard when you put your filthy hands on," he nodded at Jan, "her beautiful ass."

Jan perked up and smiled. "Thank you for almost breaking his arm, Nacho," she purred.

Gag me. We're stuck in a smelly old sailboat with a pervert and an armed drug runner, and she's flirting? And what now?

"Okay, Don Quixote, what now? I give you the wallet, and...?"

"And we take a little trip."

"I'm low on diesel."

"We don't need no diesel, we need a car. You have one? After all, you used the hell out of mine. Got it back, by the way."

"I don't got no stinkin' car."

"But, Hetta," Jan chirped, "what about the Thing? Give him the keys and let him skedaddle."

"Jan, he said *we*. *We* take a little trip. Unless he has a cockroach in his pocket, I believe that means *us*."

Nacho nodded.

"Oh. Where? And why do we have to go?"

"I need...actually, we *all* need, to get the hell out of Mexico, *pronto*."

He had that right, but not with him. No way. "Why do you need to get out of Mexico? What'd you do? Snort up all of your thuggy friends' dope? And why take us?"

"None of your business. We'll just be three tourists going back to Arizona after a weekend at the beach."

"More like two *gringas* picked up a wetback for a souvenir." Even I couldn't believe I said that, but Nacho brings out the best in me.

Nacho actually laughed and looked skyward, as if asking for divine deliverance.

"Don't bother calling on someone who doesn't know you. If you don't like our company, let us go."

He chose to ignore me. "Let's get ready to roll."

"What about him?" I pointed at the Toad.

"He's staying. And he ain't calling no *policia*, either, are you, *pendejo?*"

The sullen Herbert shook his head and his lips moved.

Nacho cupped his hand to his ear. "I can't *hear* you."

"No."

"No, what?"

"I won't be callink der cops."

"And why is that?"

Toad mumbled something unintelligible.

"I can't *hear* you."

"If I do, you'll send der video tapes to das *federales*."

"And what tapes would those be, you sick asshole?"

"Der boyss."

"The *little* boys, and *you*. Little *Mexican* boys, *cabron*. I think you know how long you'd last in a Mexican jail. They don't have no stinkin' *pervertivo* protective custody bullcrap south of the border. We Mexicans cherish our children, and not the way you and your ped friends do."

As Jan and I listened to this exchange, my stomach quivered and my nerve ends sang. We were, for reasons unknown, being taken hostage, and our only hope for rescue rested on the bony shoulders of a depraved sicko who had everything to lose if he tipped anyone off that we were kidnapped. If there was a glimmer of anything good in the situation, it was that Nacho was taking us to the border, and if anyone on earth knows how to get across without a passport, it's a drug runner.

"This is all very informative," I said, hoping my voice didn't give away the nervous breakdown I was on the verge of having, "but let's work out some plan. One that doesn't include anyone getting hurt, okay? Well, anyone except the perv, there. You can go ahead and shoot Herbert now if you like."

Herbert scowled, but Nacho actually smiled. "Too much noise. Okay, everyone to the big boat, and not one word to anyone on the dock, or that someone will not be happy. Easy does it."

He motioned for the perv to lead, then me, then Jan. Indian file, we exited the boat, then headed across the dock to *Raymond Johnson*, but someone yelled, "Hetta!"

We turned as one as Smith raced toward us. "Hetta, have you seen Maggie? I've looked everywhere. She on your boat?"

"Don't think so. I've been on *Manga Manga*."

"Can we take a look?"

I heard Jan let out a little mewl, probably because she'd been goosed with a Glock. I turned to Nacho, who was indeed cozied up to Jan's backside, and raised my eyebrows. He gave me an almost imperceptive nod.

"Sure, Smith, after you." I waved him ahead, then followed. Once aboard *Raymond Johnson*, he turned to wait for me, but I instinctively knew that Nacho wasn't about to let me go into the main saloon alone with Smith. "Go ahead, check for her. We'll be there in a minute."

Smith stepped through the open door and began calling Maggie. It wasn't unusual for her to sneak aboard. I'd found her snoozing in my bed several times. Not today, though, by the disappointed look on Smith's face when he came back out. He said a distracted, "Thanks," and took off in search of his errant pooch.

Deflated that a chance for salvation was gone, we trooped onto *Raymond Johnson*, where Nacho wasted no time. "Wallet."

Seeing no reason not to, I crossed to my desk, and handed him his wallet. He flipped it open, checked his credit cards, and for cash, which was gone. "Oops, I had to use your cash for gas. Oh, and your credit card for that new mink coat."

"I know what you used it for. I have Internet banking."

Dope dealers got Internet banking?

29

Nacho flipped his wallet shut and shoved it into the back pocket of his jeans. I noticed Jan taking note of their snug fit, and inwardly groaned. He shoved Herbert the Pervert into a chair and waved the Glock at me. "Okay, Red, let's pack up that car of yours and get ready to roll for the border. Gimme the keys."

"They're in the closet."

Jan looked longingly at the galley locker where, back in the States, I'd kept my arsenal. Unfortunately, when we decided to make a trip south of the border, our hired captain forbade us firearms on board. I considered ignoring his no-gun rule, but Jan had pitched a hissy and insisted, because of the severe penalties for possession of guns in Mexico, I leave them at home. See if I ever listen to *her* again.

Snatching the car keys from their hook, I threw them at Nacho. He handily caught them in a graceful one-handed move that reminded me of a baseball pitcher from the Dominican Republic I once dated. Oh, boy, was that Rudy a looker, in a tall, lanky, Hispanic way, much like Nac....I mentally slapped myself back to the present. "Pack, you say? What?"

"Food, water. Don't want to stop for nothin' or nobody. How much gas you have in your car?"

"Actually, it isn't my car. It's a sort of rental."

"Damn. What kinda plates?"

"Sonora."

"Double damn. Even with half of the Latino population of the US headed back north after Christmas with the relatives in Mexico, Mex plates still get too much attention at the border crossings."

"Yeah, well, so do Mexicans, so nothing personal, but Jan and I would prefer to walk across without you. Better yet, I'm getting a lit-tle tired of you, Nacho. What if we just decide, right here and now, to refuse to go with you at all? What are you gonna do? Off us right here, what with all these people in boats around us for witnesses? And what good would it do you? Just take the car and go."

"Ain't that easy, Red. For one thing, while popping you might make my day, that's not what's gonna happen. Maybe I'll just make you, or Blondie, wish you'd never met me."

"Too late. We already do."

He smiled a mean smile. "And then," he growled, "there's always Maggie."

I did a double take and Nacho nodded. "When we get to the border, I'll make a call, and Maggie gets released. If not, she goes to bow-wow heaven."

I couldn't believe my ears. Nacho somehow had Maggie? "But how—"

"I have friends."

"In very low places, no doubt? Like Herbert here? He seems an appropriate amigo for someone like you."

Nacho shook his head in disgust. "You just never let up, do you?"

"It's my nature, *pendejo*," I spat, using the word he'd called Herbert. I wasn't sure what it meant, but it sounded properly disrespectful.

Nacho threw his arm out, the gunless one, his forefinger ending up not an inch from my nose. I was proud of myself for not flinching. "That's it. From now on, Red, not one word from you, unless I ask you a direct question. Not. One. Single. Word. Keep that smart mouth of yours shut, or I *will* make Blondie hurt."

Jan's head jerked up. "Hey! How come if she mouths off, I get hurt?"

"Peer pressure, kitten. Makes it your job to keep a muzzle on your bulldog."

I opened my mouth to protest being referred to as a bulldog, but Jan stomped my foot. "If you utter a syllable, Hetta, I swear I'll borrow that gun and shoot you myself."

Like I said before, a friend in need is a pest.

Before we left San Carlos, I had a whole new appreciation for mimes. Every time I turned around, someone asked me a question I was forbidden to answer.

We packed up bottled water, clothes and all the road food in *Raymond Johnson's* cupboards. As more and more of my secret junk food stash was revealed, Jan's snidely comments increased, and I couldn't even snipe back.

"Ya know, Nacho, you may be a bad ass, but you sure know how to show a girl a good time," Jan said. "Muzzling Hetta is ever so much fun." She found a bag of Cheetos in the far reaches of a cabinet and shook it at me. "Hoarding for a bad food day, Hetta?"

I sneered, snatched the Cheetos and slam-dunked them into a duffle bag.

"Okay, you two, let's go. Single file. Hetta first, then you, Jan. Anyone does anything stupid, Jan gets it in one of her long and lovely legs."

"Why thank you, Nacho."

I made a sound that came out like "urk" but they ignored me. Nacho pointed at the door, but I refused to move. Jan gave me a shove, but I stood fast.

"Now what?" Nacho growled.

I walked over and pointed to my laptop case on the desk.

"Okay, pack up your computer and we'll take it."

I quickly loaded up my Dell, mouse pad and power supply. I also slid a letter opener into the case. Never know when you'll need to open an envelope. Or someone's throat. Computer case in hand, I nodded toward the pervert sitting on my settee, then at the door.

"You want him to go with us?" Jan asked.

I shook my head.

"You want him off your boat?"

I gave an emphatic nod.

Nacho shrugged. "Okay, perv, off the broad's boat, *rapido*."

Scoady Toad scampered off *Raymond Johnson* as fast as his little Nazi legs would travel.

"Now, ladies, can we possibly get a move on?" Nacho asked through clenched teeth.

I shook my head violently, tilted my head and daintily cupped my ear.

Jan's face lit with delight. "Sounds like?"

Yes! I pointed at the ship's clock.

"Sounds like clock. Dock?"

I turned my head from side to side.

"Sock? You want some socks?"

From the tick of his rigid jaw muscles and crimson cheeks, I ascertained that our Nacho was getting a mite impatient with our antics. Dangerous game, perhaps, but I wanted to see just how far he could be pushed. I found out.

His arm lashed out, encircled Jan's neck and he jerked her roughly against him. Pointing the gun downward with his other hand, he growled, "I hate Charades. Move, *now*, or I swear I'll pop Blondie on one of her gorgeous knees."

I saw Jan's eyes widen, but she leaned back into him and gave a little butt wiggle against his groin. Nacho looked flustered, shoved her away, and yelled, "Out! Now."

Weary of hearing about Jan's feminine attributes, I considered letting him whack one of them, but obediently did a one-eighty and stomped toward the door. Stopping dead in my tracks though, I tapped the lock.

"Yeah, yeah, yeah. I get it. I'll lock the fuggin' door. Git!"

I smiled sweetly and mouthed a silent, "Thank you," but Nacho muttered, as he herded us toward the parking lot, "Fuggin' gringas."

Yeah, well, Mr. Macho Nacho, this fuggin' gringa's got a flare pistol in her pocket and she *ain't* glad to see you.

30

When we reached the marina parking lot, Nacho was less than thrilled with the Thing. He shook his head in disgust. "You call this a car?"

"Does that qualify as a direct question, or simply rhetorical?" I ventured, testing Nacho's gag order.

Jan whapped me on the head, and Nacho growled, "Shut the hell up."

Rhetorical, I surmise. Sometimes I'm clairvoyant that way.

Nacho ordered me to drive, Jan to ride shotgun, and he opted for the back seat, no doubt to better keep my skull in his gun sights. With nothing but an overturned metal bucket to sit on in the back, I was gratified that Nacho would be less than comfortable. Had he been in my good graces I might have offered him a dollop of Prep H, but circumstances being what they were, I said a little thank you to the higher power in charge of butt pain.

Before handing me the keys, he asked, "Do you know the road to Nogales?"

No, but hum a few bars and I'll pick it up, I wanted to say, but I only nodded.

"Okay, keep it at, or under, the speed limit, which is about sixty."

If I hadn't been gagged, I might have told him the speedometer didn't work. Or maybe not.

"I figure," he continued, "we can make the border by dark. In fact, I want to cross after dark. Just take it easy, and no funny stuff. With any luck we'll all be across, and on our separate ways, in a few hours. How much gas you got?"

I pointed to the gauge, which read FULL. Jan opened her mouth to comment, thought better of it and slouched down into her seat. I started the Thing and, with a lurch, drove toward the marina exit gate.

Off in the distance, I saw Smith pacing and calling for Maggie. Only Marina, the dock dog, stood by his side while his plaintive calls went unanswered. I shot Nacho a look of pure disgust, but he only shrugged. "It's up to you two whether he gets his pup back."

I couldn't say anything, but Jan could. "Ya know, Nacho," she sneered, "it doesn't take much of a man to threaten two defenseless women and a tiny dog. Your mother must be sooo proud."

Good girl.

The Thing sputtered to a halt just on the other side of Hermosillo, in a desolate stretch of desert.

I knew, from other highway trips in Mexico, that a stalled car was a beacon to good Samaritans. Mexican Samaritans, as a rule. Unlike back home, everyone in Mexico watched out for their neighbors, because most had cars that frequently ended up stranded. No one left home without jumper cables.

Nacho cursed softly, then told us to, "Stay put," as he slid from his bucket perch. I was gratified to see two grooves in his jeans from the bucket edges, and that he'd developed a major wedgie. He tried to look cool while pulling denim from his butt crack. He no longer had a gun in hand, but he didn't need one; he waved his cell phone at us. "Remember, one call and Maggie's history."

Popping up what served as a hood, he sniffed loudly, came back to my side of the car. "I thought you said we had gas."

I shrugged and pointed to the gauge, which still read FULL.

Nacho narrowed his eyes. "If I didn't need...oh, never mind." He pivoted and stood on the side of the road, intent on waving down help. Gringo cars sped by at twice the legal limit, all headed for home after a rollicking good time south of the border. By the way some drove, they were still partying. After ten minutes, Nacho ordered Jan out of the car.

"Get us some gas, Blondie, or I'll lift the gag on your friend."

"Oh, wouldn't want that." She gave me an evil smile, hiked her shorts, pulled down the neckline of her tee, and about ten seconds later an SUV pulling a boat trailer skidded to a dusty stop. Four drunken men bailed out, offered us a cold beer, and siphoned five gallons of gas from their boat's gas can into the Thing.

I sat silent as ordered, hoping against hope they'd already added outboard motor oil into the gas can so we wouldn't get three feet farther. I wanted to scream for help, pass a note, anything, but Maggie's soulful eyes swam before me. I also really, really wanted one of those beers, but Nacho nixed their offer.

After the helpful fishermen left, I started the car.

Unfortunately, it fired right up, and at the next Pemex station, Nacho topped us off and did a quick calculation. "That should get us to Naco. Anything else I should know about this piece of junk?"

I figured he was being rhetorical again.

Naco? Naco? Where had I read about Naco? And where in the holy hell is it? I wanted to ask a couple of questions, but felt they weren't really worth getting Jan shot. Back on the boat, when I was studying the road map and trying to come up with a plan to get Jan across the border without a passport, I'd traced Mex 15 from Guaymas to Nogales. For the life of me, I couldn't remember any place called Naco along the way, but the name rang a bell. Maybe it was the sacred birthplace of guys called Nacho?

I remembered there were toll booths at Hermosillo, and near a place called Magdalena, but my hopes of getting help at either were dashed when, just south of the first toll booth, Nacho instructed me to take a right. After driving on back roads through what looked to be vineyards for thirty minutes, we returned to the main highway. We'd bypassed the toll booth. Not only was Nacho an asshole, he was a cheap asshole.

Fatigue moved in on me. The adrenaline rush, the one fueling fury over our abduction, as well as Maggie's, suddenly wore off, leaving me incapable of doing anything more than keeping us on the road. I backed my foot off the accelerator and slowed to a speed I thought I could handle safely.

"What are you doing?" Nacho demanded.

There he goes again, asking a question I'm forbidden to answer. And doing charades at forty-five miles an hour is not a great idea. I continued to drive.

"What's she doing?" he demanded of Jan.

"Uh, the speed limit?"

That stumped him, but he demanded I pull over. I did, in

the first wide spot I found. "Okay, Red, I'm going to let you say one sentence. One, only. Why have you slowed down?"

Gee, I can finally talk, and all I can come up with is, "I'm tired." I slumped over the steering wheel for emphasis.

"That's it?"

I turned to look at him and raised my eyebrows.

"Okay, another sentence."

"I'm sick and tired of you, you cowardly, lowlife son of a bitch," I spat. Nacho growled a curse word in Spanish I'd never heard before, but I think it is derived from the noun, mother. Jumping from his perch, he un-wedgied himself, and motioned me out of the car. Jan let out a fearful mewl and asked, "What are you going to do to her?"

"Put her ass on that bucket, that's what. I'll drive."

Why didn't he just shoot me and get it over with? When bucket seats come to my mind, this version wasn't one of them. But wait, if he's driving, who's manning the gun? What's to keep me from stabbing him in the neck with my secreted letter opener?

Jan must have been thinking along the same lines. She surreptitiously winked at me before I climbed into the back seat and tried to find a comfy spot on the sharp edges of the bucket bottom.

Nacho stood outside the Thing's open door on the driver's side, punched a number into his cell phone and said, "If you don't hear from me every fifteen minutes for the next two hours, shoot the mutt."

So much for removing his brain with a letter opener.

He took off at mock one, which was okay until we hit a town called Imuris and we sped onto Mex 2, which if memory served, is an east-west main highway, and a major truck route from Baja California to Juarez, across from El Paso, and points east.

Surely what must be the entire trucking fleet of Mexico was headed to Juarez, and Nacho had little patience for trailing behind the twenty-mile-per hour semis. Passing in no passing zones, barely diving in front of horn blowing semis before we had a head on with another, Nacho rarely slowed down. Jan had her eyes shut, but, somewhat like watching a train wreck, I was mesmerized. If I was going to die on this long and winding road, I'd just as soon see it coming.

Appropriately enough, it was a Tecate truck that finally called Nacho on his chicken game, and ran us off the road. After what seemed like an eternity of jolts, tips, screeching metal and screams, we came to rest in, miracle of miracles, a turnout. Several truckers, lounging next to their overheated semis, watched quietly as the dust settled, then began sauntering our way. Nacho, slightly dazed, got out to inspect the damage. Jan sat dumbly before turning to check on me. I was sprawled over the cooler where my overturned bucket dumped me. I pushed myself up and checked for broken ribs.

Nacho waved the would-be rescuers off with a smile and shrug. I managed to clamber out, grab his arm and point to his watch, then his cell. When I grabbed the arm, he made a move toward his gun, but realized I was just giving him a heads-up on his second Maggie call. He flipped open the phone and hit redial. One of the truckers yelled something I didn't understand, Nacho nodded, then spoke into the phone.

Jan finally joined us, her teeth chattering from fear and the cold. Late afternoon cast shadows into the valley we'd landed in, and a crisp breeze funneling between the mountains added to the chill factor. Although it was probably in the sixties, it felt like low forties. I grabbed a couple of sweat tops from one of the bags and helped her slip one over her head while Nacho inspected the tires. Within twenty minutes, with Nacho patiently trailing the truck parade at a snail's pace, we skirted the town of Cananea, lost the traffic, and a fast thirty miles later, took a sharp turn onto a secondary road.

A secondary road, by definition, is just that, *not* a primary road. In Mexico, however, a secondary road is one step above gravel. Yes, it was paved, but the pavement was pitted with huge potholes, washouts, and a roller coaster-like surface that put what was left of the Thing's suspension to the test. Every time we bottomed out, my bottom put a new dent in the bucket. Or vise versa. It is probably just as well I never wanted children.

Just when I thought things couldn't get worse, they did.

31

gloomy dusk fell as fast as my own gloom. Past tired, I was numb and dumb with fear, dread, and cold. Deep grooves, worn into places left better unmentioned by the bottom rim of the bucket, gave a whole new meaning to pain in the butt. On the bright side, maybe I'd permanently lose some cellulite.

On the horizon, an aura glowed, but from what city? By my calculations, we had to be nearing the border, but where? After a couple of more miles we saw what appeared to be a fairly good-sized spread of lighted houses and, strung to the left and right, a straight row of lights like those on a fence. No, a wall. The border? A little frisson of energy sat me up straight.

Nacho slowed, then stopped, consulted a piece of paper, and pulled from his jacket pocket what looked to be a hand-held GPS. "You two get out. No cute ideas, either."

Jan stirred from the zombie-like trance she'd been in since our scary unscheduled departure from the highway due to Tecate truck interference, and slowly slid from her seat as

I dismounted my bucket of doom. She looked scared silly, so I put my arm around her and patted her shoulder..

Big tears loomed in her eyes. "Hetta, I'm scared."

I wasn't feeling overly optimistic about our situation myself. More than one critter-ravaged body had been dumped in the desert by low life dope dealers. The thought of being left for buzzard food should have scared me sillier than I already am. Instead, a wave of fury swept over me and gave me the determination to survive so I could kick Nacho a good swift one in his *huevos*. Screw him and his gag order all to hell. "Look, Jan," I pointed to the row of lights, "the border. Everything will soon be all right, huh, Nacho?"

Nacho seemed to forget I wasn't supposed to talk. In the dim light I saw his face was drawn with fatigue. In a weary voice he answered, "Yes. It will soon be over."

I didn't like the sound of that. Being *all right* and *over* are not necessarily the same thing.

Still holding onto Jan, I growled, "You don't need us anymore. Leave us here, dammit. By the time we walk to the border, you'll be on the other side, safe and sound with your slimebag friends."

"No way, Red. This desert is crawling with dangerous animals."

"Ain't it though? I, for one, prefer to take my chances with *real* rattlesnakes. They, at least, only kill for food or protection."

"Stuff the National Geographic bunk. You know how to use a GPS?"

"No, I guide my boat by stars and Ouija board."

Ignoring my sarcasm, he handed me the GPS. "See these coordinates? I'm going to drive, and you are going to keep me on a straight course. Cooperate, and we'll be in Arizona in a few minutes. Screw with me and I'll drop a dime on

Maggie, then put a bullet in Blondie's leg and leave her out here to deal with the coyotes."

"Gee, I feel so left out. What you gonna do to me?"

"You don't want to know."

Gulp. "Okay, make the Maggie call and get this show on the road. The sooner we get over the border, the sooner we're shut of you. According to this," I studied the GPS, "we're only five miles, as the crow flies, from your waypoint, which I assume is in Arizona?"

"Close enough."

"Is it or isn't it?"

"You'll see. Now, load up and do what I say."

What choice did we have? "You just keep this rattletrap on the road, and I'll tell you where to go."

"Who said anything about a road?"

For future reference, a Volkswagen Thing, not all that great on the road, is pure torture off-road. To its credit, though, the tough little bugger held up for what had to be the roughest ride of its life. Certainly mine. Comparatively speaking, my trip across the Baja peninsula in Nacho's four wheel drive Toyota was like driving a Mercedes down a German autobahn.

Nacho drove fast, through the dark desert, without lights, and across terrain designed by nature to keep idiots like us from crossing it. I kept us on course, thanks to the backlit screen of the tracking device, and Nacho kept us right side up. Jan? She whimpered with each bump. I felt her pain, all over my backside.

"Half a mile, straight ahead," I yelled at Nacho. "Say, isn't that, like a wall or something?" I asked, staring at a line of lights illuminating a tall, rusty, corrugated iron fence much like the one I'd seen along the border between Tijuana and the US border.

"Yep. Runs for several miles in each direction."

"Several miles? Looks like your coordinates are off. We're headed straight for it."

"Shut up and watch that GPS." He accclerated.

"Quarter mile, straight ahead."

He concentrated on driving.

The wall loomed to the left and right, as far as I could see. The GPS said straight ahead.

"Two hundred yards. Jan, get ready to jump!"

"No!" Nacho yelled, "Do not jump. You'll be killed. You have to put your trust in me. It will be all right."

"Trust you? Are you friggin' nuts? Just because you have a death wish doesn't mean—oh shit, oh dear."

Nacho bore down on the wall, but by now jumping was out of the question, as we were surrounded by tall, spiny, spindly cactus. Nacho mowed down the ones in front, but a forest of ocotillo enveloped us on all sides, just waiting to rip tender skin to shreds. Cactus, wall? Cactus, wall?

I slipped my hand into my jacket pocket and cocked the flare gun. If I could get off a shot, at least someone would find our bodies before the coyotes did. Nailing Nacho with it would only hasten our own demise.

As I pulled out the pistol, we bore down on the wall doing about forty.

Oddly enough, what popped into my mind at the nanosecond before impact was the old engineering paradox: What happens when an irresistible force—that would be us—meets with an immovable object, say, an iron wall?

My life flashed before my eyes. And Nacho's, it would seem. "What the fu—"

Not my life flashing, after all, but a flare. In my fear, I'd pulled the trigger, sending the flare high into the sky overhead.

Just like in the song, the rocket's red glare gave proof through the night that the wall was still there.

Everything went into a surrealistic sort of slow motion. In the glow of what must surely be the fires of Hell, metal on metal shrieked. Or was that me?

From behind me, Jan chanted, "Oh, m'god, Oh, m'god, oh, m'god."

Then, in what I can only put down to Divine intervention, or maybe Divine comedy, the wall swung open, and we barreled through.

Then again, if there *is* such a thing as an irresistible force, then *no* object is immovable, ¿*verdad?*

Instead of ending up like sardines in a flattened can, we found ourselves airborne.

We'd slammed into the wall, sailed through a hinged opening, only to have the bottom drop out. There was that stomach rolling sensation of weightlessness, flight, before plummeting into what turned out to be a six-foot deep trench.

Nacho, in the middle of crowing about how good the GPS coordinates had been, was thrown forward, his head connecting with the steering wheel. As dust billowed around us, and the Thing gasped its last, he croaked, in a puzzled tone, "Well, heck, what's the ditch doing here?"

His eyes rolled back into his head and he passed out, but not before grabbing the GPS from me and stuffing it into his pocket.

Turning to check on Jan, I saw she had a death grip on the roll bar above her head, but she looked unhurt. In the flare's glow, a cloud of fine dust fluoresced, like a witch's cauldron, all around us. Behind, the hinged gate squeaked softly, slowly returning to its closed position. Guess Homeland Security sorta missed *that* little entry point.

I was squirming to extricate myself from the Thing and check on Jan when she started laughing hysterically and quipped, "Welcome to Arizona, and thank you for flying God airlines. Please check the overhead before departing the plane." I'd forgotten she once aspired to be a stewardess, flight attendant or whatever they call themselves these days, before deciding being a CPA paid better.

I laughed with relief, somewhat stunned we were still alive. I looked through the red haze, up into an inky clear sky twinkling with stars. Yep, Heaven was still up, and I didn't detect fire or brimstone pulling us under.

Behind us, the fence had ceased creaking and left no sign of ever opening. Once again my engineering background kicked in, this time with a grudging respect for the artisan who redesigned that wall. Someone very clever had, probably in the dead of night over a long period of time, and using only small hand tools, created a masterpiece of illusion. He was probably, at this very moment, either tunneling out of some prison, or starring on a Las Vegas stage.

"Hetta, you okay?" Jan, finally in control of her giggles, whispered. After our explosive entrance into the good old US of A, whispering seemed a lit-tle redundant as a means of obscurity.

"I'm fine, but we have to boogie. Let's grab our bags and some water."

As we unloaded our stuff from the Thing, Jan eyed the unconscious Nacho. "What about him?"

"Screw him."

"He could be badly hurt."

"I certainly hope so."

Nacho roused a mite, croaked, "That's not nice," then passed out again.

"Not nice at all," pronounced a deep voice from on high. If that was God speaking, He wore a cowboy hat.

Out of the red haze sauntered an apparition, making me reconsider whether we'd actually survived the crash, but in a voice that could hardly be classified at angelic, it drawled, "What in hey-all are y'all doin' in that ditch?"

"Well, heck, Jan, we've died and gone to Texas."

32

Okay, so we weren't dead, nor in Texas, but we were being pulled out of a ditch by a group of Militia Men from our home state. How lucky is that? Or was it?

After a few questions as to whether we were harmed or not, one of them cocked his head suspiciously toward Nacho. "Whut you gals doin' with the Mex?"

Jan, fully aware of the disdain many Texans hold for interracial mingling, batted her big blues in the fading glare of the sputtering flare. "He…he…kidnapped us, and threatened to shoot Maggie."

One of the cowboys put his hand on my shoulder. "That true, Maggie?"

"I'm not…yes."

After that we were treated with utmost sympathy, while the same couldn't be said for the semiconscious Nacho. They manhandled him rudely out of the Thing and roughly propped him against a rock, but they did throw a blanket over his shoulders while they called the authorities. The first official wave arrived in minutes.

"What we have here?" a Border Patrol guy asked as he speared us with his flashlight. Another reached inside their jeep and lit up the entire desert with his spots.

Head Militia Man shrugged. "Two white gals and a Mex."

"What's their story?" he asked, like we weren't standing right there.

"Claim they was kidnapped by the Mex, forced across the border."

"They were forced across the border *from* Mexico?"

"Right through yon wall, if the tire tracks tell the story."

The agent cast a skeptical eye toward the solid steel wall, but refrained from calling the guy nuts. More vehicles roared up, and men in suits and various uniforms joined our circle of light. Nacho was bundled into an ambulance that took off into the night, lights and sirens going full blast. Desert creatures scattered in all directions. Then, once again, it was quiet.

I produced a passport from a bag in the Thing. Jan, of course, could not.

We were trying to explain how it was that she lost her purse, and all her identification, without divulging our whereabouts at the time. I was in the middle of backing up her hotel theft story when, over the wall, swooped a loud and winged creature. With a mighty squawk, and a hearty, "Oh boy! Oberto," Trouble dive-bombed a couple of Militia Men, then landed on my head and scurried for safety under my jacket collar. Cozying up to my neck, he peeked out to taunt the men who had drawn their weapons, intent on blasting him from the sky. When Trouble took refuge on my shoulder, we both became a target.

Alarmed at seeing the self-appointed border guards taking aim at an American citizen, the US Border Patrol drew their weapons. Before we had an O.K. Corral kind of moment, with me in the middle, I yelled, "Hey, everybody just please chill!"

"Oh boy! Oberto," Trouble screeched. I had to teach him to say, "Cease fire."

After a tense minute, guns were holstered, and an embarrassed silence fell over the entire cadre until someone quipped, "I do declare, I think we got us an illegal avian here." He broke into a guffaw, so amused was he by his own wit, and we all followed. The tension, so thick it was palpable, dissolved.

Still chuckling, a BP officer shined his light on Trouble. "Hey, I know that parrot. He's famous. Saw him on TV."

"On TV?" I asked.

"Yep, jerky commercial. Everyone's talking about him. Best ad since they did away with that 'yo quiero' dawg. He belong to you?"

"Ye…uh, why do you ask?"

"Because famous or not, he can't come into this country. Well, he could fly in on his own, I guess, but if he was with you, we'd have to arrest you for bird smuggling. The fine is about a grand."

"I've never seen this bird before in my life."

"Good answer."

"Free at last, free at last, Thank God almighty, we're free at last," I sang after the border patrol guy, who was obviously enamored with Jan, dropped us curbside at Bisbee's historical Copper Queen Hotel. It was almost nine, and we were hungry, thirsty and dog tired, but we were free of Nacho, and on home soil.

"Hetta, I don't think you should be quoting scripture. At

least not while I'm within lightning strike distance. And I also might remind you that we are not exactly free."

"It's a hymn. Or an old spiritual. Something like that. I think it applies."

"Whatever. Let's check in, take really long, hot showers and then make a whole bunch of phone calls."

"And get us a cold beer. Several."

"Amen."

The Copper Queen Hotel, nestled into the historic mining town of Bisbee, Arizona, is indeed a courtly lady. Several stories high, over a hundred years old, and adorned in a Victorian white, green and red paint job, she boasts being the oldest continually run hotel in Arizona, and even claims an in-house ghost. I was glad she boasted a bar, which we planned to head for as soon as we were cleaned up and made a few phone calls. Jenks was first on the call list.

"Hetta! Thank God! Are you all right? I've been worried sick."

"Jeez, I've only been gone a day." I'd never heard Jenks even close to anxious, but there was definitely a panicky edge to his voice. "Are *you* all right?"

"Where in the hell are you?" he demanded, that edge inching towards anger.

Not liking his tone, I growled, "Since you ask so sweetly, Arizona."

Someone in the background asked him something I couldn't quite make out. He said, "Arizona." Then, to me, "Is Jan with you?"

"Yep. Right here."

I heard a rustling, like he was shaking his head, affirming the question. "Hetta," his voice softened, "are you…safe?"

"Far as I know. We're in a hotel in Bisbee, Arizona." *Under house arrest by several federal agencies. How safe is that?*

"Okay, stay put. Martinez can probably get to you by sometime tomorrow."

"Martinez?"

"I called him when you went missing."

"I did not go missing," I insisted. After all, I'd only left my boat this morning.

"Hetta, you need to tell me the truth. What happened?"

We were kidnapped by a drug thug, who crashed us through a US border fence, and then we were arrested for illegal entry and bird smuggling. Okay, so they let the bird smuggling thing go.

"Hetta?"

What the hell. "We were kidnapped by a drug thug, who crashed us through a US border fence. And then we were sort of put under house arrest here at this hotel. They let the bird smuggling thing go, for now."

Jan threw a pillow at me and hissed, "Have you lost what little mind you have?"

I waved her off. "Jenks, you still there?"

"Yes. I hope that was a joke."

"'Course it was."

The phone line crackled, like he was muffling it against his body. I could hear him arguing with someone, probably his brother, but I couldn't make out what he was saying. I did catch something that sounded like, "You don't know her like I do." Finally, he said to me, "I have to tell you something, but only if you promise me you will not, under any circumstances, go back into Mexico."

"Who are you talking to?"

"Lars. He doesn't think I should tell you, well, what I have to tell you. Knowing you like I do, though, you are *not* just going to follow orders and *not* return to Mexico because I tell you not to."

Orders? "That was some string of 'nots' for me to not follow. Jenks, my boat is there. I have to go back, but, FYI, I first plan to go to the Bay Area, get my car, do a down and dirty project that shouldn't take more that a month, *then* drive back to Margaritaville."

"Who did you leave in charge of the boat? Who has the keys?"

"The marina office. Port Captain. Smith, this sailor— oh, no." Maggie's sweet face suddenly popped into my mind. In all the excitement, I'd forgotten about the calls Nacho was supposed to make to keep Maggie safe. "Something has happened. What is it?"

"We don't know exactly. The marina office called my cell phone and left a message this afternoon—your afternoon—because you gave them my number as a contact in case of an emergency. When I returned their call, Isabel answered and sounded very upset, then she handed the phone to someone who identified himself as federal police. I...you're sure you're okay?"

"Yes, honest. Jan and I are perfectly fine. Are you gonna tell me what happened, or do I have to go find out for myself?"

"No! You stay put until Martinez gets there, you hear me?"

Marty Martinez is a retired Oakland cop turned PI, who lives in the Baja, and has been called to my aide more than once. Just recently he'd helped Jan and me out of a jam at Magdalena Bay. Now, it seems, he's back in the fray, thanks to Jenks. This better be good. "Start talking, Buster. Did something happen to *Raymond Johnson?*"

"Sort of. Something happened aboard. There's blood all over the deck, and inside. Signs of a struggle. The saloon door was left wide open, and you were missing."

"Jenks, we locked that door when we left. What else?"

"They...I...thought..." his voice trailed off, then he

recovered. "No one knows what took place, but whatever, it isn't good. If you go back down there now, the *federales* will most likely arrest you."

"They'll have to get in line."

"Not funny."

"Sorry. I just don't know what to say." What Jenks said was true; under Mexico's antiquated Napoleonic law, suspicion of a crime taking place can land anyone involved, or even in the near vicinity, in jail. For that reason, Mexicans, normally the most helpful people in the world, scatter like chickens when they witness any crime, even a traffic accident. Witnesses? No way. "So, all we have is an open door, and some kind of bloodbath."

"Isn't that enough?"

Jan had moved beside me. "Bloodbath?"

"That's what they told me. If they know more, they aren't saying. You were missing, that's why I called Martinez, hoping he'd go to San Carlos, get some answers. I tracked him down on his cell phone. He was in San Diego picking up supplies for his home building project in Baja, said he'd leave immediately. He left around seven tonight, your time. He's probably past Yuma right now. I think I can catch him, divert him to Bisbee. You two sit tight until he gets there."

"I don't think—."

"Not negotiable."

"I can't go anywhere anyway, until we clear up our, uh, illegal entry."

"I thought you were joking."

"Of course I was. Anyway, we will wait for Martinez, I promise."

"Cross your heart?"

Jan was jumping up and down on the bed, demanding to know the story. "Okay, okay," I said, speaking to both Jan and Jenks.

"Good. Hetta?"

"Yes, Jenks?"

"I'm really glad you're safe. You scared the crap out of me this time. You've got to stop…oh, never mind. We'll talk later, but don't leave me hanging, okay? Give me your phone number and the name of your hotel. Do you have your US cell phone with you?"

"No, I was going to renew when I get back to Oakland." I gave him the particulars of our locale, then told him I'd call him as soon as I knew more.

"I'll hold you to that."

"You can hold me any way you want."

He chuckled. "By the way, since you're in Bisbee, do you plan to check in with the home office?"

Huh? "Huh?"

"You know, the Sierra Vista Dispatch, just a few miles away. Hetta Coffey, star reporter at large? I'm sure, after your story made the big time, they'd like to meet you."

"You know how we reporters are. Elusive. However, now that you mention it, perhaps they owe me money."

"Wouldn't bank on it. Stay safe, and call me as soon as you know anything, okay?"

"Will do. Love you."

"Me, too."

I hung up and Jan pounced. "What the hell is going on? Bloodbath? Martinez?"

I told her what little I knew, then called the marina office. No answer, but what did I expect? Crime or no, they close at five. Smith didn't have a phone on his boat, so calling him was out. I tried the port captain's office. No answer. No surprise there, because I'd been told that the week before Christmas the entirety of Mexican bureaucracy goes on *alto*.

"Oh, Jan, I hope Maggie is all right. You don't think that bastard, Nacho, actually had her killed do you? On my boat?"

"I don't think Nacho would hurt a fly."

"Your judgment, when it comes to men, has to be worse than…mine. He's a drug dealer. A gang member. He kidnapped us. How can you think anything good about him?"

"Maybe he saved our lives?"

"Excuse me?"

"Hetta, your boat is bloody. Whose blood, we don't know. If he hadn't kidnapped us, it might have been *our* blood."

On that specious bit of logic, I gave up. Doing verbal battle with an unarmed blonde was beyond me at this point. Right now, I had bigger problems. Like finding out if Smith, Maggie or Captain Reyes were missing a few pints of blood. Dammit! Where was a ham radio when you needed it?

While Jan called her mom, I took a long, hot shower and then rummaged through my duffle bag for my least wrinkled pants and a tee shirt. If the hotel had a dining room dress code, they'd have to get over it. We world famous journalists travel light.

33

Since my parents were on the RV trail and steadfastly refused to get a cell phone, Jan's mother was our contact point. In the past, if they couldn't reach me, my mom called Jan's mom to track me down, and vice versa. Jan finished speaking with her mother, hung up the phone, and handed me a note written on hotel stationary. "Your folks are in Florida. Here's the number. They're in a hotel this week." She headed for the shower.

I dialed, it rang and, miracle of miracles, Mother answered. "Hi, Mama, how's Florida?"

"Hetta Honey, it's just full of Yankees. Where are you?"

"Arizona."

"Not in Mexico?"

"No, why?"

"Your Aunt Lillian has been trying to call you on your Mexican cell phone."

"Oh, no, you gave her my number?"

"She said it was urgent."

"What can be so urgent as to sell your daughter down the tubes?"

"She wants her parrot."

Too bad, Lil, your parrot's a jail bird. "I don't have him."

"I know that now, I saw him on TV. You sold her parrot?"

"No. I gave him away to a good home." *From which he escaped, but I wasn't gonna let old Auntie know that. The last thing I needed was for the old bag to show up in Bisbee.*

"Lil thinks you sold Trouble for a bunch of money, what with him being famous and all."

"Well, then, she'd be wrong. Is the old sot back home yet?"

"That's my big sister you're talking about."

"Oh, let me rephrase that. Has the aging dipsomaniac returned to the scene of her many crimes?"

A loud guffaw emanated from the bathroom, but from the silence on the other end of the line, my mother was not so amused by my keen wit.

"Mom, I gotta go. Just tell Aunt Lil that Trouble has a happy home and a good job. Something she could aspire to, by the way."

"I'm hanging up now."

"Bye. Give Daddy a —"

The line went dead.

"Ya know, Hetta, calling your aunt a drunk might not be real great for family relations."

"Spade's a spade."

"And a kettle probably shouldn't be calling the pot black."

"I need a drink."

"I rest my clichés."

* * *

There's nothing like a few ice cold beers to inspire one to greatness.

Unfortunately, the cozy and inviting Victorian bar at the Copper Queen Hotel was jammed with a private party of Christmas revelers by the time we went downstairs. The dining room was already closed for the evening.

Tromping out into the cold night in search of a warm bar and that cold beer, we were drawn by neon to St. Elmo's Bar, appropriately located in Brewery Gulch. No cowboy bar, this, unless cowboys in Arizona ride Harleys.

Eyeing the lineup of shiny motorcycles parked outside, Jan pulled on my arm.

"What?" I growled. Getting between me and a cool one when I'd been highly mistreated for an entire day is never a good idea.

"Perhaps we should find another bar."

"Guy at the desk said this is the only one within walking distance that's still open."

"Looks like trouble to me."

"Trouble's in the lockup."

"You know what I mean. I don't think I can handle much more excitement right now, and the men who hang—"

"Last guy I met on a motorcycle turned out to be a handsome, single, dentist from the Bay Area." Okay, so I don't know if Mad Dog is single, but Jan sometimes needs inspiration.

She perked up. "Oh, well then."

The minute we entered, I fell in love. Neon, smoke, beer fumes, loud music and best of all, a dog sat on a bar stool. Home sweet bar.

* * *

We made a lot of new best friends, most of them aging hippies and gays who had migrated from northern California, notably Santa Cruz, and my old stomping grounds, San Francisco. It was a slow night at St. Elmo's, according to the patrons, so we were able to secure a bar stool and suck up a few while being regaled by the locals about the wonders of Bisbee. The wonder is that we lasted until midnight before agreeing we were plumb wore out. By the time we'd stumbled back to the hotel and crashed, we'd long since forgotten about getting any dinner, and were too fatigued to worry about what the morrow would bring.

Somewhere around two a.m. I sat straight up in bed and yelled, "Stephanie!"

Jan, startled awake, sat up herself. "The hotel ghost? Is she here?"

"No, doofus. Stephanie, the ham operator. She lives in Tucson. We can call her and find out if Smith and Maggie are all right."

"Can we wait for, say, dawn?"

"No way. I can't sleep another wink. If I can't, you can't. We have to think."

Jan rolled back down into her bed, pulled a pillow over her head and shot me the finger.

Left to do all the thinking, I decided that maybe Jan was right, and Nacho wasn't all bad; he'd let me bring my laptop. Firing it up, I accessed the ham operator list someone gave me, and came up with Stephanie's phone number. On the third ring, the machine picked up. "Hello," said the recording, "we can't come to the—" "Hello," a sleepy voice answered.

"Stephanie?"

Evidently she'd had a chance to look at the clock. "Who the hell wants to know at this hour?"

"Uh, it's me, Hetta Coffey."

"Hetta! Oh, jeez, where are you? We've got the coast guard, the *federales* and everyone else looking for you."

I was starting to feel mighty popular. "I heard about my boat."

"How did you hear?"

"My, uh, boyfriend told me. He's in Kuwait, but the marina called him. Do you know what happened?"

"No details. We were all so worried about you, and feared the worst. When the phone rang just now, I was afraid they'd found your—"

"Body?"

"Well, yes. I mean, since they already found Herbert's."

"Herbert's body?" I said dumbly.

Jan threw off her covers, sat on the edge of her bed. "Herbert's body?"

I shushed her with my hands so I could hear Stephanie.

"In the desert. He's dead and it looks like someone, uh, well, cut him with a knife, then shot him. His boat is clean, well, clean for Herbert's boat, I guess. Anyhow, rumor has it someone did a serious knife job on him, then dragged him into the desert and finished him off."

"That's wonderful."

"Huh?"

I know, hearing that someone was probably butchered on my boat shouldn't be good news, but we're talking Herbert, here. "Sorry, Steph, I'm just so relieved that it wasn't someone…I was afraid it was Smith, or Maggie, his dog. Or even the port captain. They all have keys to the boat. Well, Maggie doesn't."

"Oh, I see. Far as I know, everyone else is fine, but I'll check in the morning for you. Is it okay, you think, for me to let folks know you're safe?"

"I guess, so long as you don't tell them where to find me. I have my reasons."

"Where are you?"

"If I tell you, I'll have to kill you."

She laughed. "Fair enough, but everybody is so worried."

"Tell them I'm alive and well, in Paris."

"Works for me."

Retired lieutenant, Marty Martinez, late of the Oakland Police Department, called at eight, waking me from a semi-coma. Jan answered. From her end of the conversation, I surmised he was, once again, not pleased with us. Over the past year or so he had been instrumental in bailing me out of a few situations, both when he was still with the OPD, and after he retired to Baja.

"But it wasn't her fault this time," she whined. "We were kidnapped."

I snatched the phone from her hand just in time to hear Martinez say, "Must'a been some kind of nitwit to kidnap Hetta Coffey."

"Hey, I heard that."

"Hello, Hetta. I would ask something clever, like whether or not you'd incited any international turmoil lately, but wait a minute, you have."

"I didn't do anything."

"Ha! Prove it."

"Did you call to help, or just revel in our misfortunate circumstances."

"The latter sounds tempting, but Jenks asked me to get involved in the former."

"What have you found out so far?"

"Not on the phone."

Once a cop, always a cop. "Then how do we communicate?"

"You could join me for coffee."

"When? Where?"

"Now, in the lobby."

34

"You two look like hell."

"Good day to you, too, Marty. Here's your reality check of the day. Jan and I can have our hair done and put on makeup, while you, on the other hand, will still be stuck with that face and bald spot *for*ever. And by the by, you look even worse than your usual self."

"Ignore her," Jan interjected as she put her arms around the detective. "She's had a bad couple of days and we are ever so grateful you're here."

"Had to come, missed Hetta's smart mouth. Life without Hetta? Well, it's so calm. So sane, so..."

"Boring?" I suggested.

"There's that." He opened his arms, and Jan and I melted into his reassuring presence. Jan began to sniffle, and I felt the sting of relief in my eyes, as well. The cavalry had arrived. We were safe. We were—

"—being taken into custody."

I whirled to face whoever had an iron grip on my wrist,

and found my nose pressed into a gold shield. I stared at the badge. It was shiny, with fish and ducks engraved on it. Department of the Interior, Fish and Wildlife Service. Special Agent. And it was pinned on a vest, which fit snuggly on a broad chest of someone tall, tanned, blond and outdoorsy. Not James Bond, mind you, but if I wasn't so shaken, I could have been stirred.

He had his other hand wrapped around Jan's arm. "You two, come with me." He steered us through the lobby, and outside. As we stood waiting for we knew not what, I spotted something to divert my attention. Steps led down to the next street, and sitting on the steps was a guy totally covered in pigeons. I hate pigeons.

"Bird poop man of Bisbee?" I said to nobody in particular.

The fish and game man scowled. "I should probably bust him for feeding the wildlife, but this *is* Bisbee, and I guess, technically, these pigeons aren't really wild, more like pets. We also have a guy who walks around with a mouse riding a cat riding a dog. Like I said, Bisbee."

An SUV with green Border Patrol markings pulled up and we were asked to get in. I considered protesting, but figured it wasn't worth getting cuffed.

Tourists shot worried looks our way, one of them speculating we were probably illegal Russians or some such.

Martinez, seated in the front seat, sat in stony silence, not reacting to the litany of unkind remarks I aimed at him, Jenks, and the entire state of Arizona, but Special Agent man's lips twitched a couple of times.

Fifteen minutes later, we pulled up to the border, and some familiar faces. Jan waved gaily to the two Border Patrol agents who'd taken Nacho away after our dramatic entry into the US, but as Martinez ushered us past them, they only nodded in response to her friendly greeting. Fickle, these federal types.

We were joined by a baby-faced, but gray-haired gent in a crisp United States Customs uniform. He put us into what looked to be an interrogation room. They shut the door behind us, leaving us alone to stew. "Looks like they's gonna sweat us, Guido," I snarled, trying to lighten the mood, "but they'll never get me to squeal."

"Very funny, Hetta. Ya think we're in big trouble?"

"Nah, but I'd sure like to know what that rat fink Martinez had to do with this."

"I want my mommy."

"Oh, dear. Do you think someone will contact our parents?" I was trying to remember who I'd listed as a contact on my passport.

"I sure hope not. Unless, of course, you need bail money," said the ever-practical Jan.

"We won't need bail money, we haven't done anything too illegal. Hey, hold the horses there, cowgirl, what do you mean, unless *I* need bail money? You're here, too. How did we get from *we* to *you*, Brutus?"

"Well, Hetta, far as I can tell, *I'm* not under arrest."

"Neither am I. I'm, uh, in custody." There is a difference, isn't there?

We sat in silence for a few minutes, trying to sort things out, me feeling betrayed by everyone. And hungry. Why hadn't we eaten dinner last night instead of chugging beer? Why didn't we have breakfast? For that matter, why didn't I get married at twenty-one, settle down with two kids and a mortgage?" My growling stomach interrupted this string of whys. "If this is kind of a police station, do you figure they have any doughnuts?"

"I sure hope so. Hetta, who do you think killed Herbert?"

"Anybody. If anyone ever needed killin', it was him."

"Shhh. Someone might be listening. You *are* in custody, you know."

"And you aren't? Why me and not—"

The door opened and three kinds of uniforms entered, along with a suit, and Martinez.

We needed a bigger room.

"Please sit down, ladies."

Jan sat. I remained standing.

Martinez grinned, or what passed for a grin with his phlegmatic self. "Okay," he said, taking charge of the meeting, "now that all the *ladies* are seated, I guess we can get started."

I glared at him, then at the others, who were not doing a great job of suppressing their amusement. "Gee, Martinez, we should book you at the Not Really Ready for Comedy Club. Okay, what is all this about? Am I under arrest?"

Special Agent shook his head. "No ma'am, we just need to talk with you and your lawyer here."

"My…?" Martinez shot me a warning look. "My lawyer, Martinez." I plopped down next to him. "So, counselor, what are we charging these guys with?"

The agents looked at Martinez, who gave them an, "I told you so" look, but when I opened my mouth to speak again, Martinez shot me a signal that said, "Shut up before you bury yourself." Amazing how communicative the man can get with his eyebrows. I took his silent advice and clammed up.

Customs man took over. "Okay, let's start over. Miss Coffey, we have a witness who, in his own words, indicates you have lied to federal officers, and have committed a criminal offense. We are, however, ready to hear your side of the story."

Witness? Who? Only Jan and Nacho were there. Nacho is in jail, Jan wouldn't rat on me and besides, they were both guilty of running the border. Hell, at least I had a valid passport. These guys had to be bluffing. "I'd like to hear your alleged witness's testimony first." Martinez actually looked impressed and the corners of his mouth twitched. After all, he'd taught me everything I knew about being obtuse.

Customs rose and left the room, only to return with a large cage in hand. Trouble saw me, fluffed his feathers, blushed and chanted, "Hetta, Hetta, she's our gal, if she can't do it, no one shall."

Busted.

"Do you still maintain that you've never seen this bird before, as you told these officers when you were apprehended crossing the border illegally?"

"Hey, I'm a ninth-generation Texan. How long have you been here?"

"But Texas is a whole 'nother country," he quipped, using the Texas Tourist Bureau's catch phrase.

"Very funny. You," I looked at one of the BP guys, "saw my passport."

He nodded.

"See?"

"And the bird?"

"He's crossed the border so many times he has frequent crosser miles." I then told them the rest of the story, including Trouble's Texas beginnings, me giving him to Oberto, and his obvious escape to chase me across the border. I concluded with, "So, as you can see, he's not my bird, he's a bird of the world. A veritable feathered jet setter. A—"

Martinez interrupted, just when I was getting warmed up. "How are we doing here? You guys satisfied that my client is not into smuggling birds?"

Customs shrugged. "I guess. But here's the rub. We have to destroy the parrot."

Jan and I squawked in tandem, which set Trouble off. His screeches sent men scrambling from the room with their hands over their ears. The wildlife guy waved me out, as well. I slammed the door behind me, muffling somewhat the ear-piercing screeches.

"Look, I told him," I can calm him down if you'll let me go back in. Besides, I'd like a minute to say goodbye.

He looked at Customs, who shrugged. "Okay, why not."

"Jan, stay here. You're so upset, Trouble will know something's wrong. I'll be right back."

I opened the condemned's cage and he immediately shut up and hopped onto my finger. I gave him a kiss. "Sorry, little guy, but I gave you a home and a job and you just couldn't stay put. I'll try my best to get you out of this, but for now, you gotta stay here."

I started to put him back on his perch, but spotted a wadded up net in the bottom of his cage. Furious, I snatched it out, stuffed it into my pocket, then put Trouble onto his perch. He protested quietly when I shut the door, but I draped my sweatshirt over the cage and he quieted down. I took a last look, and left the room.

Confronting the wildlife man, I shook the net in his face. "What was this doing in Trouble's cage? He could get caught in it and break a wing or leg."

Wildlife scowled at the others. "What's with the net?"

One guy looked sheepish. "Only way we could get him. He was swooping around like a hawk, so we netted him. Sorry, guess we shoulda taken it out of the cage, but that bird is a menace."

I stuck the net in my pocket again lest they terrorize some other poor unsuspecting creature.

"Never mind. He's settled down now, but the best thing to do is just leave him alone until...you do what you have to do."

Jan gasped. "Hetta, you can't mean...we love Trouble.

He's..."She broke into tears, which sent all the men scrambling for tissues.

I put my arm around her. "I'm sorry Jan, but it looks like there's nothing more we can do."

Her chin trembled. "Nuh, nuh, nothing?" Shifting her focus on the customs agent, she asked, "How will you do it? I mean, Trouble won't, like, hurt, will he?"

The man shifted on his feet, visibly uncomfortable. "I really don't know. We've called Animal Control. They handle these things." Then, he brightened and added. "Of course, right now they're up in the Huachuca mountains tracking a bear that broke into a home, probably thinking it looked like a good place to hibernate. They'll be awhile."

Jan refused to be cheered up by a temporary stay of execution. "Can't we just put Trouble in quarantine or something?" she wailed. "He's just a little gray bird. He can't hurt anyone."

Unless that anyone happens to be a Mexican male. I spoke up. "Martinez, we're obviously spinning our wheels here, and since we can't stop the inevitable, can we take Jan back to the hotel now?"

He looked at the various agents, who nodded somberly.

We rode back to the hotel in silence, then headed for the bar to begin Trouble's wake. A little prematurely, grant you.

Martinez passed on the wake, preferring to get a nap since he'd been on the road for hours on end. I'd grill him later on how he managed to become my lawyer. As he headed for his room, he tossed me the keys to his pickup. "I'm parked in a four hour zone. Before you get sloshed, will you move me somewhere legal? I was on the road most of the night and I'm flat bushed. I don't even want dinner."

"Sure, no problem. Night-night. See you in the morning, unless something comes up. I'll probably skip dinner, as well. Too tired."

I found another parking space, this time in a paid parking area, then rejoined Jan. We'd both ordered Jack Black on the rocks and she was blubbering into her second when I returned. Whiskey, straight, on an empty stomach, is a really bad idea, but neither of us were hungry, for different reasons.

Jan was mourning Trouble's loss, and I was dreading what I had to do next.

35

After three fast doubles in the hotel bar, Jan was slurring her consonants.

I, on the other hand, slowly—what a concept—sipped one drink and chased it with water. We hadn't eaten anything except stale bar popcorn and a greasy donut or two in almost two days, so Jan's drinks hit her hard, and we barely returned back to the room when she crashed.

While she snored, I packed up, then wrote a letter outlining Trouble's dire straits to the Sierra Vista Dispatch. I was picking up a WIFI signal, so I sent the letter via e-mail, then, just in case the somewhat dubious plot I'd hatched failed, I copied both CNN and Oberto headquarters. All that done, I stole a pillowcase from my bed, and slipped out the door.

In the hotel bar, I bought a couple of bottles of water to go, and stuffed popcorn into my jacket pockets. After a short pause in the park in front of the hotel, I reclaimed Martinez's Mazda pickup and headed south. One stop more and I was ready to rumble.

By late afternoon I was lurking in Naco, Arizona, slumped down in my car seat and munching on the best damned gyro I'd eaten since a brief stint on Mykonos. Who knew that Gus the Greek's Pizzarama in the San Jose district of Bisbee would turn out such a fine gyro? I'd ordered extra tzadsiki sauce and was having trouble corralling the tangy mixture of shredded cucumbers, garlic and yogurt in it's fresh baked pita bread wrapper. I regretted not ordering two.

While eating, I took in the comings and goings on the American side of the border. There were few people about, none of them interested in me.

With my hair tucked under a scarf I'd lifted from Jan's suitcase, and a baseball cap pulled low over my sunglasses, I walked toward the crossing gate, near enough so I could see there was no Animal Control paddy wagon in the border station parking lot. That, and the unearthly screeches emanating from the BP station, convinced me that Trouble was still alive and well and causing an Excedrin kind of day for all the agents. If he didn't shut up, one of the BP guys just might get tired of waiting for Animal Control and carry out the execution himself.

Back at the Mazda, I started the motor and pulled as close to the building as I dared. Still, no one paid me any mind. So far, so good. Turning on the prepaid cell phone I'd purchased at a local Dollar Store next to Pizzarama twenty minutes earlier, I dialed the number on the customs agent's card. Someone else answered, I told them who I was. After being transferred three times, Mr. Customs Man answered. I had my fingers crossed that he was still at the border station.

"Agent Charles Riley here."

"Oh, hi, Charles. Hetta Coffey here."

"What can I do for you?" I could hear screeching in the background. Good.

"I lost my ring. It was left to me by my grandmother, and I think I lost it when we were with Trouble this morning. Jan and I were so upset when we left, I didn't realize the ring was gone. Uh," I managed a voice tremble, "they haven't come for him yet, have they?" Like I couldn't hear him raising all Billy hell in the background.

"Oh, take my word for it, he's still here. He's not happy. As soon as you left, he started a racquet and hasn't piped down. Look, I'm sorry about all this, I really am. He's a cute little bird, if a bit noisy. Do you want me to see if I can find your ring?"

"If it wouldn't be too much bother."

"Under the circumstances, it's the least I can do. You want to hang on while I plug my ears and take a look?"

"Sure. Thanks."

I turned off the phone, rolled down the window and pulled the purloined hotel pillowcase into my lap. Now all I could do was wait. And pray.

The agent walked into my line of vision, making for the door behind which Trouble was raising Cain. Holding my breath, crossing my fingers, promising promises toward Heaven that I probably wouldn't keep, I drove slowly toward the Mexican border crossing, letting other cars pass me by. Doing my best to look like a lost and bewildered tourist, I stopped just short of the Mexico *entrada*, in a sort of no-man's land, and pulled out a map.

Still, no one paid me any mind.

Suddenly, there was a yell and a loud screech. I opened the pillowcase, let the two hapless pigeons I'd snagged out, then joined the short line waiting to cross the Mexican border. Once in line, I whistled repeatedly as loud as I could.

As the line of cars inched forward, I crossed my fingers and held my breath. The car in front of me was given a green light, and moved on. There was no one behind me, and no one on the Mexican side seemed to care that I had stopped altogether. As luck would have it though, a uniformed man looked up, pushed away from the official looking pickup he was leaning against, and began walking my way.

I had to make a move.

Rolling forward, hands clenched on the steering wheel, my hopes began to dwindle. Then, miracle of miracles, he was called back to his truck. The second his back was turned, Trouble sailed through my window and landed on my head. Sliding on the slick scarf, he ended up on my shoulder and squalled into my ear, "Oh, boy! Oberto."

"What took you so long? Never mind, just shut up, bird, we're almost home free."

To let me know he was not pleased with the day's events, he pulled out a few strands of my hair before hopping onto the passenger side seatback. As he roosted, another bout of yelling and cursing broke out on the US side, with what sounded like shots fired.

"Oops, look like we'd better be heading…oh, no." I'd drawn a red light that said Alto and a loud bell rang, whatever that meant. And, evidently roused by the brouhaha on the US side, two Mexican feds stood directly in my path with their hands held out in an unmistakable "halt" position. I grabbed Trouble and stuffed him into the glove compartment, where, luckily, I'd also stashed some jerky from that handy Dollar Store. After one loud squawk, he discovered the jerky bag. I turned up the radio to muffle the sound of shredding plastic.

While one officer leaned on my hood, the other strolled up to my window.

I sat in silence, leaving the ball in their court.

"*Buenas tardes, señora.* Do you have anything to declare?"

I do declare that I am scared pee-less. "I only have my clothes."

"And this is your truck?"

"Yes." My bladder constricted, like it always does when I lie. I suffer from guilty bladder syndrome.

"And where are you going?"

"San Carlos."

"On vacation?"

"Yes."

"Alone?"

"Ye...well, I am meeting my boyfriend there." No use asking for unwanted attention.

"Please, wait here."

Now what? Drug dog? Or worse, parrot dog? Having heard stories of how these border crossings work, I fished a twenty from my wallet and slid it onto the dashboard in full view. A little *mordida* in the right palm can grease a lot of skids, and if I ever needed greasing, it was now. Personally, I like a country where a small bribe works, unlike ours, where the price is much, much, higher.

The guy returned and motioned me into what I surmised was secondary inspection. I was devising a plan. Okay, get out, walk around to the other door, throw it open, let Trouble out, then take my chances they wouldn't see him fly away? Scenario two? Trouble attacks border cop and we both get shot? I was about to go for plan three, bald-faced bribery, when the man asked, "Can you give my friend a ride? He is also going to San Carlos."

Just what I needed, a hitchhiker. But then, driving through Mexico alone at night wasn't such a good idea, either. And if I refused, would they search the car? "Sure, why not." I reached over and unlocked the passenger door, then turned to the officer. Out of the corner of my eye, I saw the other one on his cell phone and hoped he wasn't chatting with US Customs, or the border patrol. I had a sneaky feeling I was a wanted woman, by both.

"Well, I guess I'd better get rolling as soon as your friend…"

The door opened and Nacho jumped in. A sharp instrument poked my ribs as, with an evil grin, he growled, "Drive, Red."

Talk about the rock and the hard place. If I screamed to the Mexicans for help, I might end up in a Mexican jail. If I somehow managed to make a successful break for the US border, I'd be flirting with a vacation at Club Fed.

I drove.

36

"Did you miss me?" Nacho asked, a grin on his handsome face. He still had a small bandage on his forehead.

"I thought you were in jail where you belong. Or better yet, dead," I said, blowing garlic breath in his direction.

He did a nose twitch. "So you *did* think of me, even though you underestimate my survival instincts."

"Likewise. Want some jerky? There's a bag in the glove compartment."

Nacho scoffed. "Oh, yeah, like I didn't see that bird of yours fly through the window? How stupid do you think I am?"

"On a scale of one to ten?"

"Just shut up an drive. Bird stays put."

"But he'll suffocate."

"Tell you what, I'll let him out, but if he comes after me again, I'm going to wring his scrawny little neck and then roast him, with a little garlic, for dinner."

I started to reach in my pocket, but Nacho grabbed my

wrist. "Not so fast, Red. How do I know you're not armed."

"Only with popcorn. If you feed Trouble, you won't have to eat him. Here," I dragged a handful from my pocket, "have some, share with Trouble. He has no morals and readily accepts handouts from even lowlifes like you."

Nacho ignored the insult. "Don't mind if I do. You always carry popcorn in your pocket?"

"Only when I'm pigeon hunting."

"I wondered how you snagged them. From where I was watching, I had a ringside seat to the little scene you set up over there. How did you know it would work?"

"I didn't. How did you know I'd be coming across the border?"

"I didn't. It's pure karma. So how did you spring the bird?"

"They let me visit with Trouble alone this morning, and I slipped the lock on his cage."

"So, when they opened the door to the room, out he flew. The pigeons were diversionary. Brilliant."

I shrugged. "It was worth a try."

"Well, it worked out, for both of us."

"Karma sucks."

"How Zen of you. Oh, Hetta Coffey, why didn't we meet under different circumstances?"

"You mean, like, when you weren't a slimy meth dealer? When was that? When you were, like, ten?" I dug into my other pocket. "Here, more popcorn. Let the bird out."

Trouble blinked a couple of times, let go of a piece of jerky he'd been shredding and hopped onto Nacho's outstretched, popcorn-filled, hand. I held my breath, waiting for a howl of pain, followed by flying feathers, but Trouble grabbed a piece of popcorn and flew onto Nacho's shoulder. Nacho flinched, but Trouble didn't attack. Both Nacho and I breathed a sigh of relief.

"Afraid of a little bitty bird, big bad Macho Nacho?"

"No, but you scare the hell out of me. Pull over."

"So you can off me in the desert? I think not."

"Hetta, pull over, now. We have to talk. Believe me, it's in both our interests."

I found a wide spot in the road. There was little light left, but I could still see Nacho clearly enough. He turned to face me and his hand shot out. I winced, but he only handed me a breath mint, then he gently stroked my cheek.

"Like I said, Red, different time and place…."

"You have *got* to be kidding. Are you putting a hit on me? After kidnapping and terrorizing Jan and me? Are you nuts?"

"You're right. Look, I'm sorry I put you through so much, but right now I'm going to level with you. I'm not a drug dealer."

"Yeah? And I'm Julia Roberts."

"I like you better. You're sassy."

Jeez, I was starting to like this lying sack of crap. Okay, this lying, charming, sack of crap, handsome in a criminal sort of way. With whom I was parked in a dark car, in the middle of the Mexican desert. "Convince me."

"That I like you better than Julia?"

"That you're not a drug slug."

"I can't right now. You have to, well, trust me."

I snorted. "Sure I will, what with all you've done for me in the past."

"Actually, I've done more than you think. I've gone to bat for you at least three times."

"Like?"

"Like, at San Francisco Island? Paco wanted to off you and your boyfriend, right then and there, just for some gasoline. He was tweaking on meth, almost losing it by the time we got to your boat. To make matters worse you could be the poster child for how *not* to deal with a tweaker. You pushed his buttons like you do everyone else's. Not a loveable trait, by the way. If I hadn't gotten us out of there, I would have had to blow my cover to save your ass."

"Why should I believe you?"

"Okay, how about this? Why do you think no one came after you when you motored out of Agua Fria? You saw something you shouldn't. We had fast boats and guns. Would have been a turkey shoot."

Don't bet on it. You haven't seen Jenks in action. "You said three times."

"San Carlos. My guess is Paco found your boat. My, uh, sources, tell me there was an incident. "

"Incident? *My* sources tell me there was a murder. Herbert bought it. Probably on my boat, which, I might add, you led both Paco and Herbert to. Coincidence? Let me be the judge."

"Okay, okay, so maybe not three, but now we gotta team up to save both our butts, and some other innocent folks."

"Gee, Lamont, why don't you just conjure up The Shadow?"

"Caught that one, huh?"

"You think you're playing with kids here? Pray tell, Mr. Cranston, why should I be interested in saving your butt?" *Cute as that butt may be.*

"If I tell you, I have to kill you."

Trouble liked that. "Kill you. Kill you."

"Put a lid on it, Trouble." I handed him a jerky strip. "Very dated and overused catch phrase, Nacho, you can do better than that." *Besides, I like to use that one myself.*

"You know, Hetta, I don't think jerky is that good for parrots."

"Gee, of all the scuzbuckets, in all of Mexico, I have to draw the one with a degree in avian nutrition. Okay, back to what we're doing. What are we doing? Or rather, what are you doing that makes me a necessary, albeit reluctant, part of a team. I thought I was, once again, your hostage. Or is that *not* a pistol in your pocket?"

"Oh, it is. But I am also very, very glad to see you."

"Be still my heart. Not mutual."

"That could change. After all," he practically purred, "the Shadow has hypnotic powers, able to cloud men's, and perhaps women's, minds."

Doodness dwacious. "Ha!" was my clever retort.

"I could grow on you."

"Kinda like fungus?"

"I give up. Just drive."

"Where to?"

"San Carlos. We need your boat."

"What for?"

"We're going to Agua Fria."

37

"You want me to take my boat, and you, to Agua Fria? Hey, I have a great idea. I drop you off in Hermosillo, you grab a plane to Loreto, then rent a car, and drive to Agua Fria. Be sure to use Budget Rentals and give me as a reference. They love me there. Oh, wait, I forgot, the road is mysteriously blocked. Wonder how that happened?"

"Dynamite, works every time."

"Just for laughs, mind you, say I do decide to go along with this insane plot of yours—and this is assuming my boat isn't impounded or some such—don't you think old Paco will recognize *Raymond Johnson*? What with him leaving blood all over her decks and all?"

"We're gonna sneak up on him."

"Oh, of course. A forty-five foot motor yacht won't be noticed in the Agua Fria harbor."

"Leave that part to me. Look, Paco's a loose cannon, trying to cover his ass before the big boys at Agua Fria find out he managed to lose his…never mind."

"He lost his never mind? I hate it when I lose mine. Let me take a wild guess here, if you tell me what he lost, and evidently you found, or took, you'll have to kill me."

"You're a fast study."

"You want to know *how* fast? Give me one good reason why I should not just stop this car, and get out. You won't do Jack-do-do, will you? I think you're full of it."

He grinned. "Pot calling the kettle black, if you ask me." That was the second time I'd heard that recently, first from Jan and now Nacho. I tried to think of a suitable comeback, but failed.

Nacho seemed to ponder his options, then sighed. "Okay, there is nothing to stop you from walking away. I won't kill you, or even hurt you, but if you don't help me get Paco, you will never be able to sleep another night without fear."

"That a threat?"

"No, *querida*, that is the truth."

Querida? Beloved? Yikes, did that sound sexy or what? I acted like I didn't hear that little term of endearment and scoffed, "Your version of the truth."

"No, Paco's. There is nothing more dangerous than a psychopath on meth. If somehow Paco offs me, he'll come after you on general principal. In his fried brain, you are a loose end. No logic, no reason, that's just the way he works. He leaves nothing to chance, no witnesses. The gang he came from, and still has ties to, MS-13, is the most dangerous in the world. They never, ever, stop until they get someone if that someone has been fingered for execution."

"Execution? Me?"

He nodded. "And me. My guess is he hasn't dared call for help from his *compadres* yet, because if he tips his hand, they'll want details. Once he talks, though, even if they kill him for what he's done, they'll *still* come after me. And you.

And your entire family. That is the way they work. Help me get Paco first, and our troubles are over."

"What the hell is MS-13?"

"Mara Salvatrucha 13. Started in El Salvador, apparently at that address, 13 Mara Salvatrucha, then branched out all over. They even have ties to al-Qaeda, with plans to smuggle members into the US. Recently, they've been making a strong play in Baja, in the meth trade, but we won't let that happen."

"You have a mouse in your pocket? Or do you actually have backup? *Other* than me."

"Royal we. Never you mind. We're not totally alone in stopping MS-13, but it when comes to Agua Fria and Paco, we're pretty much it for now. Let's go get Paco."

"By get, I assume you mean kill."

"Without doubt. No other choice. And I have to do it very soon. Before Christmas."

"Killing someone right before Christmas could put you on Santa's naughty list, you know."

He grinned. "I'll chance it. There's so much more to this whole thing, but first things first. Paco."

"So you are sure he ran this little murder mission on his own."

"For both our sakes, I hope so. Actually, I'm banking on it."

"And you claim to be some kind of undercover cop or something?"

"I made no such claim."

"You said, and I'm quoting here, 'If I hadn't gotten us out of there, I would have had to blow *my* cover to save *your* ass.'"

"Don't miss a thing, do you?"

"Cover from what?"

"Look, I really can't tell you, for your own good, I swear it. Also, you have to let me drive, because time is short and you drive too slow."

"I have a strange sense of self-preservation. Besides, the last time I gave you the wheel, you drove us through a steel wall."

"Exactly. The wall opened, didn't it?"

Just like he knew it would. "How come you didn't know about the ditch?"

"Turns out those yahoos from Texas, the Militia dudes, just dug it for the land owner. Who knew?"

The Shadow, *quierdo?* "Watch it, buster, those are my home boys. Not my fault they didn't like you."

"They didn't like me because I'm Hispanic, pure and simple. Let's not get into a political debate here. I got you and Jan across, unharmed."

Jan. "Nacho, I have to call Jan and let her know I'm not in danger."

"You are in danger, though. I said if you and I can get to Paco before he gets to us we should be home free, but it's a big if."

"I know that, and you know that, but Jan can be kept in the dark. I'll call, and lie. Tell her I left for, say, San Francisco, before she realizes I'm AWOL and alerts every law officer in the entire free world?"

"Sorry, cell phones don't work out here."

"Bummer. Okay, as soon as we get—wait just a damned minute—didn't you call someone from right about here," we were once again snaking along Mex 2 through surprisingly heavy traffic, "and tell them to off Maggie if you didn't call every fifteen minutes?"

"I lied."

"You mean you really *don't* have anyone backing you up? Holding Maggie hostage?"

"Nope. Just me and thee against the bad guys, for now."

"Then why did you say you had the dog?"

"Opportune coincidence. I wanted to get you and Jan out of Sonora, dog was missing, it worked."

"Bastard! I've been worried sick about her."

"Sorry. Sometimes you gotta do what you gotta do."

As relieved as I was that Maggie was most likely safe, I was furious with Nacho. Whatever he was, he was a devious, underhanded, jerk. Albeit, a handsome, charming, underhanded jerk. Before I met Jenks, I'd considered jerkism a plus.

We switched seats. He picked up the pace, zigzagging around cars and trucks while explaining that the Christmas rush into Mexico was at fault for all the traffic. Jeez, I'd almost forgotten that Christmas was less than a week away until Nacho mentioned it. Hardly of any importance at this point. Which was what? Exactly what point were we at? Maggie was no longer a factor, Jan was safe in Bisbee with Martinez there to watch her. Uh-oh.

"Nacho, if we don't want anyone to know where we've gone, we'll have to ditch this truck."

"Why, you steal it?"

"Sort of."

"Shit, I was kidding. Where did you get it?"

"It belongs to a cop friend of mine."

"Cop? Oh, that's just great. Not that it matters. They take pictures of all the license plates when they cross the border now. If he's sharp, he'll be checking with the border station."

"Oh, he's sharp all right, but I don't think his truck or I will be noted as missing until tomorrow morning. Jan's out like a light, and Martinez planned to sleep for the entire afternoon and night. They are pretty much both down for the count. Martinez asked me to move his truck, so he won't know where to look. I don't think, though, he meant for me to move it into Mexico."

"You think? What kind of cop?"

"Retired. Oakland Police Department. We have a history."

"Oh, that Martinez."

"You know him?"

"No, but when I had you checked out, his name popped up. The OPD has quite a file on you."

"I never did any of it."

"Not what I hear. Given your background, you wouldn't, by some chance, have a gun or two on board your boat, would you?"

"Of course not. They're illegal in Mexico. I left them all at home."

"All? Sounds intriguing. Oh, well, we'll make do with what I've got."

"I had a potato gun, but it kinda blew up when we launched a Molotov cocktail at some guys in a panga."

Nacho boggled the wheel a little.

Good, I like 'em off balance.

38

It was almost two a.m. when we finally pulled into the marina parking lot.

Nacho had me slide down and pull the hat over my face when he went through the guard gate, just in case the Mexican police had posted a lookout. He chatted briefly with the sleepy guard, then, as we drove in, he started laughing.

"I'm glad you find some humor in all this. What did the guard say? I couldn't get a word of it."

"He's from down south, and they talk really fast and use a lot of slang. You're gonna love this."

"Good, I'm truly tired of stuff I don't love."

"Like me?"

I ignored his fishing expedition. "What did the guard say that I'm gonna love?"

"The Mexican authorities have come to the conclusion that Herbert committed suicide."

"What? Just like that, in one day?"

"Just like that. Guard says they found the kiddie porn on

his boat and decided he wasn't worth investigating. Case closed."

I guess my mouth fell open, because he continued. "Don't look so surprised. Maybe we need a little more of that kind of police work up north. Bad guy gets offed, no great loss."

"In Texas we say some folks just need killin'."

"For once, Texas is right."

He killed the motor and we sat quietly, watching the boats and the lot for activity. *Raymond Johnson* sat in her slip, darkened. The intermittent blink of a dock box light going bad was all that illuminated the boats in their slips.

"I see *Manga Manga* is still here, Nacho. So's Smith's boat."

"You know what *Manga Manga* means?"

"Isn't that a Japanese comic book, or something?"

"Yes, but it is also a term for lolliporn."

"And what, pray tell, is lolliporn?"

"What Herbert liked."

"That's disgusting. He had the nerve to advertise? I'm glad he committed suicide."

Nacho chuckled quietly. "See? Justice is served." He unscrewed the overhead light bulb in the Mazda and opened his door. "Stay here while I check things out. Give me your boat keys."

"No."

"No? Why not?"

"I want to stay with you."

Nacho's teeth, like those of the Cheshire cat, glowed in the dark. He reached out and brushed my cheek with the back of his hand again. "I told you I'd grow on you," he said, his voice a little husky.

I'd like to say he had no effect on me at all. I'd like to say that the soft graze of his hand on my cheek didn't give me a little thrill right where— "No, that's not what I meant. Not at all."

He seemed amused by the uncertainty that I'd tried to keep from my voice. "Okay, come on, but stay right behind me, and no noise. Not a peep. How's security around here?"

"There's a security guard who makes his rounds, but it's awfully cold tonight, so my guess is he's holed up in his office."

"Okay, then, let's go."

He started to step from the car, but I grabbed his arm and jerked him back in. "Quick, shut your door."

"Wanna make out?" he teased.

"In your dreams. Look," I pointed to a dark shape moving our way. The marina dog, aptly named Marina, slinked towards us, hesitantly wagging her tail and no doubt wondering if there was food in the offing. She often met cars as they returned from forays into the local restaurants, and was usually rewarded with leftovers. Problem is, Trouble was in the car and had a nasty habit of attacking poor Marina on sight. All we needed was a noisy dog and bird altercation.

Explaining the problem to Nacho, I grabbed Trouble, stuffed him back into the glove compartment, and jumped out of the pickup to give Marina a couple of pieces of popcorn before she started barking at us. She was as grateful for the stale popcorn as if it were Chateaubriand. Hoping for more, she trailed Nacho and me down to the boat.

As we approached *Raymond Johnson*, Nacho stopped, motioned for me to stay put while he boarded. He reached out to unlock the door, found it open an inch or two, and backed off.

"It's open."

"Maybe the cops left it that way. Wouldn't you think there would be, like, yellow crime scene tape all over the place?"

"Case is closed, remember? Stay here, I'm going in."

Marina and I stayed put. I found a few morsels of popcorn deep in my pocket lining, buying her company for a little longer. Not that she was worth a damn as a guard dog; she'd been kicked and rocked too many times. Marina avoided danger at all costs, having learned that people offer food, but also pain. Incompetent attack dog or no, she was still a comfort.

"Come on in," Nacho whispered.

I reluctantly boarded, and even more reluctantly stepped inside the dark saloon. I expected to smell…what? Mayhem? Blood? What I got was a snoot full of Pinelen, the Mexican version of pine-scented disinfectant that, like most Mexican household products, was over the top, smell-wise. My sniffer also detected Zote, a bar soap advertised to serve a dual purpose as catfish bait. Go figure.

"Someone has cleaned your boat," Nacho whispered.

My eyes stung from the fumes, and I could hardly breathe. "Let's open some windows before we pass out. I have to get Trouble, but I need his cage so he doesn't go after Marina. Oh, hell, I gave his cage to Oberto's guy."

"How about we lock Marina in one cabin and Trouble in the other?"

"I don't think I can get Marina on the boat."

"Let me handle it." Nacho rummaged in the fridge, then under the sink and left me to open hatches. He was back in a flash, with poor Marina struggling to escape a garbage bag. Why she wasn't squealing to high heaven, I don't know, but all she did was kick and whimper.

I put a bowl of water and an open bag of potato chips in the forward cabin. When Nacho let her loose she went for the chips, evidently forgetting she was captive, for not another sound was heard. Probably the luxurious experience of a carpet under her for the first time was enough to set a stray to dreaming.

I went after Trouble, who was getting cranky by now. He was tired of being stuffed into the glove compartment, and protested when I tucked him in my pocket. Luckily there were tiny crumbs of popcorn left to keep him busy until I reached the boat again.

As I stepped aboard, Nacho grabbed my arm and put his finger to his lips.

"What?" I whispered.

"Listen."

From behind my master cabin door came a scratching sound, and what sounded like heavy breathing.

"Someone's in there, Nacho. Think the cops left a guard?"

"Not a very good one, judging by the snores. Stay back, I'm going in."

"Be careful, they may have a gun."

"Worried about me, *corazon*?"

"No, I just don't want more blood on my carpet."

He grinned, opened the door and stepped inside.

With a huffy hiss, something very large ran between his feet, slithered over mine, and into the saloon. Stunned, I shrieked, pushed Nacho forward as I jumped back, almost mashing the popcorn out of Trouble when I collided with a wall.

Trouble squawked, Nacho cursed, I squealed, and something hissed.

Much as I didn't want to, I turned on a light.

In the center of the main saloon, a furious five-foot, spiny iguana was letting us know he meant business. Spines on his back stood straight up, sharp teeth glinted in his open mouth. As his head bobbed rapidly, his pendulous dewlap swayed. Worse, his long striped tale whipped from side to side. As he gave us the evil eye, he turned his flank towards us and bowed up, his dewlap puffed even larger. This was one pissed off lizard.

Nacho and I practically tripped over each other in our hasty retreat. We backed into my darkened master suite and slammed the door.

"What in holy hell *is* that?" Nacho asked. "Some kind of dragon?"

"Iguana. Big one. Had one as a pet when I was a kid, but much, much smaller. I can't figure out how he got into the boat."

From behind us came a growl. We froze. Now what?

I snaked my hand along the wall, found a light switch, and flipped it.

"Oh, God, turn it back off, or blind me," Nacho wailed.

I turned to find my Aunt Lil, buck naked, sprawled on the bed and snoring to beat the band. One hand was still wrapped around an empty Bacardi bottle.

"What, or who, is that?"

"My aunt." *And my worst nightmare. Could I end up like this? Old, drunk and alone?*

Nacho had his hand over his eyes. "For God's sake, cover her *up*."

I threw a blanket over my least favorite relative. She never stopped snoring. On the floor next to the bed was a leash attached to a rhinestone studded collar. I picked it up and handed it to Nacho.

"Here, take her iguana for a one-way walk into the desert."

Nacho demurred on getting a collar on the large and angry lizard, so I coaxed the reptile back into my bedroom with a long line of lettuce leaves.

Trouble, cowed by such a ferocious looking creature, clamped his claws into my shoulder and stayed put.

I considered dumping Aunt Lil on the dock, but Nacho was afraid she'd roll into the water and drown. Not that I would mind, but Mother would never forgive me, and two bodies connected to my boat in less than two days might incite even the ever-so-practical Mexican judicial system to action.

"Looks like the old bag and her lizard are in for a boat ride, Nacho. When we start up these engines, half the residents on the dock are going to peek out to see what's going on, and with what went down here recently, some will investigate."

Nacho seemed lost in thought, then his face lit up. "How many gringo boats, with people on them, are in this part of the sea at this time of year?"

"Oh, I don't know. Say, twenty here, another twenty-five at the other marina, a few at anchor. On the Baja side, another fifty or so scattered between Santa Rosalia and Puerto Escondido."

"And, if they had to, how many could, and would, come to Agua Fria if asked."

"Depends on the reason. Free beer works. Cruisers love a beach party."

"How would we contact them?"

"Ham radio. I can put out a call on the Sonrisa Net tomorrow morning, but why? What do you have in mind?"

"Safety in numbers. The boats can be a diversion, much like your pigeons, while I get to Paco."

"Are you sure they won't be like sitting ducks, instead."

"I think not. There is some element of danger, but not if I succeed in my plan. I have been working on this for weeks, before I was forced to change my original mission."

Now it's a mission? What am I getting into? "Lucky for us, my tanks are topped off, and all systems were checked out before you kidnapped me."

"I did not really kidnap you."

"Oh, yes you did. And I don't intend to forget, or forgive."

"Hetta, haven't you ever heard of Stockholm Syndrome?"

"Nacho, does the phrase, 'Remember the Alamo' have any meaning for you?"

39

I started the engines and, just as I predicted, lights popped on in nearby boats. Within seconds, Smith was dockside, with, thankfully, Maggie trailing along behind. He spotted me on the flying bridge.

"Hetta? You're here? And all right? Where have you been? Better yet, where are you going?"

"Agua Fria. Can't explain right now, but we might need a little help over there. If we're not in touch within twenty-four hours, call out the gendarmes and send *them* to Agua Fria."

"Wait, I'll go with you."

"It would be better if you bring your boat over."

"Can't. Engine trouble."

"Okay, then, hop aboard. Time's awastin' and we have to leave, pronto."

"I'll be back in a flash," he said, jumping onto the dock. Then, back over his shoulder, he asked, "Don't you want to take *Se Vende?*"

I looked over the side at my panga. "Nacho, do we need my skiff?"

"We'll need something to get to shore."

"*Se Vende* will slow us down, I have to tow her."

Smith turned back and yelled, "Follow me. We'll grab my dinghy and throw her on deck."

Nacho and Smith were back in five minutes with the dinghy, and a little something else.

"Oh, no, you don't, Smith. I'm allergic to cats."

"Hetta, we can't just leave him here. Mr. Bill's boat trained, never leaves. And now that his owner is gone, there's no one to take care of him. I have his litter box."

"Where's her owner?"

"Dead. She was Herbert's."

Nacho, having finished lashing down the dinghy, interceded. "We gotta go, cat or no cat."

"Oh, ok, put him in…" I had a really mean thought, "my cabin. And Smith, just crack the door and toss him in."

Nacho tilted his head at me, and I gave him a wicked smile. My aunt abhorred cats and with any luck at all, Mr. Bill had a hankering for lizard. From the size of him, I figured that fat cat could handle an iguana, no problemo.

"Can we please go now?" Nacho growled.

"Yep, help Smith with the lines." Smith had boosted Maggie to the flying bridge, so I put her in the captain's seat behind me. Not to be left out, Trouble joined us, giving the dog an affectionate peck on the nose when she sniffed him in hello.

With all the commotion, any vestige of a stealth exit was long gone.

Several other sleepy-eyed boaters emerged from their bunks, and as I was backing out of the slip, Smith yelled to them, "If you can come to Agua Fria, get underway. Hetta needs help. We'll monitor channel eighty-eight if you want details."

Nacho joined us on the bridge. "Will they come?"

"Some will," I reassured him, "but remember, I can do ten, twelve knots and most of them can only do five, unless there's wind. Which, right now, there isn't."

"But in the morning, after you ask for help, others will come from Puerto Escondido?"

Smith nodded. "My bet is there will also be boats from Conception Bay, and even the islands north of La Paz. Problem is time. When is it that whatever's going to happen, well, happens?"

"It is imperative that we act before, or on, Christmas Eve." He fingered my Christmas lights. "Can you turn these on?"

"Now? Sure, if you want us to cross the sea lit up like Las Vegas. That's why Christmas boat parades are so spectacular, they light up the night sky."

"Christmas boat parade? Do the other boats have lights?"

"Most. Why?"

"That is what we will have, a parade, right into Agua Fria harbor."

"Gee, and here I was afraid that, after being rudely snatched by a crazed Mexican, I'd miss the parade. Now, I guess, I get to lead one."

"Yes," Nacho seemed pensive and answered as though talking to himself, "that will work very well. I can think of no better way to interrupt Weeweechu."

"Weeweechu?"

He looked a little startled, as though he'd forgotten we were not privy to his innermost thoughts. "It is a code name. When will we arrive on the Baja side?"

"Never, if you don't start talking. When I ask for help,

boaters will come, but we have to warn them there may be an element of danger involved."

"What kind of danger?" Smith asked. Maggie was tucked into his jacket, and Trouble sat on his shoulder, gently grooming the dog's ears.

I looked at Nacho. "Yeah, Nacho, I think it's time we knew what we're getting into, so start talking."

Nacho sighed. "You are right. The villagers at Agua Fria are being held captive, forced to manufacture crystal meth in a super lab behind the village."

"What?" Smith and I cried in unison.

Trouble stopped nibbling Maggie's ears and perked up. "What? What?" he screeched.

I recovered a little from the shock. "And you want us to drive right into this disaster? I think not."

"Where's your Christmas spirit? " Nacho quipped, trying, unsuccessfully, to insert a little humor into the situation.

"I gave at the office."

"Look, it's not as bad as you think. I already decided, in advance, and by myself, to stop the, uh, mayhem the gang has scheduled. With your involvement, though, my plan—"

I put my hand to my ear. "Hello? Professor Whitman, from Planning 101? He's on the phone and wants you back in class, Nacho, for it is *you* who got *me* involved."

Smith threw up his hands. "Hetta, shut up. Nacho, explain."

I shut up, and Nacho 'splained. "The villagers are being paid quite well for their work, but they still have no choice but to cook meth. The gang in charge of the operation has created, as Hetta well knows, a landslide to block the road so relatives cannot visit. The only phone line is cut. Anywhere else besides Baja, this would raise questions, but it is not unusual for villages to be cut off after natural disasters. The problem is, another disaster, far worse, is about to befall this village."

"What more can happen to these poor people?" I was thinking of Chino's grandmother.

"This gang knows they cannot hold off outsiders indefinitely. They will, very soon, leave for good. Christmas morning, as a matter of fact. Most of them have already split, overseeing the second half of the scheme."

"Isn't that good?"

"Not if they leave no witnesses."

Smith's mouth dropped open. "You're shittin' me. How many people are we talking about?"

"Maybe a hundred or more."

I re-hinged my own jaw. "How can they get by with killing so many folks?"

"As far as we know, it is the first time anyone has planned to make an entire village disappear, but with the new government crackdown on crack, the guys running the lab plan one last, big shipment in many, many separate loads. And this stuff is ninety-percent pure Mexican ice. We're talking not hundreds, but *thousands* of pounds. By the time it gets to the end user in the US, we're talking a billion dollars here. And this outfit controls its own chain of distribution. No outsiders, no sharing the wealth."

"And over a hundred innocent people die."

"Not if we get there in time."

"The drug slugs are just going to stand by while we anchor off their beach and, like a grade B movie, save the villagers?"

"Actually, most of the bad guys are off on Christmas vacation."

"Say what?"

Nacho shrugged. "Christmas is a big deal down here. I, myself, am supposed to be in LA. As is Paco. That is why the time is perfect for us to make a strike, because, starting Christmas Day, the village of Agua Fria goes up in smoke, and operation Weeweechu begins."

"Weeweechu?" I asked for the second time, but was ignored.

Smith looked from me to Nacho. "Who's Paco?"

Despite Nacho's warning glance, I answered. "Probably the guy who killed Herbert."

"Well I'm confused all to hell."

"Ain't we all? Nacho, want to fill our friend in? After all, he volunteered to get in on this little counterplot of yours. Oh, wait. If you tell him, you'll have to kill him."

Nacho narrowed his eyes at me, then gave Smith the story he gave me about Paco, and his murderous mission.

Smith took it all in, then asked, "If this Paco was over on the Sonora side of the sea, and killed Herbert, why would he be back in Agua Fria now?"

"Because he didn't find *me,* and now he has to cover his ass. How, I'm not sure. He didn't get what he came for, so he has to create some sort of story before the boss finds out he's lost his…"

A little light went off in my head. "GPS?"

Nacho actually smiled. "I didn't say that."

"So, since you didn't, I get to live?"

Smith lost his patience. "What are you two talking about?"

Nacho clammed up, so I elaborated. "Our friend Nacho here, who claims he's not a member of the drug gang, but has yet to prove it, has a GPS, which he took from Paco. In this little device is a list, with coordinates, of all the safe places to move drugs across the border, into the States. Even through iron walls. This Weeweechu is going to be something like the Berlin airlift of meth, except on foot, by truck, and maybe a mule or two. Am I getting warm, Nacho?"

"You are very, very warm." He said it all sexy-like, making me blush.

Smith was too worried to notice our little flirtation. "I'm still a little lost here. Won't the border patrol stop them?"

I had the picture now. "Oh, Smith, I think we're talking blitzkrieg here. Hundreds of crossers, all at once, on a major holiday—Pearl Harbor comes to mind—along the entire border. Safety in numbers, right? With all those runners, more meth will get through than not. Right, Lamont?"

Nacho grinned. "'Who knows what evil lurks in the hearts of men? The Shadow knows!'"

"You two are nuts. Okay, I'm in, because it's not like I have a choice right now. What's the plan?"

"Nacho don't got one, and we're sticking to it."

40

What we needed was a plan not to stick to.

I peeked in on old Aunt Lil, who was, unfortunately, still breathing. Mr. Bill sat on her chest, purring in unison with her snores. The iguana was stretched out on the end of the bed, unharmed, and asleep. That cat obviously has no taste when it comes to people, but then he did belong to Herbert. Any hopes I'd had for feline lizard control were dashed.

I rejoined the men and looked behind us as, even from almost mid-sea, first light silhouetted the tips of the Tetakawi mountains against the eastern sky. We were over forty miles out, but the lack of air pollution in this part of the world makes for spectacular visibility.

As the sun rose, Nacho, Smith, and I pored over a charts of the middle sea. Nacho tapped Agua Fria, then asked, "Is there another place, near by, but not visible from Agua Fria, where we can rendezvous with the other boats?"

"Here," Smith pointed. "If this weather holds, and it is supposed to, this little anchorage is good. Only two miles or so north of Agua Fria."

"What's it called?"

"The cruisers call it Vagabond Cove, after a boat that sank there."

"Okay, so we want the cruisers to rendezvous at Vagabond Cove by tomorrow afternoon, right?"

Nacho nodded. "Yes. When will we arrive there?"

I punched a few buttons on the GPS, brought up the menu of preloaded waypoints and cursored down to Vagabond.

"At this speed, late afternoon. I can put on a few more turns, get there earlier."

"Perfect. That will give us almost twenty-four hours for the other boats to arrive, for you to organize your parade, and for me to, uh, do what I have to do."

Nacho and I went topsides, leaving Smith to catch a nap on the settee. The morning air was chilly, but windless, and the Sea of Cortez was as glassy as I'd ever seen it. Nary a ripple or swell disturbed the surface. To the northwest I could make out the outline of the Three Virgins, the volcanoes near Santa Rosalia. We were joined by a huge school of dolphins, probably a hundred or more, that chattered, jumped and entertained us for a good twenty minutes before getting bored with our relatively slow speed, and going about their business.

The dolphins gone, I turned to Nacho to share my thoughts. "Let me summarize this brilliant plan of yours. We all get in a little straight line, with me out front standing in for Rudolf. We turn on our Christmas lights, blast Elvis singing "Blue Christmas" on the loud hailer, and cruise right into a drug lord-controlled harbor. With a fleet about as militarily effective as the Swiss Navy. What's to keep said bad guys from blowing Dancer, Donner, Blitzen and Raymond plumb out of the water?"

"Me, of course. I—."

"Hetta! Help! I need you down here," Smith hollered.

Nacho and I ran down the stairs, expecting to find the boat filling with water or smoke, but it was worse. Auntie Lil was awake.

Wrapped in a bed sheet that she was having trouble holding onto, she was bent over, her head in the fridge and her withered hindquarters bare.

"Aunt Lil, for heaven's sake, go get dressed. There are men here."

Without changing position, she asked, "Where's your tomato juice?"

"I don't have any."

"Oh, well, then. Just get me the vodka. Cut out the middle man, so to speak." She straightened and turned to face us. The sheet, thank all the stars in heaven, did its job. Her steely gray hair stuck out in all directions. Black mascara smudges bruised her cheeks and she had, apparently without benefit of a mirror, smeared bright red lipstick across her lips. Alice Cooper would no doubt applaud her maquillage.

Incongruously, a Queen Elizabeth-style handbag hung from her way-too-bare arm. Her jaw worked and she smacked her lips in a way I knew all too well, an involuntary movement, the result of popping pills. That handbag held an addict's dream list of pharmaceuticals, most of them prescription from a plethora of doctors she played like the lottery, and undoubtedly enhanced by an all inclusive trip for two to a Mexican *farmacia*. I would have dumped the bag's contents overboard while she slept, but I had no way of knowing which pills were recreational, and which were actually necessary to keep her alive. It's against my nature to waste a perfectly good recreational drug.

"No vodka," I stated, drawing an amused look from Nacho.

"What kind of ship is this?" my aunt wanted to know.

"A dry one. No booze on board. I'm trying to quit," I lied. During the night I had cleared every single bit of booze from the main saloon into the far reaches of the engine room.

"Well, then, I insist that you take me to shore."

"My pleasure, believe me. In a few hours you'll have all the shore you can stand." *In the middle of nowhere Baja.*

As if her vision suddenly slammed into focus, she noticed Smith and Nacho. Putting on what she thought was a coquettish smile, she batted her eyelashes. "My goodness, Hetta, I sure like the looks of your crew. But you really must remove your cat from my room."

"It's not your room, and it's not my cat. Now, please, go get dressed."

"I can't find my clothes. I must have left them in the taxi. I had a most dreadful row with the driver over Iggy, who escaped his duffel bag when I wasn't looking, and climbed into the man's lap. Gave him quite a start. The taxi man, not my iguana. Man almost wrecked us. Such a careless driver."

"You were naked in the taxi?"

"Of course not. That taxi driver dumped us in the parking lot and took off with my suitcase."

"Then put on the clothes you arrived in."

"They're soiled. I have no idea how."

Oh, I do. "Then I'll give you some sweats. Come on."

I led her into my stateroom where Mr. Bill and Ignacio, Iggy, were curled up together, still napping. I felt a familiar tickle in the back of my throat and headed for my medicine chest, and the antihistamines. Unless I dumped Mr. Bill soon, I would be flirting with a full blown asthma attack. As much as I liked cats, an extreme allergy to them was the only thing I had in common with my aunt. Too make sure my dear aunt didn't take all my medicine when hers ran out, I stuffed my inhaler and meds into my jacket pocket. When this little caper was over, I would have to de-cat my quarters.

I threw a pair of sweats at Lil. As my mood darkened, my already stretched tolerance for my least favorite relative thinned. "Here, put these on, and stay out of the way."

"Your mother would be appalled, you talking to me that way. You have no respect for your elders."

"Respect is earned."

"You've always hated me, and now you've stolen my sweet little bird and sold him off."

"Trouble!" I yelled. He sailed into the room, but took one look at the now awake iguana and cat, and sailed back out. "See, he's here, and he's all yours. I've waited years to give you the bird."

Okay, lame and immature, but it made me feel better.

Back on the flying bridge with Nacho, I sulked. What I wanted was a drink, but could I have one? No. And why? Because I had to keep booze from a woman I hated. I wanted Jenks, but where was he? In Kuwait, while I sailed into disaster. And why? Because that's what I do.

Nacho, wisely, kept silent while I steamed. The antihistamine hit my blood stream, and empty stomach, taking the edge off my anger and making me a little high. Runs in the family, I guess.

"Nacho?"

"Yes?"

"What are you going to do when we get to the other side?"

"I told you."

"No, you gave us a vague indication. I want details."

"No you don't."

"Then give me one good reason to put myself, and others into danger."

"Okay, I will. When this is over, you'll be glad you did. For the rest of your life, you will know that you unselfishly put yourself into danger to save others."

"That is the worst reason I've ever heard. I am selfish, and I want to stay that way."

"Then do it for me." He said this softly, not looking at me, but at the horizon. "Help me save you. I don't want you on my conscience."

"Like you have one."

He didn't answer.

Something in his manner set me to ruminating on the past three dizzying days. Seemed that one minute I was worrying about getting Jan *across* the border, and the next I was running *through* it. I'd committed several punishable crimes. I was consorting with a known drug dealer, pursued by another, I'd…a little light went off in my head. "Nacho, you rat bastard. You sicced Paco on me, didn't you?"

"I'm afraid so. At the time, I didn't think it would come to this, but it has."

"You owe me the story."

He sighed. "After you took my truck, Paco realized the GPS with all the border crossing waypoints was missing. I told him it was in my truck."

"But it wasn't."

"No. I had hidden it until I could get it into the hands of the right people."

"Which you did."

"Yes. All the drugs will be stopped, and the carriers arrested."

"Why did you need me?"

"Paco traced the truck to Lopez Mateos, then learned you had left in it. These small towns, people talk. By the time he arrived in Santa Rosalia, you were gone. He returned to

Lopez Mateos and began stalking Jan, hoping she would lead him to you. In a way, she did."

The idea of a psychopath stalking my best friend turned my blood cold.

"While Paco was in Lopez Mateos, I decided to make a run for it. Take the GPS and hightail it for the border. I was in Santa Rosalia to catch the ferry when I spotted Jan at a pay phone. I maneuvered close enough to hear she was talking with you. When she headed for the marina, I followed. I was sure Paco was nearby, and I couldn't just leave her unprotected."

"How gallant of you."

He ignored my barb. "You know the rest. We were lucky to escape Santa Rosalia. Paco must have nosed around and learned where we went, and by then he knew I was...well, not one of them."

"But he couldn't blow the whistle on you without getting himself in deep caca."

"Correcto. Now I will finish off the villain, save the villagers and, more importantly, my Marlo Lane."

"Oh, gosh, Lamont, I'm sooo relieved."

"You know, Marlo, sarcasm is the lowest form of wit."

"I tailor my wit to suit my audience."

41

Super hero on board or no, I had no intention of staging a one-boat parade, just in case The Shadow got his cape shot full of holes.

Smith, unlike *moi*, was a legally licensed ham operator. He tuned in the Sonrisa Net and pleaded for other boats to join us at Vagabond for a parade into Agua Fria.

"Think they'll come?" Nacho wanted to know.

"Some will, for sure," Smith reassured him. "Even if we only have five boats with lights, we'll make a splash. Hetta, do you really have Elvis's Christmas music? I'm impressed."

I nodded, and said, "Let's hope we don't impress a bunch of bad guys into blowing us out of the water."

Nacho grinned. "It will not be that way. By the time you enter the harbor, I will have neutralized any serious firepower they have."

"How about the *un*serious firepower? And how do you plan to disarm them?"

"I will walk from Vagabond Cove to," he tapped the chart,

"here. I stashed a few heavy duty weapons near this spot. If all goes well, and I'm sure it will, I will at least have the few men at the lab under control. It is the guards in the village that you need to distract, and there are probably only about three or four. They will be as astonished as the villagers when your parade arrives."

"I'll go with you, Nacho," Smith offered.

"No, I need you for another operation. While everyone is watching the parade, a volunteer, namely you, will go ashore and bring as many willing villagers as you can out to the boats. Tell them it's a party."

"And what, pray tell, will keep the guards from grabbing Smith?"

"Their job is to intimidate the locals, not engage outsiders."

"How do we know the people will be willing to come to our so-called party?"

"You will offer them gifts for their children."

"I do have a few things onboard that Jenks suggested I bring. Crayons, pencils, writing tablets. We trade them for fish and lobster."

"Perfecto."

"Other boats will have stuff, as well. If these folks are virtual prisoners, though, won't the guards stop them from leaving the beach? If folks can just up and leave, why haven't they?"

"The guards know that the villagers will do nothing to jeopardize the children. The people have been told that, after Christmas Day, it will all be over, but for now, all of the children under twelve are held at the school. They live and sleep there, under guard."

"This just gets weirder and weirder. This meth gang is planning to wipe out the entire village? Kids and all?"

"Oh, no. After the adults are murdered, the children will be transported out. Kids are valuable commodities on the black, or should I say, white slavery, market. The lolliporn trade sells pornographic photos, and even the children themselves, to people like that," he looked like he'd bitten into a lime, "Herbert."

Smith did a double-take. "The Herbert who was murdered?"

"No," I drawled, "the Herbert who cut his own throat on my boat, then dragged himself into the desert and put a bullet in his pervert brain. These Nazis really know how to commit suicide." This drew a bark of laughter from Nacho.

"You two, though, think it was this Paco character who killed Herbert, right?"

"You can take it to the bank, Smith," I said. "Small world, ain't it? Ironical that Paco knocked off a potential customer."

Nacho shrugged.. "His people skills suck."

Iggy the Iguana, after his initial angry posturing, turned out to be docile, and even a little endearing, if that's a word you can possibly associate with a five-foot, spiny reptile. I let him out of the aft cabin and he waddled after people like a pet poodle, patiently waiting for someone to scratch his head and dewlap. He was easily put to sleep with a little petting, and even gave up threatening the other animals. Maggie and Trouble initially gave him a wide berth, but soon grew used to him and, while not bosom buds, they reached détente, leaving each to his own.

We also allowed Marina into the main saloon, but she took one look at Trouble and that dragonlike reptile and hid under the galley banquette. Mr. Bill stayed sprawled out on my bed, permeating my sheets and pillows with enough cat dander to insure sending my body into respiratory arrest.

After our Sonrisa Net announcement, Stephanie agreed to put out a call for boats on all of the other nets, letting all within cruising distance know that there would be a rendezvous at Vagabond, followed by a lighted boat parade to Agua Fria to cheer up the impoverished villagers who were trapped by a landslide. It was just the kind of call that rallied cruisers in force, and I felt guilty that there was a possibility of more adventure than they were banking on.

Stephanie also told us Jan had called her an hour earlier, wanting to know if she'd heard from me. "Jan said, and I'm quoting here, 'If you hear from that blank, Hetta, you tell her to get her big blank back here, and bring Martinez's blanking truck with her.' I added the blanks, cuz I can't say some things on ham radio without losing my license."

Nacho and Smith burst into laughter while I asked Steph to call Jan, fill her in on my whereabouts, and tell her I'd be back in Bisbee within two or three days, suitably contrite and ready to face up to my crimes. Whatever they were.

As a matter of fact, just what were they? Okay, so I ran the border, but they didn't press charges on that because we were kidnapped. Bird smuggling? Nope, I convinced them he'd just flown over on his own. Aiding and abetting a jail bird break? No proof, no witness, unless they sweated the pigeons. Car theft? Martinez wouldn't rat me out, would he? So all I really did was to leave Bisbee when requested by the authorities to stay put. How serious can that be? Heck, they couldn't touch me.

"Hetta? You still there?" Stephanie asked, blasting me from my self-righteous reverie.

"Roger."

"I just talked with Jan again, gave her your message. She

says you should not, repeat not, set one foot into Arizona. Some folks here are pretty ticked off with you, and are putting together a list of charges a mile long."

"For what?"

"Dunno, but she said you needed a lawyer, and to stay south of the border for now."

"Touchy these Arizonans. Okay, message received. Thanks."

"Oh, thank *you*."

"What for?"

"Entertainment. Before you came to the sea, all we had to deal with were the normal things. Boats sinking, storms brewing, dinghies stolen. Now we have you."

"Glad to be of service. Out."

Aunt Lil tottered into the saloon in time to hear that lawyer thing, mumbled something like, "I knew you'd come to a bad end," and retired to my quarters. Two seconds later, Mr. Bill was tossed out the door. I was tempted to break out the booze, because as insufferable as my aunt is drunk, she's more so sober and grouchy.

Mr. Bill landed on his feet, shot a dirty look in the direction of the slammed door, then regained his dignity and strolled forward, tail up, to grace us with his presence. I'm sure he'd been kicked out of better cat houses.

We reached Vagabond with enough afternoon left for Smith to take Maggie and Marina for a pit stop on the beach. Nacho left with him, taking my handheld VHF radio. We agreed to talk on channel seventeen, coordinate our movements for what we now deemed Operation Weeweechu Two, since the drug lords had conjured up the name, Weeweechu, for their border running operation.

Before the men and dogs left, though, Nacho pulled me into the forward cabin. "Hetta, I want to tell you something before I leave. For many years I harbored anger and hatred for another. It clouded my judgment, and hurt me far worse than it did the other person. Until I learned to forgive, that anger poisoned my very soul. You need to let go of your anger for your aunt. She is old and will soon die, probably because of her own inner hatred. Do not follow in her footsteps, for if you do, she will have won. I do not doubt your assessment that she harms others, but do not let her harm you."

Of all the drug dealers in the world, I draw one who thinks he's Dr. Phil? Before I could reply, he said, "*Vaya con Dios.*"

"This sounds like a fairly final *adios.*"

"Perhaps, but I mean it. Go with God." His big brown eyes watered, he kissed my cheek, and rushed past me to get into the dinghy with Smith. I recovered from my shock at his touching goodbye and followed to watch him and Smith load the dogs into the dinghy.

Marina did not go easily into the skiff. Only after Maggie whined, then barked at her in some kind of dog talk that must have said, "Move your butt, gal, I gotta pee," did she jump in.

I was tempted to bag Iggy and send him ashore to be let loose, but I feared he'd been raised as a pet and would never survive in the desert alone.

Okay, so I'm soft on large lizards, and handsome Mexicans.

42

The Sea of Cortez bestowed a magical Christmas Eve upon our little fleet. No wind. Flat seas. Almost balmy air. Mother Nature, according to Smith, who follows these things, was set to throw in a waxing gibbous moon, which meant more than half full. With a moon rising well before the sun set, we were to have excellent visibility.

Fifteen boats arrived by four that afternoon, all of them with at least a string or two of Christmas lights. When we paraded into Agua Fria, we were gonna make one hell of a target.

As the afternoon waned I became more and more anxious to hear from Nacho. He made it clear, before he left, that we were to wait until we heard from him before sailing within firing range of the village. We wanted to round the point just at dusk for maximum effect. In a place like Agua Fria, with no electricity and, therefore, no ambient light other than that promised moon, we would look like the city of New York cruising into their harbor.

I paced and fretted, tempted to call Nacho on channel seventeen, but he'd told me not to. My voice booming out of the radio, he said, might jeopardize everything. Too much was at stake for that kind of snafu.

Tension mounted on *Raymond Johnson* as the sun sank in the West. The animals picked up on the nervous strain, and became increasingly restless. Aunt Lil, cranky by nature, unbearable in withdrawal, grated on my last nerve with her ceaseless bellyaching. She'd discovered my confiscation of her drug stash, and tried to convince me certain pills were necessary to sustain life. Like I care? In an attempt to shut her up, I fired up the Satfone and checked out her pharmaceutical's names on the Internet, gave her back everything that did not contain a controlled substance. Didn't work, of course. I considered popping a couple of the stronger ones myself, but vetoed the idea until this evening had passed, and we were all safe.

"Hetta?"

I dove for the mike. "Nacho, thank God. Are you all right?"

"Yes. It is comforting to know you care."

"Yeah, well I don't. I just want to get this night over with."

"Chur you do. Are you ready?"

"You bet."

"Okay, then, here goes," and he sang:

"Weeweechu a Merry Christmas;
Weeweechu a Merry Christmas;
Weeweechu a Merry Christmas;
And a Happy New Year."

Smith, myself and even Aunt Lil broke into laughter, theirs a little more enhanced than mine. I suspected they'd shared a joint when I wasn't watching.

When I caught my breath, I answered, "Very clever. Okay, Operation Weeweechu is officially underway."

I switched to channel sixteen and announced, "Ladies and gentlemen, start your engines, please. And weeweechu a very Merry Christmas."

I would like to say we sailed into the Agua Fria harbor, easily rescued the villagers, and saved the day without incident.

It actually looked that way for the first hour.

We rounded the point looking much like an electrified centipede. Elvis, his moanful crooning cranked to the max my speakers allow, lamented having a "Blue Christmas Without You." People soon gathered on the beach, gawking as we formed a huge raft-up. To my mind, tying all of the boats together only made us a larger target, but that's what Nacho wanted.

With our lights, and the moon's glow, there was a fair amount of visibility on the beach. Smith dinghied to shore while I held my breath. When he wasn't blown out of the water, he signaled for others from the boats to join him.

Dinghies were launched, and headed in, but no amount of cajoling or bribery enticed the villagers to leave. As long as those children remained hostages, they refused to budge. Of course, they didn't know that I knew about the kids, and I had not shared that info with the other boaters. Nacho said he had a plan, and I had to trust him.

Smith returned empty, so I left him on the boat and went in myself. My plan was to ferret out Granny Yee, see if she had any influence over the others.

An ancient fisherman stood at the water's edge as I eased the dinghy onto the sand. He made no move to help me pull the boat ashore, and for a moment I feared he was one of the guards Nacho had warned me about.

"*Hola, y Feliz Navidad,*" I offered.

He only nodded.

"*Uh, por favor, señor, yo quiero…*" I ran out of words. What is the verb for "to find"? *Encontrar*? Screw it, I'd stick with the basics. "*¿Esta Señora Yee aqui?*"

He only stared.

Frustrated, I brushed by him, but he reached out and grabbed my arm. Alarmed, I spun to do battle, only to meet a sweet, if toothless smile. He pointed to his ears and mouth, and I understood he was a deaf mute.

"Just great," I muttered under my breath, "now what?"

He pulled me towards a group of others who had ventured out to watch our parade, and prompted me to ask the question again. A small, attractive woman stepped from the crowd and said, in perfect English. "I am Senora Yee."

"Oh, that's great," I said, trying to sound casual, even though I feared I was in someone's gun sights. "I bring Christmas greetings from your grandson, Chino Yee. He is my friend."

She looked alarmed and shot a furtive look back into the darkened village. "You must go."

I ignored the warning, and blithely gushed, "Gosh, I just arrived. I'd like you to come out to the boat, so you can call Chino on my satellite phone. I know he'd love to hear from you."

"Oh, no, I cannot do that."

Others began nervously asking her what we were talking about, and whatever she said sent them skittering back towards their homes. With a quick bob of her head, she followed them. So much for saving the villagers.

Frustrated, I tailed Granny Yee. We had just reached her house, or what I assumed was her house, when something akin to a nuclear blast almost flattened us. A red cloud rose from behind a hill to the west, followed by even more explosions. It was then that I saw two men with guns take off in the direction of the blast. Nacho said there were three or four guards. Two gone, one or two to go.

"Where is the school house?" I asked Chino's grandmother.

Shaken, but suddenly understanding that I knew more about the situation than she'd thought, she scooped a terrified, bleating goat kid from her yard and yelled, "Follow me."

As we ran through the village, Chino's grandmother told others to follow, and they did. Some brandished machetes, and a pitch fork or two put in mind an old vampire movie where the villagers finally get up the gumption to storm the monster's lair. Problem was, our monster was probably packing an AK-47.

Granny Yee stopped suddenly and motioned for quiet, then she waved me forward. The explosions had stopped for the time, and it was eerily silent except for the distant croon of Elvis. The red glow of the fire in the hills painted our faces red, bringing to mind a Heironymus Bosch rendition of Hell.

I could no longer see the fleet, but hoped they were rapidly breaking ranks and heading for sea. As I crept behind Chino's grandmother, my knees quaked and our footfalls, to me, sounded like drumbeats. No, wait, that was my own heartbeat drumming in my ears.

Stopping again, my guide pointed. "There."

The schoolhouse was a small square building surrounded by a chain link fence. Ominously, the top of the fence, normally angled to keep out intruders, was reversed to detain the occupants. The windows were boarded shut. From within, we heard children wailing with fright and beating on the door.

With a huff of disgust, Granny ditched the goat, scaled that fence like a mountaineer, and dropped to the other side. I followed. After getting cut all to hell, I plummeted ungracefully into the school yard, and was gasping for breath when I saw, a little late, that Grans Yee had unlocked and opened the gate.

Parents rushed through the gate and pried the schoolhouse door open. No guards appeared, and within minutes we were all sprinting for the beach. Bless their souls, the boaters had separated from the raft-up, but waited in the harbor. Within minutes, all the children and some adults were headed for the boats. I estimated there were about twenty-five kids, and nearly a hundred adults. We had fifteen dinghies, with the average capacity to safely carry four people. The math told the story; it would take awhile to get everyone off the beaches and onto the boats.

The first group had barely reached the cruisers when we heard a burst of gunfire. It was then I learned that most Mexicans, especially those from fishing villages, don't swim.

"We live on the water, around the water, but few of us ever learn to swim. We rely on our pangas," Granny Yee explained when the people refused my suggestion to swim for it. "You go. We will wait for the boats to return."

"Truth is, I can't really swim, either." Which is true, but more importantly the idea of getting into that dark water, scratched and bloody, had little appeal. Not only would it sting, I'd be like so much chum.

Her face broke into a brilliant smile. "Maybe you are Mexican and don't know it."

I laughed and petted her goat. "Actually, my family were Mexican citizens at one time. Maybe that's it. I know I like *cabrito*, roasted slowly over mesquite," I teased.

She held her goat tighter. "Not this one. He is my pet."

Our light patter took my mind from our plight, and after all, what could I do, anyway? I only hoped that Nacho had taken care of business and offed the bad guys. I was sure he was the one who blew the lab, a mite ahead of the drug lord's schedule. Weeweechu a Merry Christmas, indeed.

Smith returned to the beach on one of the first dinghies, and took on a load of folks destined for Raymond Johnson. I groaned inwardly when Granny Yee stepped in with her goat, followed by the toothless old man cradling a chicken under one arm and a duck under the other. Was there a forty day and night rainstorm in the offing?

As the other dinghies took on passengers and left, I was soon alone, waiting for Smith to return. In truth, I had waited to see if Nacho would appear. Not that I really cared, of course.

Another series of smaller explosions startled me. I turned to look in the direction of the noise and saw, coming toward me from the houses, a man. Backlit by the fires raging over the hill, I couldn't make out who it was, but I could see, from his silhouette, that he was packing. Frightened, I backed toward the water, determined to swim for it if I had to.

Something large splashed behind me. Now scared out of my wits as the dark figure approached, I was still even more afraid of whatever sea monster lurked in the dark depths behind me. I'll take a known threat to an unknown threat any day.

"Stop," I yelled, "I have a gun." I held out my hand and pointed my finger.

"Don't move, Hetta." Nacho ordered.

Relieved, I took a step toward him.

"I said, stay where you are," Nacho growled, and pointed his weapon straight at me.

"Gee, I think I'll return your Christmas present," I said, trying to sound tough, but my voice quavered, betraying my bravado.

"Shut up." He raised the gun and fired.

My last thought as a tremendous blow slammed into my shoulder and the sand came up to meet my face was, "Men are scum."

43

"Hetta? Hetta, wake up." Someone gently patted my cheek and flicked cool water onto my face.

"Can't. I'm dead. Nacho shot me."

A familiar voice asked, "Who's Nacho?"

Another answered, "Drug dealer friend of hers."

I shook my head, still refusing to open my eyes. "No friend, he shot me."

"Hetta, this is Jan. You aren't shot. I think you fainted."

I raised my arm and groped my shoulder. "Is that blood I feel?"

I sensed a flashlight beam aimed at me. "Yes, but not yours."

Covering my eyes with my hand, I peeked between my fingers. Hovering faces came into focus. Jan, Chino, Martinez, and Jenks. Jenks?

"Jenks? You're really here?" I put my hands on his face, then grabbed him in a neck lock that threatened to topple him headlong into the sand with me. He got his balance and pulled me to my feet. I hung onto him as if he would disappear if I let go.

Jenks gave me a light kiss on the cheek, but I wanted more. I traded the neck lock for a lip lock until I heard Jan say, "Oh for heaven's sake, get a room."

I broke off the smooch, but still kept a steel grip on Jenks. "How did you get here? And what took you so long?"

Jenks rolled his eyes and shook his head. "Sorry I was so late to your latest disaster, Hetta, but I just spent over twenty-two hours in the air and, thanks to Chino, arrived just in time for your little fireworks display."

"It wasn't my fireworks display. Oh, never mind, I'm just glad you're here. I'm sorry I dragged you into another mess."

"Apology taken, for now. Hetta, listen to me. Did you shoot this guy?"

"What guy?"

Jan piped up. "Paco. He was laying right next to you, hole in his forehead. Jenks dragged him down the beach. We're afraid the Mexican navy is going to show up any minute. We heard them talking on the radio. They are sending boats to investigate the explosion, so we gotta scram. But first we need to get rid of Paco, and the gun. Where is it?"

"I didn't shoot him. I didn't even know he was— Oh."

"Oh, what?"

"Nacho. I thought he nailed me, but he must have seen Paco coming up behind me and shot him, instead. Maybe Paco, when he fell, pitched forward, collided with my shoulder on his way down. I felt the blow and thought I was shot. I guess I did faint, after all. Lord knows I was scared enough."

"I didn't think you had it in you to carve him up like that."

"Carve? I thought he was shot."

"And whittled. Someone sliced a big Z in Paco's back, and I don't think Zorro's anywhere around here."

I struggled to my feet and walked over to check out Paco's body. Sure enough, he was on his stomach, his shirt gone, tattoos showing, and a bloody red Z was cut into his back.

Chino knelt next to the body. "I think it is a Zeta sign, a warning from a gang member to others. This Nacho, do you think he did this?"

"I don't know why he would."

"Gang members leave signs like this as a warning. Or a message."

Aha! I smiled. "Yes, I think it means I can sleep at night."

Jenks looked puzzled, but I didn't feel like explaining right now. "Let's douse the lights on the boats and get the hell out of here. Leave Paco lay, the Federales will deal with him. I think it's safe to bring back the people who live here, then we need to boogie."

Epilogue

My boat smelled like a zoo.

Auntie Lil agreed to turn both Iggy and Trouble over to Rancho Oberto. She returned to Texas to do volunteer work at the VA Hospital. No doubt to be near a good source of drugs and husbands. Her latest amour she'd gone to Mazatlan with, Fred, returned to rehab, graduated, and decided she was a bad influence.

Granny Yee stayed aboard with her goat until we reached Puerto Escondido, then returned to Lopez Mateos. Said she'd grown tired of *her* new love interest, who didn't have the balls to stand up to a bunch of LA punks. On top of that, he didn't like goats. She and Auntie Lil traded notes on finding love on the Internet.

Trouble got his wings clipped. It took four of us, and a few of Aunt Lil's more potent prescriptions, but we did the deed. No, we didn't give them to *him*. Although he can no longer fly around at will, he is a TV celeb with his own fan club, and an unlimited amount of jerky. Because he frequently appears at children's functions and fund raisers, he is undergoing etiquette lessons from a world renowned bird trainer. The trainer is on Valium.

Marina and Mr. Bill also found a new home at Rancho Oberto.

Jan and Chino reconciled their differences and returned, with Grans Yee, to Lopez Mateos. Jan will remain on the dive team, but all talk of marriage is out.

Martinez, after reluctantly telling me Arizona no longer had any interest in my so-called crimes, presented me with a fat bill that included a ferry toll to retrieve his pickup from San Carlos, and travel expenses to get back to his new home in Baja. He didn't invite me to visit.

There was nothing in any of the newspapers about the incident at Agua Fria. Bad for tourism, you know.

It was CNN International that broke the story following an anonymous tip. A four-state border bust netted hundreds of meth-smuggling illegals, along with millions of dollars worth of drugs. Many of the hapless illegals reported horrible abuse at the hands of the gangsters who told them when and where to cross the border. Some of the smugglers were taken to US hospital and treated for knife wounds, most notably Zs carved into their skin.

Another agency reported a shootout between the Mexican army and hired hit men from a drug cartel calling themselves Zetas. Over a hundred gang members were killed, but not before they branded Zs onto the backs of their hostages.

News agencies speculated the two incidents might be related. Duh.

Jenks and I, after fumigating *Raymond Johnson*, are taking some time to cruise around the Sea of Cortez until we both have to go back to work. To keep the peace, we agreed not to discuss my activities over the past month. He did mention that I seemed to go to great lengths to get a New Year's Eve date, though.

And Nacho? Only The Shadow knows.

Weeweechu a Merry Christmas, and a Happy New Year.

~End~

About the Author

A ward-winning author Jinx Schwartz has spent most of her life traveling the world for work and pleasure. She spends as much time as possible afloat in the Sea of Cortez and pulls adventure from her boating experiences there. She also writes destination articles for boating magazines, and is a member of Mystery Writers of America and Sisters in Crime. When not in Mexico, Jinx finds herself high and dry in the charming desert town of Bisbee, Arizona.

Visit Jinx's Web site: www.jinxschwartz.com

11-4-22
1-24-24